A SMUGGLER'S CAVE AND A WATERY GRAVE

Shiraz Jones Marine Rescue Mysteries
Book Four

*Dedicated to Sisters Florrie and Marie
of Somerset, England;
two very Christian people.*

Copyright

CONTENTS

AUTHOR'S NOTE

Shiraz Jones Marine Rescue Mysteries are set in England and written by an English author.

*In this book, Oscar carries a torch.
US readers may prefer to call it a flashlight.*

Either way, it's the item you grab during a power failure only to discover it has flat batteries.

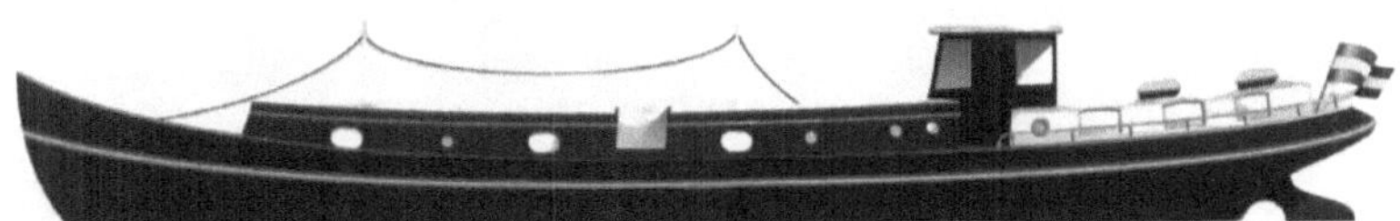

CHAPTER ONE

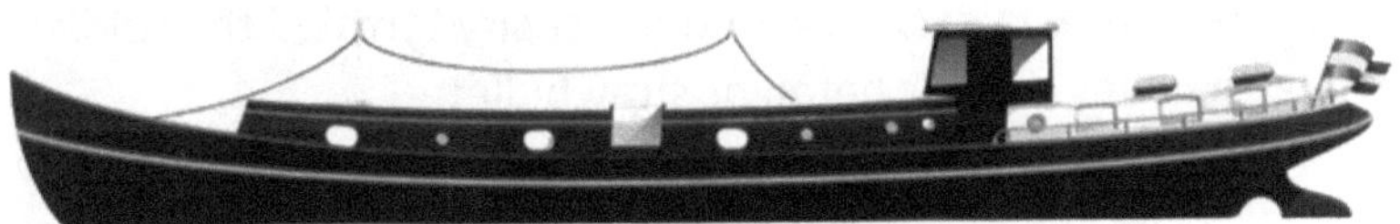

Kabul, 26th October 2014

The soldier hadn't been trained for this situation.

Trained to fight—yes.

Trained in explosives—of course.

Trained to evade the enemy, battle with knives in close combat, to resist interrogation and torture—definitely.

But not for this moment.

Not for the final day of British military presence in Afghanistan.

The soldier sat on a Bergen backpack, waiting with hundreds of other combatants to fly home.

Home to what?

Home had been a hostile environment for so long, the soldier had forgotten benign, ordinary life.

Some boring nine-to-five job? Two weeks summer holiday in Spain? Grocery shopping? Gardening?

How was anyone supposed to adjust?

The excitement, the battle, the not knowing. The constant reminders in the flashes and explosions that it was either the other person's life, or yours.

The mundane existence of domesticity terrified the soldier more than any mortar bomb or stray bullet.

Thank goodness for the plan.

The proposed operation.

The operation which would not only give the soldier a combat-like thrill in its execution, but also would bring sufficient riches not to have to worry about whose turn it was to clean the car or walk the dog.

The soldier could wait.

Wait for years if necessary.

All that remained was to choose the date and the location of the battle arena.

CHAPTER TWO

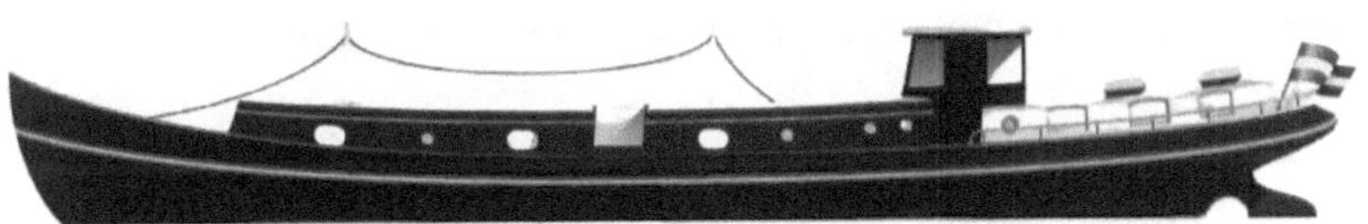

Redcliff-upon-Sea, present day

"Man overboard! Starboard side."

I jumped at Murph's voice.

He jabbed his finger. "Eyes on the casualty, Shiraz. If you lose sight of them, even for a split second, you might never find them again, and they'll drown."

"I have visual," yelled Emily. "Dead astern." She held her arm horizontally towards the distant head which appeared and disappeared between the waves.

Jules, the qualified crew on this shift, grabbed a safety harness and clipped it onto me. I hadn't worked with her before and, considering she was much younger than my 38 years, her professionalism impressed me.

"When we're pulling the person on board," she explained, "the last thing we want is for one of us to fall in. This time, you're going to be the crew member performing the recovery. What's the next step?"

"Open the boarding door?" I unlatched the section of the boat's side, which would allow me to pull the person from the water onto the deck easily and swung it open.

"Stop!" Murph's voice boomed. "Splintering shipwrecks. What d'you always say before you open the boarding door?"

I slapped my forehead. "Ask your permission. Sorry. In the heat of the moment, I forgot."

"Correct. Always ask the skipper first."

"Man overboard visible thirty feet off the bow," yelled Emily.

I knelt with my head and arms inches from the sea with Jules behind me.

"Ready to retrieve the casualty," I shouted. I reached towards the waves, and the reassuring restraint of the harness tugged on my back.

"D'you have visual?" called Murph.

"Yes. I can see them."

"Tell me. Communicate with your skipper. I can't see what you're seeing."

"Sorry. I have visual. Five feet, three feet, and... I have hold of them."

I grabbed the casualty's arm and fought against the waves to prevent them being swept under the boat and into the engines. Jules's arms reached over me, and between us we heaved the man overboard onto the deck.

"Report on casualty's condition," demanded Murph.

"Dead."

"Dead?"

"Yep. Dead. Because they're a bright-orange rescue dummy with a luminous yellow head."

Emily giggled. Jules hid a smile.

"Thank you," said Murph, "for your brutally honest summation of the situation. What would you have done if this had been a real person we'd pulled out?"

"Check for vital signs and commence CPR if needed."

"Very good, Shiraz. You're doing well. Close the boarding door, and we'll try the exercise again. This time, Emily can pull them in. And remember, if you're doing this in real life anywhere except this boat, you won't have a harness. It's essential you remember how to tie a bowline knot to make one out of a rope."

"I have a very important question before we swap roles," said Emily.

"Yes?"

"The rescue dummy's called Ruth Lee. It's written on the side. And every member of crew on the boat today apart from you is female. So why did we call 'man overboard' and not 'woman overboard'?"

"I'd never thought of that," said Jules, "and I must've pulled her from the water dozens of times."

Murph rolled his eyes. "Shivering stowaways. The reason we say 'man' and not 'woman', for your information, Emily, is not because Redcliff Marine Rescue is some kind of chauvinistic, male-centric organisation. Quite the opposite.

As you've observed from the composition of today's crew, under my leadership our female membership numbers have increased significantly. Nope. The reason's simple. It takes longer to say 'woman' than it does 'man'. And, one day, somebody's life could be saved because you didn't have to yell an extra syllable."

We were excused from debating this matter further by the crackle of the radio.

"Marine Rescue Redcliff, Marine Rescue Redcliff, this is Coastguard Headland Bay. Come in, please. Over."

Jules responded into the handset. "Coastguard Headland Bay, this is Marine Rescue Redcliff receiving. Over."

"We've had a report of two children on an inflatable being blown out to sea from Redcliff Main Beach. Proceed to the scene immediately and begin a search. Over."

"Received. D'you have a more detailed description? Over."

"Negative. We'll contact you if we get more information. Please advise when you are on scene. Over."

"Roger. Marine Rescue Redcliff heading for Main Beach to search for two children on an inflatable. ETA fifteen minutes. Over."

"Thank you, Marine Rescue Redcliff. Coastguard Headland Bay out."

Murph wedged himself behind the rescue boat's wheel. "Unclip that harness, Shiraz. Everyone in the cabin, please, and holding on."

"Holding on," we responded, as he pushed the throttles forward.

I braced myself as we bounced across the waves. April marked my fourth month as a marine rescue volunteer, and I had absolutely no regrets about my decision to move to Redcliff-upon-Sea. The vapid party world of London, and my former life there seemed like a dream; something that had happened to someone else in a parallel universe. This was where I belonged, on this boat, saving lives at sea, making a difference. Not on a red carpet posing for a stupid photograph.

"Ten minutes to destination," yelled Jules.

We rounded the promontory from West Cove, passing the harbour on our port side, and Redcliff town came into view.

"What should we expect?" asked Murph. "It's the Easter school holidays, the weather's mild for April, the sea temperature will still be very cold, and all we know is that two kids have been blown out to sea from Main Beach. We don't know their ages, what they're wearing, the colour or size of the toy they're riding on; anything. Shiraz, how should we best use this time to prepare?"

"Grab the blankets out of the forward locker to keep the kids warm," I said. "And towels, in case they're wet."

"Yep, do that. While you're finding those, Emily, what else could we do?"

"Pull out the binoculars?" she replied.

"Definitely," said Murph. "We can stop the boat and have a look around, although binoculars can be ineffective for searching for something as small as a person in the water. Hopefully, the kids are still on the inflatable. With this stiff northerly breeze, we'll need to find them before they're blown to the horizon."

The vessel completed its curve around the harbour wall and approached Redcliff Main Beach, then the radio crackled.

"Marine Rescue Redcliff, Marine Rescue Redcliff, this is Coastguard Headland Bay. Come in, please. Over."

Murph slowed the boat, so we could hear the communication clearly, as Jules grabbed the handset. "Coastguard Headland Bay, this is Marine Rescue Redcliff receiving. Over."

"We have further details about the casualties. Are you ready to write them down? Over."

Jules slipped a pen out and poised it over the boat's log. "Ready," she said. "Go ahead. Over."

"The children are a boy and a girl aged eight and five. The girl's wearing a pink swimsuit. They're riding an inflatable whale directly offshore from the Smuggler's Tavern. Their mother's waiting on the beach. Over."

"Received," said Jules. "Two children, eight and five years old. Girl in pink swimsuit. Riding a whale. What colour is the whale? Over."

"Sorry, we don't have that detail. Please advise when you have an update. Over."

"Redcliff Marine Rescue commencing a search directly in front of the Smuggler's Tavern. We will advise when we have an update. Over."

"Coastguard Headland Bay out."

"I'll bet you anything that whale's blue," said Murph. "And therefore impossible to see against the ocean."

We motored slowly parallel to Redcliff's main beach, roughly half a mile offshore and paused opposite the seafront pub called the Smuggler's Tavern. To the port side, the golden sands shone, mixed with patches of pebbles, punctuated by beach towels and umbrellas. Easter was in the middle of April this year, and the holiday crowds were enjoying the early-season sun, although not too many folks were braving the still-chilly water.

"Is that them?" asked Emily. She held the binoculars to her eyes and pointed. "It's hard to focus these when we're bobbing up and down."

"Where?" asked Murph.

"Off the port bow, eleven o'clock."

Murph swung the boat, so the bow aimed where she'd indicated. "Let's look," he said, as he pushed the throttles forward slightly. We approached the object Emily had seen which turned out to be an orange rubber dinghy containing two teenage girls.

"I'm pretty sure this isn't what we're looking for, but we've had misinformation before. It's best to check." Murph slowed down as he came alongside the dinghy, and he slid open his cabin window. "Excuse me, girls, did you call for assistance?"

"No, we're fine," replied the older one. She raised her phone and snapped a picture of the rescue boat.

"Have you seen two young children on an inflatable whale?"

The younger one shook her head.

"No problem," said Murph. "Be careful out here. You should be wearing lifejackets." He closed the window, shook his head minutely, and we motored further towards the shore.

"There's no one else floating on anything," I said, as I shaded my eyes and scanned the water. "I can see a person in a rowing boat near the harbour, but not two kids on an inflatable."

"Someone's waving at us on the beach," called Jules, pointing at a figure sweeping one arm backward and forward. "Could you steer close enough so we can talk to them?"

"Yep. We'll go in slowly. Everyone, eyes on the water. The last thing we want to do is run over a swimmer. Or those kids."

We drifted towards the beach. People stared at the rescue boat, and some took photos. The figure waved an arm harder. They held something against their body.

"That's as close as I dare," said Murph. "There's a submerged ledge here, and I don't want to run aground."

"Hello," yelled Jules.

"Help!" the woman called back, as I observed the bundle in her arms was a baby snuggled against her chest.

She gesticulated out to sea. "My children. Out there. Please help."

"Were you the person who called the coastguard?"

"Yes. Quick. Save them. My daughter can't swim well. She's only five. Please be quick."

"Are they floating on a toy whale? What colour is it?"

"Blue," said the woman. "They sailed off in the wind. I lost sight of them. Hurry, please."

"We're on to it, Madam. We'll find them. Don't worry." Jules turned to Murph. "Did you catch that?"

"Yep. I knew that whale would be blue. Hold on. Going up."

"Holding on," we all said, as Murph swung the boat away from shore directly out to sea and pushed the throttles forward.

"We'll head one mile offshore and commence a parallel search," he said. "But eyes on the water all the way out. We don't want to pass them."

We all scanned the waves as the boat cruised slowly.

"Flickering fathometers," exclaimed Murph, as he scoured the sea ahead of us. "If I become Prime Minister, I'll make blue inflatables, khaki kayaks and grey paddle boards illegal. Every human-powered floating object will have to be painted luminous yellow or orange. It's impossible to see these dark colours in the ocean until you're on top of them."

We peered at the whitecaps. Even though Redcliff town with its sandy beach, ice cream parlours and souvenir shops lay close by over our shoulders, there was nothing ahead between us and the English Channel. We had to find the children before it was too late.

CHAPTER THREE

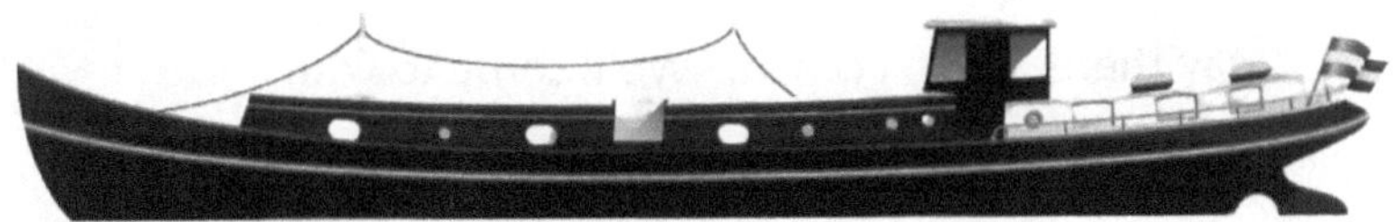

"Object directly off the starboard side," I yelled.

"Where?" asked Murph, as he pulled the throttles back, and the boat stopped.

"I can't see it now. It might be a false alarm. No. There!" I pointed. "Three o'clock. I saw something light-coloured."

Murph turned the vessel through ninety degrees. "Are you sure it wasn't a breaking wave?"

"It was a man-made object; I'm sure of it. Now it's dead ahead."

"I think it's them," called Emily, leaning out and peering through the binoculars. "Poor mites, they must be frozen."

"Good spot, Shiraz," said Murph. "Prepare the deck to retrieve man overboard. Open the boarding door. Shiraz, harness up. Emily, don't take your eyes off them. Keep your arm extended in their direction. Jules, grab the blankets and help Shiraz."

The children came into view, clutching a floppy, tablecloth-sized piece of blue plastic which might've once been an inflatable whale. The blond-haired boy was lying on his back and kicking, and he had his arm around his sister, who gripped a doll.

"Stay there, kids," I called. "We'll come to you."

"Engines in neutral," called Murph.

We drifted slowly towards the children. I knew how enormous the boat looked when you were in the water under it, and I realised this experience must've been terrifying for them. As they came within reach, I grabbed the girl by the arm and pulled her up onto the boat, which definitely wasn't the way I'd retrieved the rescue dummy, but, fortunately, she weighed less than half its weight.

"Emily, take her from me, quick. I'm going for the boy."

Two small white hands appeared on the sill of the boarding door. "Up you come," I said, and pulled both his arms. "Both children on board," I called to Murph. "Conscious and breathing."

"Good job. Dry them off and wrap them in the blankets. Check there were only the two of them. Jules, get on the radio to the coastguard and tell them the good news. Request an ambulance to meet us at the car park by the Smugglers Tavern. I'll start heading back to shore, and we'll find Mum."

Emily and Jules rubbed the kids dry with towels and wrapped them in our warm blankets.

"Are you two okay?" asked Jules. "What are your names? Were there any other people with you?"

"Just me and my sister," said the boy. "I'm Hunter, and she's called Gracie. It's a good job I got my lifesaving certificate from school last term. And my one hundred yards swimming medal. I was the best swimmer in my class."

Gracie clutched her doll and sucked her thumb. Emily held her tightly inside the blanket.

"What happened?" I asked Hunter.

"We were playing on our whale close to the beach. Mum told us not to go far; to stay where I could stand. But then the wind started blowing, and my feet couldn't touch the bottom anymore. I yelled for Mum, but she didn't hear me because Angus was making too much noise."

"Who's Angus?"

"My baby brother. I thought it would be great to have a brother to play with, but all he does is scream and be sick. Anyway, by the time she saw us, it was too scary to swim back. She shouted at us to hold on to the whale, and said she'd call for help. We held on, but then the whale started to go soft and sink."

"Poor Whaley," said Gracie, briefly removing her thumb from her mouth. "She wanted to dive under and find her whale friends."

"I was really brave swimming and holding Gracie," said Hunter. "Although I was scared of sea monsters. And sharks."

"I don't think there are any of those in Redcliff," I said. "Have you ever seen a sea monster?"

"Loads," said Hunter. "With tentacles that would drag a man under as big as Lance."

Gracie extracted her thumb again. "You're always making up silly stories, Hunter. Mummy and Lance aren't here, so I'll have to tell you off for them."

I grinned at the exchange between the siblings and briefly closed my eyes in relief that they didn't appear to be harmed.

"Coming down," called Murph. The anchor chain clattered, and the rescue boat stopped a few metres from the beach. The woman with the baby had removed her dress, and she began to wade towards us in her swimsuit. She had broad shoulders and a very toned body, and I wondered if she was a gymnast, or possibly a fitness coach.

"Stay where you are, Madam," called Jules. "We've got the kids, and we'll bring them to you. Wait on the beach, please." She turned to Emily and me. "I'll hop into the water and check I can stand safely. Shiraz, could you pass the boy to me?"

"I can swim," said Hunter. "I've got my certificate."

Jules laughed. "I'm sure you have, but I think you've done enough swimming for one day. Shiraz will carry your sister. Emily, pass her down once Shiraz is in the water. Permission to open the boarding door, Murph."

"Go ahead," Murph called from the cabin.

Jules swung the door open and eased herself over the side, where the water came to chest height. I passed Hunter to her, then jumped in myself. Even through my bright-yellow dry suit, the cold water formed goosebumps on my skin, and I shivered at the thought of being immersed wearing nothing but swimwear, as the kids had been.

Emily passed Gracie to me, still wrapped in the blanket, still clutching her doll and sucking her thumb. We waded onto shore and put them down on the sand next to their mother.

"Mum, Mum!" yelled Hunter. "I was really brave. The whale began to sink, and we couldn't stay on it anymore, and Gracie was scared, and I saved her, and I remembered my lifesaving, and there might've been sea monsters, and and and..." He paused to take a breath as Gracie clutched her mother's legs.

"You don't seem any the worse for wear," said his mother. "What about you, Gracie?" She tilted her daughter's head upwards with the hand that wasn't holding her baby.

"I'm sad for Whaley," said Gracie. "She's going to miss us. But she'll be with her whale friends. Dolly was very brave." She held the plastic doll in my direction. It had brown skin and wore an Arabic-style outfit.

"Thank you so much," said their mum to me. "I should never have let them go on that inflatable by themselves. But when you take kids to the seaside, they'll always want to go in the water. Lance, my partner, is in Redcliff on business, and I struggle to keep an eye on these two when I've the baby to care for as well. I was going to swim after them, but I had no one to look after him."

"Of course," I said. "Ah, here's the ambulance. We need to take you two to see the paramedics."

"Will I get to ride in the ambulance?" asked Hunter. "Cool. Will they put the blue flashing lights on?"

"They won't have to go to the hospital, will they?" asked their mum. "We should return to our bed and breakfast to meet with Lance."

"Probably not," I replied, "but they ought to be checked out."

"Look," said Gracie. She removed her thumb again and gripped my hand in hers. "My doll has the same colour hair as you. What's your name?"

"I'm Shiraz. This is Jules. The other girl with the blonde hair's named Emily. And the big guy with the beard on the boat's called Murph."

Gracie grinned. "I'm going to name my doll Shiraz, after you. D'you like Easter eggs?"

"Of course. Who doesn't like chocolate?"

"Will you come with me to the Easter egg hunt tomorrow?"

I began to say that I couldn't, when her mum spoke. "Gracie, these people are emergency service workers. They won't have time to hunt for Easter eggs. They've more important things to do, like saving little children who don't listen to their mothers."

Gracie shoved her thumb back in her mouth, clutched her doll and gave me the saddest expression I'd ever seen. I turned her request over in my mind and failed to find any reason to refuse.

"I don't have any plans tomorrow," I said. "Do you, Jules?"

"Nothing that can't be moved."

I bent down to Gracie's level. "It's a date."

Her wide eyes met mine, and her thumb exited her mouth with a pop. "Is that grown-up speak to say you'll come?"

"It is."

"Yaay. Mum, Mum, they're coming. They're coming, Mum. Hunter, they're coming to the Easter egg hunt tomorrow."

I turned to their mother. "It'd be our pleasure. Where and when do you want us, Mrs…?"

"Evans. Chloe Evans. You're so kind. These two seem to have taken to you. It's in the vicarage garden of All Saints Church at two o'clock. D'you know where the vicarage is?"

"I do," said Jules. "Kids, we have to go now, and we'll leave you in the capable hands of the paramedics. But we'll see you tomorrow."

"Pinky promise?" said Gracie.

"Pinky promise." I linked my little finger with hers.

"Cool," said Hunter. "Last time we had an egg hunt, I found millions."

"Excuse my son," said Chloe. "He always exaggerates everything. Such an imagination. See you tomorrow. And thank you again."

"I'll bet you didn't expect that when you turned up for training this morning," said Jules, as we climbed back onto the boat.

"No. Hey, Emily, d'you want to come with us to the vicarage Easter egg hunt tomorrow? The little girl invited us."

"Easter egg hunt? You won't have to ask me twice. Although I don't think they let adults do any of the hunting."

Jules laughed. "Give me your phone number, Shiraz. I'll come tomorrow but I won't eat any eggs. I don't like chocolate."

Emily and I stared at each other, and our jaws dropped. "Don't like chocolate?"

CHAPTER FOUR

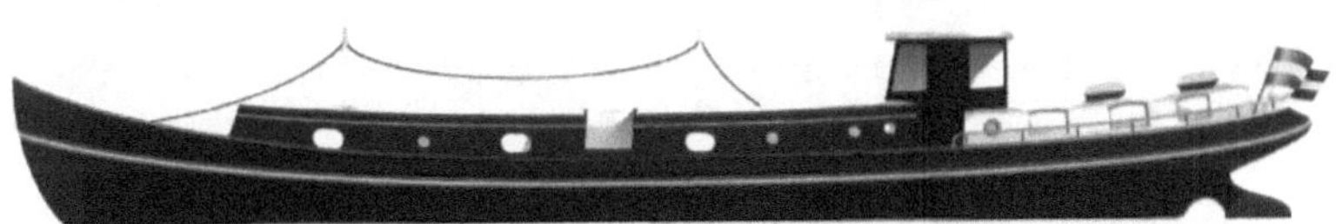

Two years previously

The woman stood with her mouth open. Her face froze, as if a photographer had captured her in an awkward pose. No tears came, but they would fall soon.

"What d'you mean, dead?"

The Casualty Notification Officer stood silently to one side.

"Are you sure it's him?" The woman bit her knuckles, and her upper body shook. "How? Where? Why?"

"I'm very sorry, ma'am. An accident during a training exercise. The army's investigating, and I'm sure they'll take steps to ensure this never happens again."

"An accident? In training? Are you telling me his own side killed him? Friendly fire, you people call it? Hah! Isn't that the deadliest oxymoron ever?"

The Casualty Notification Officer stared directly ahead. He didn't meet her eyes. "The V.O. will be the single point of contact between you and the army at this difficult time. And the padre can provide support as needed."

"Padre!" She spat the word. "Why would I need a padre? A padre can't bring him back." The woman swept papers onto the floor and smashed her fist into the table repeatedly. "This is their fault. Those politicians. They'll never serve on the front line like he did. They're nothing compared to him. Nothing. They're the ones who should die. Not brave fighters like… You people make me sick."

The Casualty Notification Officer remained silent. He'd witnessed this scene play out many times. But his was a short role to play in the theatre of grief. He'd depart, and the V.O., or Visiting Officer, would live the trauma with the bereaved, while the Casualty Notification Officer moved onto the next widow.

"The V.O. will be in touch today," he said, finally. "Is there anyone we can call for you?"

"D'you honestly think I want you people to do anything else? You've done enough. Out. Get out. Get away from me. Leave me alone."

CHAPTER FIVE

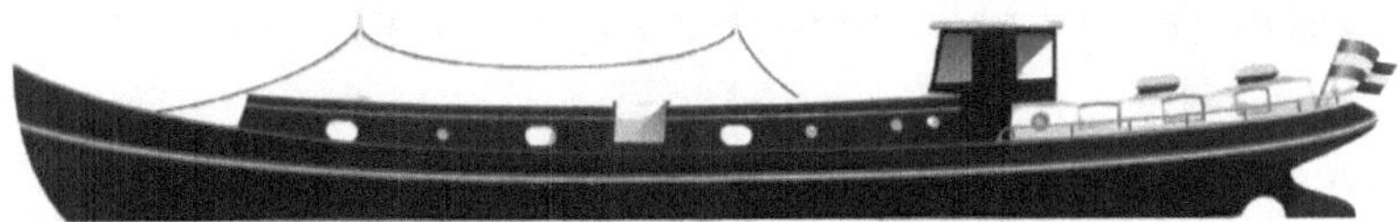

Redcliff-upon-Sea, present day

"Have you done today's Wordle?" asked Emily.

"Yep. Got it in three."

"I'm stuck. What does it end with? Is it 'Y'?"

Emily's apartment above the Wicked Whelk café provided cosy shelter from the stiff sea breeze which had blown up that evening. We sat on her couch, sharing a selection of Dairy Milk chocolates concealed in the Easter egg I'd bought for her and sipping Cabernet Sauvignon. I glanced sideways at the shapes of milk and dark deliciousness lying on a cushion between us and desperately hoped she wouldn't choose the last caramel. Although I'd had the other one of that flavour, so by all rights it was hers.

Emily pored over the puzzle on her screen while I considered for the tenth time whether I was taking advantage by living in her spare room. She refused to accept any rent from me, despite the fact she knew I could afford to pay. And she'd put a stop to our arrangement for me to help out in the café. I didn't mean to be hopeless in the kitchen, but I was no Nigella Lawson.

The final straw had come the previous week when I'd accidentally filled the salt cellars with sugar, and the customers had complained about sickly sweet eggs and bacon.

"It's unbelievable Jules doesn't like chocolate," she said, selecting a lump of light-brown joy with a hazelnut inside it.

I glanced at her sideways and grabbed the caramel quickly. "This is one of my favourite times of the year. When I lived in London, a television personality called Troy Mortlake used to host a party every Easter on his boat at Chelsea, and Monty and I always attended. Invitations were so coveted; relationships were founded on someone having a golden ticket to his extravaganza."

"I'm still amazed you wanted to abandon that life and come to little old Redcliff. Surely you loved that glitz and glamour? Did you ever meet any royalty? Like King Charles, or Prince William and Princess Kate?"

"I shook their hands at film premieres. But I'm sure they wouldn't have recognised me in the street. People I met were mainly in the film or modelling industry."

"Industry? You make it sound like it was a job. Like being in the building industry, or the farm machinery industry."

"Trust me, Emily; it's a job. A job with benefits, granted, but imagine if, right now, you had to spend hours putting on makeup and choosing clothes, styling your hair immaculately, all to attend some event you didn't want to go to, meet boring people who talked non-stop about themselves and pretend they were your best friends. When all you wanted to do was sit on your couch and share an Easter egg full of Dairy Milk chocolates."

"Yes, I suppose so. Did you really have to spend hours getting ready? With your looks, it wouldn't have taken you long."

"Paparazzi, Emily. The scum of the earth. Photographers desperately waiting for a photo of me with my hair messed up, or me looking hungover, so they could sell the pictures to some cheap magazine. Then an article would appear with a corny headline, like, 'Has Shiraz had too much Shiraz?' or, 'Look! Shiraz has been on the Raz again'. Genuinely, I'm so much happier here. It's a weight off my shoulders. The papers don't care about me anymore."

Three sharp raps sounded from the street door downstairs.

"That must be Oscar," said Emily. "He mentioned he'd pop round while taking Cadbury for his evening walk. Boots isn't here, is he?"

I searched around for the Redcliff Marine Rescue communal ginger tom, who spent most of his life either asleep on Emily's couch or miaowing at top volume until he was fed. "Nope. He must've gone out for his own evening walk."

Emily nipped down the stairs, and Cadbury's paws scrabbled as he ran up them. He greeted me by slobbering over my hand and licking melted chocolate off my fingers.

"Cadbury! Get off. Leave Shiraz alone." Oscar jabbed his arm. "In the corner. Lie down. Sorry, Shiraz."

I laughed. "All good. My hands must've needed a wash. He is a chocolate Labrador, after all. Although he's probably not supposed to eat actual chocolate."

"No, indeed; it's poisonous to dogs. There's so much of it around this weekend. That's why I've dropped in. I wanted to give you these." He reached into his shopping bag and produced two identical small boxes, each with an illustration of the rescue boat. "Redcliff Marine Rescue Easter eggs," he said, as he handed them to us. "I sell them in the gift shop."

"Thanks, Oscar." Emily held her stomach. "Although we don't need any more chocolate right now. Shiraz and I just polished off both the eggs we bought each other. You might need to help us."

"We must leave room for chocolate eggs tomorrow," I said. "Don't forget we're going to the vicarage Easter egg hunt."

"The kids can hunt for the eggs. I'm happy to watch."

"Ah, the annual vicarage egg hunt," said Oscar. "My wife will be there helping out with refreshments. She told me the vicars are expecting two hundred people. But why are you going? Unless there's been a happy event you've kept secret from me, neither of you have any children."

"No children here." Emily laughed. "We rescued two kids who'd drifted out to sea, and they invited us to go along."

"Is it one of those big, old vicarages, with loads of rooms?" I asked.

Oscar nodded. "It is, but they run the egg hunt in the garden. The vicars have a number of valuable antiques, and they won't want kids running around the house breaking them. Sadly, I attended a burglary there when they lost several valuable clocks. It was one of the last cases I worked on before my retirement, and we never traced the thieves. So now the churchwarden keeps an eye on the place if the vicars are away."

"Vicars? There's more than one?" I asked.

"Two," said Oscar. "Both female, and both in their sixties. Florence, or Florrie, as she's known, and Marie. Totally opposite characters. Florrie's an exuberant, over-the-top personality. A tall, plump, rosy-cheeked, jolly woman. It won't matter if you've known her for years or you're meeting her for the first time; she'll envelop you in a crushing hug and threaten to suffocate you with affection. Marie's more reserved. A slightly built person, with a dead-straight haircut like an upside down pudding bowl." He laughed. "The entire act resembles Laurel and Hardy."

"Two hundred people are a lot for them to deal with," I said. "And who supplies all the Easter eggs?"

"The wholesaler in Headland Bay donates them," said Emily. "Last year, his van broke down, and I had to cart three thousand Easter eggs of various sizes in my little old Morris Minor late into Easter Saturday. It took me three trips along the dark country lanes."

"Yes, I remember the lights on that car aren't too bright."

"Talking about lights," said Oscar, "sorry to change the subject, but has anyone at Marine Rescue mentioned this strange, sweeping beam off our coast? It has local residents puzzled."

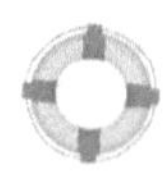

CHAPTER SIX

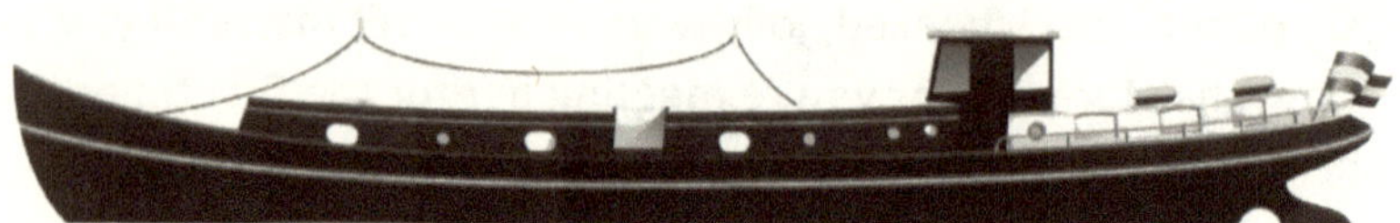

"Lights off Redcliff?" asked Emily. "What lights?"

"I haven't seen them myself," said Oscar, "but people have reported a strange light on the sea close to Smuggler's Cove. The beam swings around like it's looking for something or signalling to someone, then extinguishes. I wondered if Marine Rescue had been asked to investigate? Probably not, if no one's reported anyone in danger."

"I haven't heard any mention," I said, "but I'll ask Murph next time I see him."

Oscar stood. "Right, I'm heading home. I'll be manning the gift shop all day tomorrow. Now it's the school holidays, we're busy. Tomorrow's weather forecast is warm and sunny, so I'm expecting the town to be packed."

Cadbury stood and shook himself, and Oscar clipped his lead on.

"See you, Ladies. Enjoy your Easter egg hunt."

"Bye, Oscar," said Emily. "Thank you for the eggs."

Cadbury tugged him downstairs out into the night, and simultaneously I heard a loud miaow behind me.

"Boots," called Emily. "Where've you been? Were you hiding under the couch the whole time Cadbury was here? You're a clever clogs, aren't you? You knew exactly when he'd left."

Boots rubbed around her legs and yowled at top volume.

"All right, you've been very patient. Time for your dinner. Tuna, tonight, sir?"

The vicarage stood at the end of a long, gravel drive; a square, Georgian, stone building with ivy growing across the outside. Together with All Saints Church next door, it commanded magnificent views over a dramatic part of Redcliff's coastline, where crashing waves sprayed over gigantic, dark-grey rock formations.

"Do the vicars live here by themselves?" I asked Emily. "This place is massive."

"I think so. It's a wonderful location for public events. Every year, they have this Easter egg hunt, then, in the summer, there's a church fête. During December, we have the Marine Rescue Christmas dance in the huge barn." She pointed.

"That barn belongs to the vicarage too?" I stared at an ancient building with a steep roof, joined to the house with stables in between.

"Yep," said Emily. "It's rustic inside, with an earth floor and stone walls, but once we've decorated the interior for Christmas, it's absolutely magical. I feel excited and Christmassy already. You'll love it."

"It's only Easter. Christmas is months away. Let's get through this egg hunt first. Ah, here's Jules."

Jules waved and strolled up to us.

"I love this warm weather," she said, swirling her cotton dress. "An early taste of summer. The beach is full of tourists. I hope the pager doesn't go off so I can enjoy afternoon tea."

We queued behind several families at a trestle table, where a middle-aged woman took money and handed out tickets. Everyone had small children with them, and I felt conspicuous without any, a bit like you'd experience if you went to the cinema alone to see *Chip 'n Dale: Rescue Rangers*.

"Good afternoon," said the ticket vendor. "Three adults? Six pounds please." She tore off three tickets. "The kids' Easter egg hunt will start in a few minutes." She peered behind us. Do you have children with you? Help yourselves to one of these paper carrier bags each for them."

"We don't have kids," I said. "We're meeting people here."

"No problem," she said. "Our volunteers are serving hot and cold drinks, and we have cream teas available for a very reasonable price. Who's next, please?"

"A cream tea sounds scrumptious," I said. "We didn't have lunch."

Emily licked her lips. "Let's grab one and then find Chloe Evans and the kids."

Trestle tables covered in white paper tablecloths had been arranged in the lee of the vicarage garden wall, and groups of people who clearly knew each other well chatted animatedly. One table had three people sitting at the end of it, including a clean-cut man in his fifties. He wore a polo shirt with a nautical design which immediately interested me. His companions were a lady in her sixties caked in makeup, her lips smothered in a thick line of dark-red lipstick. She wore a fake-fur coat despite the warm day and a hat designed to appear fashioned from exotic animal skin. The man opposite her was older, and he wore overalls and a flat cap.

We were about to take a seat at one end of the table, leaving a strategically polite distance between ourselves and the other three, when Hunter and Gracie rushed up to us.

Hunter thrust a Rubik's cube at me. "Look, look. I can do two sides. Can you do the cube? My friend can do it in eight seconds."

"No, he can't," said his mother, pushing a pram behind them. "Stop telling fibs. Hello, Marine Rescue team. Thank you for indulging my children. I'm sorry, I've forgotten your names."

Gracie removed her thumb from her mouth and held my hand. "This one's called Shiraz; I named my dolly after her." She pointed. "That's Jules, and the girl with blonde hair's named Emily. But where's Murph?"

I laughed and crouched to her level. "What a memory you have. Murph isn't here today, but we can't wait to see all the eggs you find. Are you excited?"

"I'm going to find thousands," said Hunter.

"You *always* exaggerate," said Gracie, in an echo of one of her mum's expressions.

"This is my partner, Lance." Chloe indicated a slim man who stood behind her. He had a crewcut hairstyle, a military-style moustache and seemed very preoccupied with something on his phone. He waved one tattooed arm without looking up from his device.

"Please excuse him," said Chloe. "He's in the middle of organising something for work, and he's immune to distractions."

"Have the kids recovered from their experience yesterday, Mrs Evans?" asked Jules.

"Oh, please, call me Chloe. Yes, thank you so much. Hunter spoke to his cousin on a video call this morning and, the way he described it, you'd have thought he'd been shipwrecked for months. Gracie, let go of Shiraz. She might not want to hold your hand the entire day."

Gracie looked up at me and smiled shyly. "Did you get any Easter eggs?" she asked. "I got three. But Mum said I was only allowed to eat one."

"I was given two," I said. "But I expect you'll find loads here."

A female voice sounded through a loudspeaker, but I couldn't see who was speaking behind the throng of adults and children.

The first words didn't seem to be for general consumption. "Marie, Marie, is this working? Can you hear me?" The voice became clearer. "Ahem. Good afternoon, ladies and gentlemen; boys and girls. My name is Sister Florrie, and I'd like to welcome you to the annual All Saints Church Easter egg hunt."

The voice became slightly more distant, and I imagined her holding the device away from her mouth. "Marie, Marie, are we ready?"

The broadcast returned to its original volume. "When I say 'Go', and not before, young man, fill your bag with as many chocolate eggs as you can find. And don't worry; there are plenty for everyone. A big thank you to Headland Bay Catering Wholesalers who've donated no less than three thousand eggs of all sizes which we've hidden in the shrubbery behind me."

The crowd clapped and cheered. The kids resembled greyhounds in starting gates.

"There are only three rules," continued Sister Florrie. "If you're under eight, you get a three minute head start."

"Aw," said Hunter. "That's not fair."

"Yes, it is," argued his sister. "You always take the best chocolates or cakes. I'm going to fill my bag with the biggest eggs and find them all before you get any. And then I'll share them with Shiraz, Jules and Emily. Not you."

"Quiet, you two," said Chloe. "Listen to the instructions."

"Second rule," said the crackly voice through the speaker. "Don't go inside any buildings. None of the eggs are hidden indoors. And the final rule…"

The crowd hung on her every word as if she were announcing the lottery numbers.

"The final rule is, have fun. Under eights, are you ready? Marie, Marie! Have you got the starting siren? Are you ready to press it? Three, two, one, go!"

TOOOOT

Around forty small children fanned out among the trees. Gracie sprinted with them, paper bag in one hand, dolly in the other. I wondered which she'd release first to pick up the eggs.

"Is it three minutes yet, Mum?" asked Hunter.

"No. It's about one. Be patient."

Hunter watched the smaller children scream with delight as they searched under plants and trees. We sat down, and Chloe pulled the baby from its pram, tugged her top up and began to breast feed.

"Would you like me to fetch you a cream tea?" asked Emily.

"No, thank you," said Chloe. "I'm full from eating the kids' leftovers. They were so excited about the egg hunt; they hardly ate any lunch."

Hunter pulled at his mum's skirt. "Is it three minutes yet, Mum?"

"Not yet. Wait. The vicar will announce when you can start." She turned to me. "How's life in marine rescue? It must be very exciting."

"Yesterday was. That's the first time I've pulled a child out of the water, although, as the weather warms up there are bound to be more jobs like that. What d'you do, Chloe?"

"As well as bringing up these three, I help Lance in his import export company. We live in London and distribute goods from overseas around the country."

"Oh, wow. I used to live in London, although I'm well out of it now. You mentioned you were in Redcliff on business?"

"Apparently." She jabbed a thumb at her partner who was still transfixed by his phone screen. "Lance does all the deals. I don't know anything about that side of it. This is a nice holiday for me. Such a beautiful town you have. The bed and breakfast we're staying in is wonderfully cottagey and cosy; we can hear the river rippling past our room. And the High Street's so well provisioned. Yesterday morning, we spent ages in Hatcher's Book Emporium. What an amazing place; I've never seen so many volumes in such a small shop. The kids didn't want to leave the children's nook. You have so many famous authors who hail from Redcliff. There's an entire section devoted to local writers, which is marvellous. I browsed books I'd never have found online."

"Mum, it must be three minutes now."

"Almost. Please have patience."

"Marie, Marie, is it time? Where's the siren?" said the voice through the loudspeaker. "Right, kids, if you're eight or over, grab your bags, and off you go."

TOOOOT

Hunter sprinted away from our group and disappeared into the maze of shrubs, trees and bushes that formed the vicarage garden.

"Welcome, everyone." A tall, stout woman wearing a long, grey robe stood over us. This could only be Sister Florrie.

"How lovely to see all you angels here. I'm Sister Florrie, one of the vicars."

"Shiraz Jones, with Redcliff Marine Rescue." I held out my hand to shake, but instead of taking it she enveloped me in a crushing hug which knocked the wind out of me and flattened my face against her chest.

"Oh, you absolute cherub. Thank you for all you do for those in peril on the sea." She glanced over her shoulder. "Marie, Marie, where are you? Come and meet our local heroes."

A tiny, bird-like woman with a pudding-bowl haircut joined us and stood with her hands folded in front of her. She was concealed by Sister Florrie's tall, wide form, and I tried to include her.

"These are Emily and Jules, my colleagues," I said. "And the lady with the baby is a visitor here; Chloe Evans, and her partner, Lance."

Chloe recoiled from Sister Florrie, clearly concerned that she'd embrace her too, and the baby would be suffocated.

"So wonderful of you all to come," said Sister Florrie. "Let me introduce you to the people on your table. Shuffle up, everyone. Make friends. Don't be shy. We're all the Lord's children."

Emily, Jules and I smiled and closed the gap on the bench slightly.

Sister Florrie held her arm towards the heavily made-up woman. "This is Betty Stanton, stalwart of Redcliff Women's Institute. Hello Betty, how wonderful of you to grace us with your presence. Is that a new hat?"

"It is. How clever of you to notice. Not, I suspect because someone in your vocation would be familiar with high fashion. I bought it in Oxford Street on a weekend trip to London. It came from Liberty, a very exclusive store."

My ears pricked up. Liberty wasn't on Oxford Street; it was on Regent Street. I had an account there. Perhaps Betty was simply mistaken?

"And, for your information,"—Betty glared at Sister Florrie—"I'm not merely a stalwart of the Women's Institute. I'm the chair."

"Of course," said Sister Florrie, the welcoming smile remaining fixed on her face. "And you're a published writer too, aren't you, Betty? Tell everyone about your book."

Betty turned left and right to ensure everyone was listening. "*Uncommon Household Articles of the Middle East.* It's a full-colour, hardback, professionally published volume about some of the bizarre items I observed during my tour of the Arabic region last year. I expect to see it in libraries and bookshops worldwide once my publishing house broadcasts its availability. The subject is fascinating; the locations where Islam and Christianity collide. Similar religions in more ways than you'd think, yet historically at odds with each other. In many cases, it's hard to discern which are Muslim designs and which are Christian. It takes an expert eye such as mine to tell."

"Quite," said Sister Florrie. "We're all equal in the eyes of the Lord."

"Which publisher released it?" I asked. "I know a little about Muslim design, and I'll look for it in bookshops."

"You won't know as much as me, dear," said Betty. "Author Support Press approached me to write it. They've been so good to work with. I only had to send them a small advance of eight thousand pounds, and they even shipped me twenty-five boxes of my book as part of the package. It'll be a bestseller, mark my words. You're very lucky to have met me. I may be able to spare you a signed copy, which'll be a collectors' item in years to come."

"A wonderful achievement, Betty," continued Sister Florrie. "Redcliff loves our writers. Now, opposite Betty is Jack Walter, churchwarden of All Saints." She threw her arm around the shoulders of the man wearing overalls and squeezed him towards her. "Jack's a treasure, aren't you, Jack? He keeps everything at the church shipshape and Bristol fashion, as you, Shiraz, might say in your work."

I wasn't sure I'd heard this expression before, but then I'd only been in Marine Rescue for four months.

"Never enough money, that's the problem," grumbled Jack Walter. "There's always something which needs repairing. Last year, it was the roof. This year, it's the boilers. What are the chances of this Easter egg hunt raising fifty thousand pounds? We could do with that sum right now."

"The Lord will provide; the Lord will provide," said Sister Florrie, throwing her arms wide.

"The Lord needs to take a good look at our bank balance and provide a little more," said Jack. "It's not only the church; the vicarage and its outbuildings need substantial renovation to prevent them falling into disrepair. That barn"—he pointed—"is one of the oldest buildings in Redcliff. It'd be a grave shame if this year's Marine Rescue dance couldn't take place because the barn was condemned." He frowned at the nautically dressed man at the end of the table, who had remained silent until now. "I was hoping for a significant one-off donation, but that's been very slow in coming. If that building"—he jabbed a finger—"was still a tithe barn, we wouldn't have these financial issues."

"Tithe barn?" asked Emily. "I've never heard that expression. What's a tithe barn?"

CHAPTER SEVEN

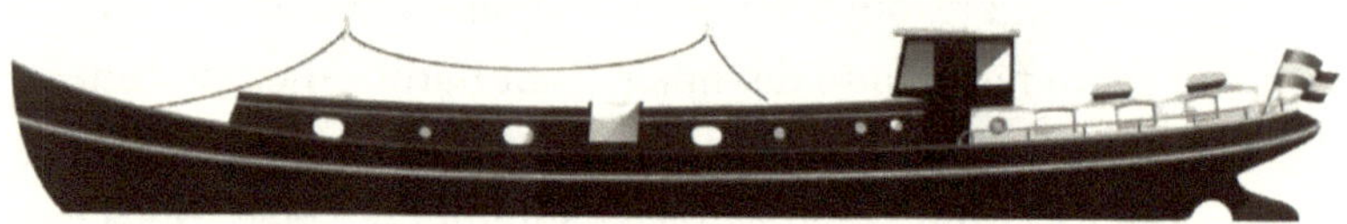

"In the old days, clergy weren't paid," Jack explained. "Instead, the church demanded farmers give one tenth of their produce to the vicar in return for prayers for whichever weather they desired that season. Rain in spring, sun at harvest time and so on."

"The barn stored all these goods the farmers handed over?" I asked.

"Correct. Handed over or 'tithed', hence the name 'Tithe barn'. The barn would've been full of hay, vegetables, chickens, even livestock for the vicar to use as he wished. He might feed his own family, give it to the poor, or sell the produce to fund renovations such as the work we need to do now. Of course, it wouldn't have mattered one bit whether the farmers donated one tenth of their stock or all of it, the weather was going to do what it wanted. But, for centuries, the church maintained this arrangement. Folk were more superstitious then."

"As a well-off member of the community," said Betty, "I've made a generous allowance to All Saints Church in my will." She leant across the table towards us and wagged one finger. "Not that I've any plans to pass away yet. But once I do, the church will be well taken care of. Until then, I intend to spend my retirement travelling and enjoying the proceeds of my book sales. Next month, I'm taking another trip to the Middle East. Such a fascinating region, on which I'm becoming an acknowledged authority."

"All Saints is very grateful for any donation," said Sister Florrie. "And finally, at the head of the table is Captain Harry Salisbury, ex-naval officer and expert on local maritime history."

"Absolutely wonderful to meet you ladies," he said, addressing us in a clipped, educated voice. "We must exchange notes about our jolly old marine experiences. I live on a boat myself."

Now this man is someone I'd like to know.

"You live on a boat?" asked Emily. "But not in Redcliff. I don't think we've met before. I run the Wicked Whelk café by the harbour, and I'm sure I'd have recognised you."

"You're most perspicacious," said Captain Salisbury. "My home and business are in Brighthaven Marina, further along the coast. I acquire decommissioned Dutch barges, sail them across the English Channel from Holland and turn them into luxury on-water homes."

"I knew a man who had one in London," I said. "A film director named Troy Mortlake. He kept it moored on Chelsea Embankment and held a party on board each Easter."

"My first customer," said Harry. "The good sport which he was, he spread the word, and now I have a waiting list. I wish I was able to convert the barges as fast as people want to purchase them." He lowered his voice. "They're popular with wealthy, separated people whose circumstances mean they, how shall I express this, no longer inhabit the family residence."

"Troy would definitely fall into that category."

As do I.

"I've always been terribly keen on the ocean," continued Harry. "I had a yen to be a naval officer, ever since I was a boy. And now, I retain my links to the good old briny deep by converting barges. People are fascinated by life on board. Plus, I have a keen interest in maritime history, including naval battles that took place off our coast, and folklore about jolly old pirates and smugglers."

"You must address the Women's Institute," said Betty Stanton. "I'm sure our members would be fascinated to hear what it's like to live on a boat. I'll book you in as the guest speaker at our meeting next Thursday. 3:00 p.m. Don't be late."

"Let me check my calendar," said Captain Salisbury.

"No need. I'll write it in mine." She pulled a small, leather-bound book from her handbag and jotted a note. "Coincidentally, I'll be in Brighthaven tomorrow morning meeting a friend for lunch, Harriet Marsh. She's sub-editor of *Educated Traveller* magazine, and she's agreed to feature my book in a forthcoming edition." Betty glanced around the table to ensure we were all suitably impressed. "She's taking me to *L'Escargot D'Or.* None of the eateries in Redcliff are up to my standard."

I noticed Emily's cheeks turn red, and she opened her mouth to object, but she was prevented from responding to Betty's acerbic comment by Captain Salisbury.

"If you're in Brighthaven tomorrow, may I invite you for a whistle-stop tour of my floating residence?"

"Hmm," said Betty. "I might fit you in. It'll have to be in the morning; I mustn't keep Harriet waiting. But visiting your yacht is an excellent suggestion. It would give me ideas, and I'll instruct you on the content of your speech. 10:00 a.m. tomorrow? That's settled," she said, before Captain Salisbury had a chance to counter-offer.

"You're awfully welcome, Betty," he began, "but…"

"Mrs Stanton, if you please, until I allow you to be more familiar."

"Ahem. Mrs Stanton. I was about to say, it's hardly a yacht. More of a…"

"Excellent. I'll see you tomorrow at ten. Don't be late."

"Right. Understood," said Harry, who was obviously too well-mannered to object. "I'll put the kettle on."

"How wonderful our little Easter hunt's brought us together in fellowship," said Sister Florrie. "Now that you all know each other so well, I'll leave you to chat so I can round up the children. If I don't set a finish time, the hunt will go on all day." She held her stomach and laughed generously. "When we were hiding this year's eggs, we found a few which the kids hadn't discovered from last Easter." She turned and yelled, "Marie, Marie! Do you have my megaphone?"

She wandered off, and I giggled to myself at the thought she didn't need one.

"The hunt is over," said Sister Florrie's voice through the loudspeaker, once Sister Marie had found it for her. "Would all the children please return to their parents? Thank you so much for coming, and don't forget Evensong is at 6:00 p.m. I hope to see you all there. The Lord is risen indeed."

Adults linked up with their excited, chattering offspring and left through the vicarage gate. Volunteers cleared away the refreshments and began to fold up the tables. The crowd thinned, and we stood. Chloe Evans sat with baby Angus on her lap, who chewed on the ear of a soft toy.

"Time to hoist the mainbrace," said Captain Salisbury. "Jolly marvellous to make everyone's acquaintance."

"I must be leaving too," said Betty Stanton. "You may expect me tomorrow morning."

"My waking hours will be spent anticipating your visit," said Harry, his sarcasm completely lost on Betty, who grabbed her handbag and marched away with her nose in the air.

"I suppose I must prepare for this evening's service," grumbled Jack Walter. "With the boilers not working, I've hired three commercial heat blowers, and they're anything but ideal. They're expensive to rent, expensive to run, and I must light them an hour before the service, then watch to ensure they don't burn the place down. I don't want to be remembered as the churchwarden who set All Saints Church alight."

He pushed his chair in and limped away.

"Where are Hunter and Gracie?" asked Emily. "All the other kids have gone."

"All of them?" asked Chloe, turning around to survey the garden. She began to call out, "Hunter, Gracie, time to go now. Come on."

"Hunter, Gracie," I cupped my hands around my mouth and yelled. "Where are you?"

"They're probably playing hide and seek," said Chloe. She stood, and passed me baby Angus, which surprised both of us. I hadn't had much to do with babies, and I wasn't sure which way up I should hold him.

"Kids, don't make me angry," yelled Chloe. "Where are you? We're leaving now."

Sister Florrie marched up to us, her megaphone in her right hand. "Everything all right here? Do we have some mischievous children hiding in the shrubbery? Here, let me help."

She raised the megaphone to her mouth and blasted from it, "Darling children, time to come out. All the eggs have been found. The hunt's over."

No response.

CHAPTER EIGHT

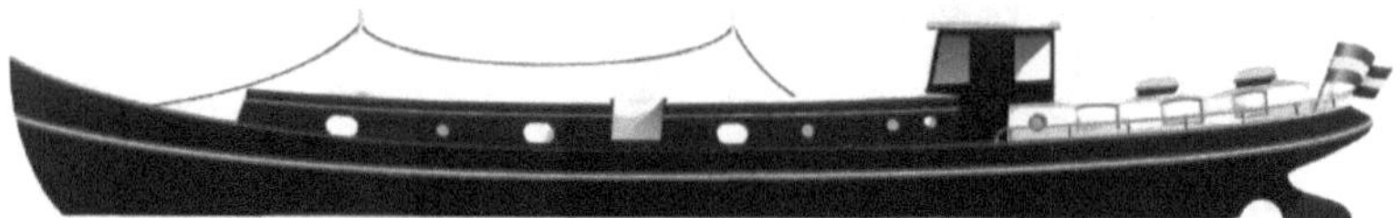

"Lost children?" Captain Salisbury stood ramrod straight. "Time to mobilise the troops. Immediate response required. Assemble a search party. I'll appoint myself on-scene commander."

"We three are trained in search and rescue," I said, indicating Emily and Jules. "We'll help."

"And us," said Sister Florrie. "Although, I know the Lord will care for the little ones. Marie, Marie, where are you?"

"Jolly good," said Harry. "Beastly occurrence, this. One of you rescue people come with me. We'll search the left side of the shrubbery. You other two search the right side, and we'll meet in the middle. Sister Florrie, you search inside the vicarage in case they went in there. Is everyone clear on their roles? Mr and Mrs Evans, remain here in case the kids return by themselves. Don't worry. We'll find your children and return them safely."

I gratefully passed the baby back to Chloe.

"Hunter. Gracie. Coo-ee," I called in a voice which I hoped would attract children, although this wasn't an activity I was at all rehearsed in. "Time to go home. Come out. Everyone else has left."

Nothing.

I heard Captain Salisbury shout from the other side of the shrubbery where he was searching with Emily. The kids didn't know him, and I hoped his booming, stentorian voice didn't frighten them into remaining hidden, imagining they were in some kind of trouble.

"Maybe they climbed a tree?" suggested Jules. "We haven't been looking upwards."

"Good thinking." I stared into the branches and called, "Hunter. Gracie. You're not in trouble. Come out. Mummy's worried about you."

Silence.

"Should we search the barn and the stables?" asked Jules.

"Why not? We've looked behind every bush and up every tree."

We approached the barn. The stone walls were held together with rusty pieces of iron, crosses and S-shapes which had been fixed into them to provide primitive strengthening. A pair of green, wooden doors nearly twice as tall as me provided the only entrance. I pushed them, and they swayed against their locks. There was no way two kids under ten would've opened them.

"Could they have crawled under?" asked Jules. She knelt, switched on her phone torch and stuck her head in the gap under the doors. Her voice echoed from inside the barn. "Gracie, Hunter. Are you in here?"

She withdrew her head, stood and brushed herself off. "I don't think they're in there. But we'll ask Sister Florrie for the key."

Emily and Captain Salisbury approached.

"Any sign?" I asked. "We've checked the bushes and up in the trees. We even looked under the door of the barn."

"The barn?" asked Harry. He glanced in the direction of the large double doors. "It's locked. They won't be in there."

"They could've crawled under the doors."

"Never," he said. "Completely impossible."

"They might really be in trouble," said Emily. "Someone might have taken them."

"How?" I asked. "No one can get into or out of this garden except through the front gate. It's surrounded by high walls."

We were interrupted by a piercing, bleeping sound.

"Pager," said Jules, tugging the black, plastic device from her handbag. "Got to go. Someone else needs help." She turned around and sprinted towards the vicarage gate.

I envied her urgency. "I can't wait until I've completed my qualified crew certificate, and I'm allowed to respond to the alerts."

"Rather." Captain Salisbury stood with his hands on his hips. "Regroup, everyone. We need to be more organised. Where's Sister Florrie?"

"Here I am," said a sing-song voice behind us. "Have you found those darling children yet?" She marched up to us, tailed by Sister Marie and two other ladies.

"No. Have you?"

"We've searched the entire vicarage. The ground floor, the first floor and even the attics. Nothing."

"Have you looked in the rest of the gardens? We've been focusing on the shrubbery, but they may be anywhere."

"Not yet. We thought you might be doing that."

"Take your team and search the back lawn, the vegetable garden, the greenhouses; everywhere. You two marine rescue people search the stables. Sister Florrie, d'you have a key for those?"

"And the barn?" I said.

"There's really no need to search there," said Harry. "We mustn't waste time."

"Jack Walter has the barn key, anyway," said Sister Florrie. "I never go in there except for the Christmas dance. Marie, Marie, fetch the stable key, please."

"As I was saying," continued Captain Salisbury, "Shiraz and Emily will search the stables. I will perform a second sweep of the shrubbery. Everyone, report back at"—he looked at his watch—"seventeen hundred hours."

I raised my hand. "Excuse me, Mr On-scene Commander?"

"Yes? What is it?"

"Who will keep Chloe Evans updated? You told her to stay at the table in case the kids came back, and she'll have no idea whether we've found them yet, or what our plans are."

"Right. Hmph. I'll do that, then continue with my allotted search area. Is everybody clear about their responsibilities? Good. We'll rendezvous here in twenty minutes. And, good luck, team. Absolutely ghastly, this."

"Push, Shiraz. Push the door while I'm turning this." Emily wrestled with the iron stable key.

"I am pushing."

"This is ridiculous. Why is it so hard?"

CLUNK

"Goodness. The key almost snapped off."

Emily and I swung the stable door open and peered in.

"There's no way the kids entered here," said Emily. "How would they have opened the door?"

"Hunter, Gracie," I called. "Are you in here? Come out."

I followed her gaze towards the roof, where cracks of light showed through the ancient tiles.

"They're not in here, Emily. It's empty. Now what do we do?"

"Report back to the commander-in-chief or whatever he's calling himself, to say we haven't found them."

"Let's hope someone else has, then. Chloe must be frantic."

We left the stables and latched the door behind us.

"I'd better lock it again, Emily. Throw me the key."

Emily took a swing like a cricketer throwing a ball underarm and jettisoned the key beyond my right shoulder, where it disappeared into an overgrown bush. I heard it clink several times, like it was falling down a staircase.

"Sorry," she said. "Where did it go?"

"It fell down here. Help me find it." I pushed a path through the foliage and found myself at the top of a flight of moss-covered stone steps.

"Where are you?" called Emily.

"I'm on the other side of the bush. I've discovered steps going down to a little room under the vicarage. A cellar. I'll check to see if the kids came in here."

I descended the steps, crouched down and poked my head through a tiny entrance at the bottom. Light from a ceiling-height window revealed a bare room too low for me to stand up straight. The walls were stark and whitewashed, surrounding a flagstone floor covered in dust. Emily pushed up behind me.

"Are they in here?" she asked.

"There's nothing in here. The room's empty. Let me switch on my phone light and check all the dark corners."

"This is scary," said Emily, grabbing my arm so hard I winced. "I'll bet there are spiders. And bats."

"Neither of those are going to eat you, Emily. You're safe with me."

We swivelled around the room, glancing in all directions. Our feet scuffed on the floor, then echoed as we walked towards the middle.

"There's nothing here, Shiraz. I'm leaving. This is too scary. Did you find the key?"

"Not yet. Help me look around."

An object scudded across the floor.

"Hang on, my foot kicked something."

"What?"

I shone my phone light at the floor. "Here's the key. Oh. And Gracie's doll."

CHAPTER NINE

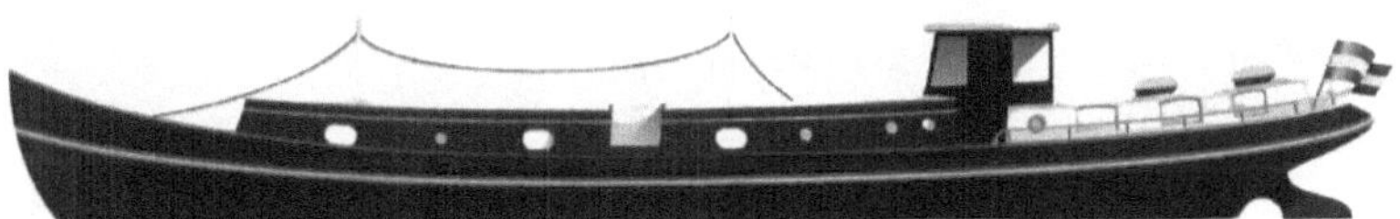

Captain Salisbury attempted to reassure Chloe Evans, as Sister Florrie and Sister Marie looked on.

"Mrs Evans, please don't distress yourself about this beastly business. We will find them, I promise. I'm sure they're merely playing a jolly jape."

I pushed past him and waved the doll. "Mrs Evans, is this Gracie's?"

She bit her lip and stared at me. The colour drained from her face. "Where did you find that?" she asked.

"In a cellar under the vicarage. Hang on, my phone's ringing." I tugged my device from my pocket, desperately trying to press the green button before it went to voice mail. "Hi, Jules. What d'you mean, you've got the kids? Are you sure it's the same ones?"

Chloe gazed up at me. Her lips trembled. Everyone else waited for my phone call to end.

"That's fantastic news, Jules. Well done. We'll see you here in five minutes. Bye."

The group stared at me.

"That was Jules, my colleague at Marine Rescue. The shout she went to was two kids on Smuggler's Cove beach who appeared lost and by themselves."

"Hunter and Gracie?" asked Emily.

"That's what she said. Murph's bringing them here now in his van."

Chloe took sudden, shallow breaths and grabbed the edge of the table.

"Praise be that the children have been found," said Sister Florrie. "The good Lord had them in his hands all along."

"But how did they get there?" asked Emily. "I suppose they must've nipped out of the vicarage gate when everyone was doing the Easter egg hunt and ran down the path to the sea."

"That's definitely what would've happened." Chloe clawed her hands down her hair, and tendons stood out in her neck. "That boy. Here you all are, frantically searching for the last thirty minutes; I'm dreading the worst, and he just wanted to play on the beach. He's in so much trouble."

"The main thing is, they've been found," said Captain Salisbury. "How absolutely marvellous. Stand down, team." He glanced at his watch. "Golly, I must be off." He shook my hand. "If you're ever in Brighthaven, do pop in. I live on the first barge down the second jetty in the marina."

"Thanks," I said. "It'd be fascinating to see what life's like on your boat."

"I'm sorry my children put you to all this trouble," Chloe said to Emily and me. "The plan was to buy them fish and chips tonight, but with their behaviour, bread and water'll be on the menu, followed by an early bedtime."

The sound of an approaching engine made us turn towards the vicarage gate, and a white van with a ladder on the roof pulled up. Murph climbed out of the driver's side, and Jules hopped out of the passenger door with Gracie in her arms, followed by a grinning Hunter. Each child clutched a brown paper carrier bag weighed down with Easter eggs. Lance strolled up to us from the direction of the barn, and I presumed he'd been searching for them.

"Mum, Mum, guess what, guess what?" yelled Hunter. "We were looking for Easter eggs and we found this secret staircase, and then we found a secret room. And in the room, there was a hole in the floor. And...and...and."

"Stop that rubbish right now," yelled Chloe. "No one wants to listen to any more of your stories. You and your sister are going home immediately for an early bath and bed. We've been worried sick. Everyone's been looking for you. I don't want to hear another single one of your fibs."

"But there was..."

"But nothing. We're leaving. Now."

Hunter's face reddened, and he stuffed his hands in his pockets. Gracie sucked her thumb and clutched her doll. Chloe pulled the pram's hood up and marched away with her children as Lance followed, still studying his phone.

Murph shrugged. "I don't know what all that was about, but I can tell you, this is the first time in my career I've rescued the same people twice in such a short time."

"What a good thing the kids were found," I said to Emily as we strolled back to her flat above the Wicked Whelk. "I was really worried someone had taken them. Who'd want to be in Hunter's shoes tonight? Chloe was angrier at him than she was with Gracie. I suppose he's older, and he's meant to show an example to his sister."

We passed the Marine Rescue gift shop as Oscar was locking up.

"Good evening, Oscar. Did you have a profitable day?" I asked.

"Very busy, thanks. The warm weather brings everybody outside. I've completely sold out of Easter eggs, and I'll need to order more mugs and keyrings. How was your Easter egg hunt?"

"Definitely eventful," said Emily.

"Eventful, hey?" said Oscar. "Don't tell me you found another skeleton?" He laughed.

I shuddered. "No, thank goodness. But we did have a mystery."

"Would you like to pop up for a quick glass of wine?" asked Emily. "I think we need one after that, don't we, Shiraz?"

"A mystery?" asked Oscar. "I do love a good mystery, so I wouldn't say no to a wine. Then I must give Cadbury his evening walk."

Emily unlocked the door beside the café, and the three of us trooped up the stairs. She uncorked a Pinot Noir and produced three glasses. Boots objected loudly to being disturbed during his pre-dinner nap, as I moved him off the sofa so there was enough room for all of us.

"How was Sister Florrie?" asked Oscar. "Last time I saw her, she hugged me so tightly, it felt like she'd broken one of my ribs."

"She was in fine spirits. They must've had over two hundred people to the egg hunt."

"And your mystery..?" said Oscar, leaning forwards.

I sipped my wine and puffed. "Yesterday, as I mentioned, we rescued two children who'd been blown out to sea on an inflatable."

"Very common in the summer," said Oscar. "When I was a skipper, the inflatables tended to be rubber dinghies and lilos. Not all these pelicans and flamingos we see now."

I laughed. "Anyway, while we were at the vicarage egg hunt, the same kids went missing."

"Gosh," said Oscar. "They sound like a handful."

"I think their mother's at her wits' end. Not only does she have these two, but also a baby to look after, and she needs eyes in the back of her head."

"Is she a single mum?"

"No. She's with her partner in Redcliff on business."

"On business over Easter?" said Oscar. "What sort of business would that be, I wonder?"

Emily laughed. "Can I hear those retired detective's cogs turning?"

"Sorry," said Oscar. "The kids went missing?"

"They did. We spent half an hour looking for them; us, the ladies from the church and this ex-naval chap called Captain Harry Salisbury."

"Can't say I know him."

"He comes from Brighthaven. Anyway, we looked all through the vicarage shrubbery where the eggs were hidden, which is very overgrown. Then we expanded the search into the house and the outbuildings. Jules' pager went off, so she had to leave."

"You saw the barn where the Christmas dance is held? The social highlight of Redcliff's calendar."

"We couldn't enter it, because Jack Walter had the key, and he'd left. We looked under the door. Then we searched the stables, but the children weren't in there. Emily threw me the key, and it fell into a bush. While looking for it, I found a flight of stone steps which led down to a cellar under the vicarage. We walked down them looking for the kids. But they led into an empty room."

"So you didn't find the children in the cellar?"

"No," I said, "But we knew they'd been there, because we found the little girl's doll. We rushed back to their mother to tell her, but then Jules rang me to say she'd found the kids on the beach at Smuggler's Cove, directly below the vicarage. And she and Murph brought them back in his van."

"The kids had decided to take off in the middle of the Easter egg hunt to play on the sand? Without telling anyone?"

"It looks that way. I'm just glad we found them."

"Hold on a minute," said Emily. "What did you do with Gracie's doll?"

"I gave it to her mother. Why?"

"I'm visualising the scene in my mind. And I'm sure that when Jules lifted Gracie out of Murph's van, she had her doll in her hand then."

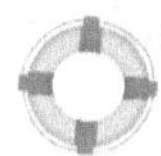

CHAPTER TEN

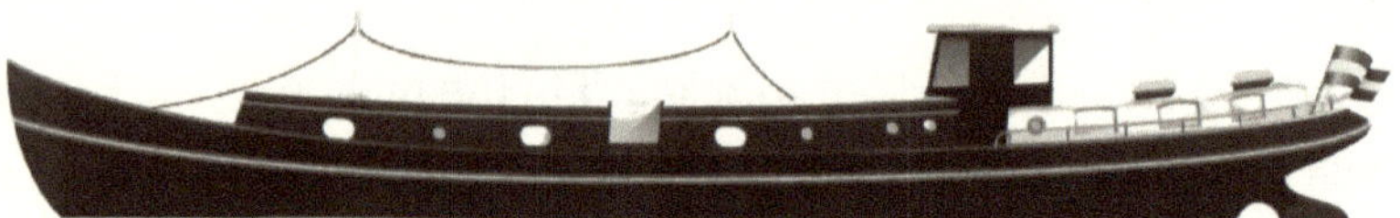

The soldier had never led a failed operation, and this one would succeed too.

Other participants caused operations to fail.

Other participants' actions, inactions, stupidity or treason.

Not the soldier's.

This operation would succeed, and nobody would stop it.

Because the soldier had insurance.

If anyone threatened this operation, they'd feel the cold, sharp blade of a knife.

Many had died by that instrument. None had lived. And anyone sabotaging this operation wouldn't either.

The soldier unsheathed the weapon, inspected it and wiped both sides of the blade.

Insurance.

CHAPTER ELEVEN

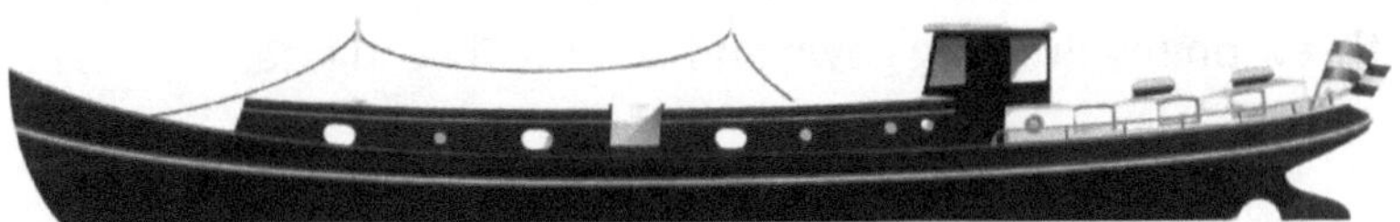

"What d'you mean Gracie had the doll?" I said. "I gave it to her mother."

"Nope." Emily squeezed her eyes closed. "The more I think about it, the more I'm sure she was in her usual pose, sucking her thumb and clutching her doll."

"Could it be she has two identical dolls?"

"It doesn't sound like anything important," said Oscar. "The main thing is the children were found. Running a search operation on Easter Sunday doesn't sound like my idea of fun."

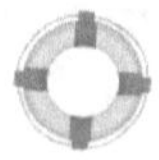

The morning sun kissed my face before I opened my eyes. Warmth on my cheek was magnified through the bedroom window, and I squinted and pulled my covers up to shield my face. My hand groped for my phone on my bedside table, and I grimaced as I heard it fall to the floor. Once I'd retrieved it, I swiped up and discovered the time was 8:15.

The sound of a tap in the kitchen concerned me. Emily would've tripped downstairs to the café before 6:00 a.m. on a Monday, so who was running water? Plates and glasses clinked, and I decided it wasn't burglars. Nobody robbed your house and paused to finish the washing up. I pushed myself out of bed, threw on my dressing gown and went to investigate.

"Morning, Shiraz."

"Oh, hi, Emily. Why aren't you in the café? It's Monday, isn't it?"

"Easter Monday. I don't open on public holidays. The money would be tempting, but I tried opening all four days one year and completely exhausted myself."

"Of course. Silly me."

"And it's a stunning day." She pointed out of the window. "How d'you fancy a day trip?"

I blinked. "Day trip?"

Emily laughed. "You haven't had a coffee yet, have you? I'll switch on the dripolater. I thought we might head off for a drive and find a pub lunch. It's a perfect day to give the convertible a run."

I'd spent the last three months enduring Emily's insistence at always removing the roof of her vintage Morris Minor, disregarding the temperature, the rain and, on one memorable occasion, driving snow. Today, no clouds decorated the sky, and I reckoned the experience would be significantly more pleasant.

"A pub lunch sounds good. I'll buy. Although, you're right. I need at least one coffee before I can even think about lunch. No wonder I forgot it was a holiday today."

Emily placed a steaming cup on the table, and I sat and wrapped my hands around it. Coffee made in her flat wasn't quite up to the standard of her all-singing all-brewing ama-a-zing machine in the Wicked Whelk, but at least it wasn't made from those revolting instant granules. Boots performed a feline pre-wash on an empty breakfast bowl which Emily had abandoned.

"We could go somewhere you haven't been before," she said. "Not Redcliff, or Alnchurch, or Headland Bay. Is there anywhere else you'd like to visit?"

I sipped the coffee. The first taste of the day was always the best. That feeling would never change. "Where did that ex-navy chap live?" I asked. "Brighthaven? Is that somewhere worth seeing?"

"Yes. It takes around an hour to drive there, and it's bigger than Redcliff or Headland Bay. There's a cobbled high street with every kind of shop, plus cafés, restaurants, and I think even a cinema. And the marina, of course, where he keeps his boat. I remember there's a pub overlooking it which does lunches."

"Why don't we drop in on him? I love seeing anything to do with boats, especially if someone lives on board."

I cast my mind back to my ex-husband's company yacht, which was big enough for people to live on, although nobody did. They'd have had to cope with mirrors covering every wall, and a fully stocked cocktail bar where the cooking facilities should be.

"I think you quite like him," said Emily. "Are you sure there's not an ulterior motive to our outing?"

"Definitely not. I've never gone for forces types."

The little Morris Minor zipped through the country lanes, and we noticed the signs of spring everywhere. Green shoots sprouted from the fields, wild flowers bloomed from hedgerows on both sides, and my heart melted at the sight of a field full of sheep, accompanied by tiny white lambs. The sun warmed the top of my head as my hair blew in the breeze and, for the first time this year, I was overjoyed Emily owned this car.

"This is so special," I said. "With the top off, you feel so much closer to nature. You can smell spring."

"I knew you'd grow to love her. All those times you complained about the roof being down."

"Like I said, I love convertibles. I had one in London, remember? But this is the weather for them, isn't it?"

Emily turned right, and we crested a hill. From the top, we glimpsed a distant view of the ocean shimmering in the sunlight, then we descended the other side, and the vista disappeared. I was reminded of childhood seaside holidays, where I spent the entire car journey desperate to see the water. After another fifteen minutes, we entered a built-up area and passed a sign saying, 'Welcome to Brighthaven.'

The ticket machine in the beachfront municipal car park confused us, and we completely failed to decipher if we had to pay a fee on public holidays. I tapped my phone on it and received a slip of paper which allowed us to stay four hours.

We strolled across the sand between the car park and the sea, weaving through beach umbrellas and towels laid on the beach. A wooden hut stood at one end of the beach with deckchairs and little boats to rent. I crouched and dipped my hand in the salt water.

Emily looked at her watch. "We were lucky to find a parking space. Four hours gives us until 3:15. Plenty of time to wander up the High Street and grab lunch at the pub."

"Let's start at the marina and see if Captain Salisbury's in. We could invite him to lunch with us."

"You like him, don't you?"

"He's a good conversationalist. Very interesting. And, after lunch, why don't we rent one of those pedal boats? I haven't ridden one since I was a little girl."

"How do we get in?" Emily shook the metal gate at the entrance to the marina. A sign affixed to it said, 'Boat owners only beyond this point'.

I peered through the grey metal mesh. Through it I observed a criss-cross of jetties with boats of all sizes tied up, from gigantic cabin cruisers like my ex-husband's company yacht and sailing boats which looked capable of taking part in around-the-world races, to smaller family motor cruisers and day sailers. Each jetty benefited from a metal cabinet at one end advertising the location of water and electricity. This marina was significantly better equipped than Redcliff's quaint, homely harbour.

"His boat must be one of those." I pointed at three black barges moored alongside the far end of one gangway. "All the rest have masts and sails, or they're cabin cruisers."

A man wearing overalls and Wellington boots clanged up the pontoon behind us. He brandished a key in one hand. "Morning," he said. "Are you looking for someone?"

I nodded. "We wanted to see if Captain Harry Salisbury was at home."

"The barge chap? No idea, but I'll let you in, and you can check."

"Thank you."

He unlocked the gate and swung it open. It clanged shut behind us, and the man clumped away down a jetty with sailing yachts of different sizes attached to it.

"That was easy," said Emily. "Security's not great."

"We don't look like boat thieves, do we?"

"What do boat thieves look like?"

"They have stockings over their heads and stripy jumpers with 'Boat Thief' embroidered on them, obviously."

We dissolved into laughter and headed towards the barges.

"Here," said Emily. "This one's his. It's the only one with curtains in the windows and a TV aerial. The door's open."

"Let's knock and see if he's home." I stepped onto the deck and banged on a wooden door which led into the wheelhouse.

Nobody responded but, even though the door was ajar, I didn't want to walk into someone's home who I hardly knew, so I banged again. "He's not answering," I said, "although I can hear voices inside." I turned my ear towards the gap in the door. "I think it's a TV show. Maybe he only popped out for a few minutes?"

"Shall we grab a pub lunch, then? The Brighthaven Arms looks over the marina. If we secure a table by the window before other diners come in, we'll be able to see when he comes home."

"It's only 11:30. Not lunchtime yet. Let's wait to see if he appears." I peeked as far as I dared into Captain Salisbury's home. "These barges are fascinating, aren't they? They'd be a great place to live. I hope he surfaces, so we can be nosey."

Emily scanned the barges next to Harry's. "No one lives on these two. He must be in the process of converting them into homes."

Fenders made from car tyres separated the vessels, and I glanced down at the black shadowy sea between them.

Something wasn't right.

"Emily, something's in the water. Come here."

I stepped off the barge onto the dock.

"Look." I pointed. "What's that dark shape?"

"Is it an old coat? Oh, no. I think there's someone inside it."

CHAPTER TWELVE

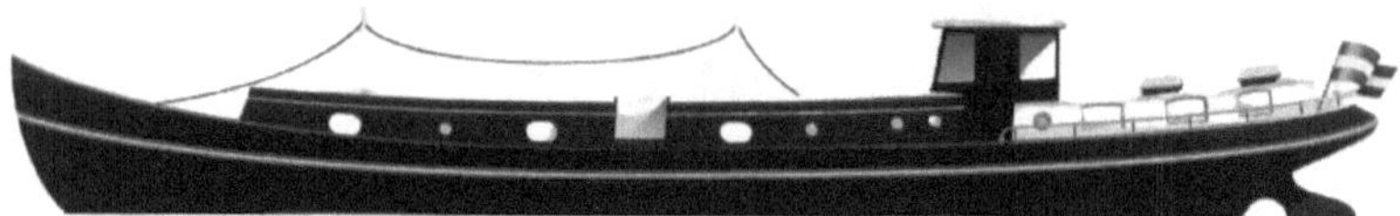

"Help! Anyone," I yelled, but no one was close enough to hear me. "Quick, Emily. Man overboard training. We don't have a safety harness, so we'll have to improvise. Find a rope. Can you remember how to do a bowline knot?"

"Yes. I've been practising."

"Great. Make it strong enough so I don't fall in. Then tie the other end to the barge railing. Hurry."

Emily grabbed a rope from Captain Salisbury's barge and wound it around me twice. I felt a tug as she tied something behind me.

"Done." She yanked twice to test it.

"Wrap it around that bollard and hold on. I'm going to lean over as far as I can and try to grab the coat. Ready?"

"Ready."

I lay down on the edge of the dock and leant outwards between the two barges. All I saw below me was a raincoat and what looked like a light-coloured wig.

"I can't reach them. Is there anything lying around we could use?"

"There's a pole mounted to the side of Harry's barge. I'll have to let go of you to fetch it."

"Wait. Let me shuffle backwards. Okay. Let me go."

I felt the tension release as Emily dropped the rope, and I turned around to see her fetch a long pole.

"This is actually a bargepole," she said. "You know that saying, 'I wouldn't touch it with a bargepole'. This is what it means. See how long this is?"

"I don't care what it's called; pass it to me. Hold the rope again."

The rope pulled on my stomach like a pair of jeans the morning after a huge meal. I stretched out and poked at the coat, gradually bringing it nearer until I could grab it.

"Okay, it's up against the dock. Lean over with me and help me pull it up."

"Is it definitely a person?"

"I think so. But we have to pull them out. Help me; I can't do it by myself."

"It's not Captain Salisbury, is it?" asked Emily. "Perhaps he stepped out to adjust his TV aerial and fell in?"

"We'll never find out if you don't give me a hand. All I can see is a dark coat. Two people for a man overboard, remember?"

Emily lay beside me, and we grasped one arm each.

"Goodness, this is heavy."

"That's because their clothes are saturated. Can you pull any further?"

"No. I can't hold on. I'll have to let go."

"Wait. I hear footsteps. Hello! Help. Over here."

The sound of boots clanked along the jetty, and I heard Captain Salisbury's voice.

"What's going on? What on earth?"

"Someone's fallen in the water. Help us pull them out, quick."

Captain Salisbury peered over the edge of the jetty to see what we were holding. He crouched next to me, leant over and seized the lapel of the coat. Suddenly the weight felt much lighter.

"On my signal," he said. "Heave."

We tugged together, and the dead weight lifted partly out of the water.

"And again. One, two, three, heave."

We pulled until Captain Salisbury slipped his hands under the coat's arms.

"Last one. Heave."

We pulled. Captain Salisbury fell backwards, with the body on his legs.

He panted. "Golly gosh. I haven't had to deal with this type of situation since my time in the Gulf."

Emily turned white, and I felt decidedly queasy. I couldn't bring myself to look at what we'd retrieved.

"D'you know them?" I asked.

Captain Salisbury wriggled out from under the body and knelt beside it. Its face was a grey colour, and water drained out of its mouth.

Emily glanced sideways and gasped. "It's the woman from yesterday who wrote the book. Betty Stanton."

"By Jove; I'll summon an ambulance," said Captain Salisbury, "though she's not going to need a medical professional to pronounce her dead, is she?"

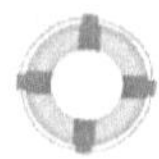

We stood a polite distance away in case the paramedics needed to speak to us as they completed their assessment. Two policemen arrived accompanied by a pair of men who removed Betty's body. One of the young constables took our details.

Emily blew her cheeks out. "No pub lunch for me. I don't feel hungry now. This wasn't what we had planned."

"Ghastly business," said Captain Salisbury. "But why are you here? I wasn't expecting to see you today."

"We thought we'd drop in on you," I said, "and then this happened."

"Jolly lucky you visited, what-ho. Golly, she could've been blotto and tumbled in? Bit early in the day for that, mind you.

Would you two like to come aboard? I've provisioned with refreshments." He brandished a pair of supermarket carrier bags.

"I'm not sure we could eat anything after that experience," I said, "but I'd love to see how you live on the water."

"Did you mean to leave your boat's door unlocked?" I asked, as we followed him onto his barge.

"I often leave it open when I pop out. No one should be able to enter the marina without a key. Although you two did.

"A man opened the gate for us," said Emily. "I wish he hadn't, now. Nothing against you, but I didn't plan on seeing a body today."

"That must've been Doug. He's always coming in and out repairing his jolly old sailing boat, but never takes it to sea. I'd prefer it if he didn't let people in; this is supposed to be a private marina. All the security in the world, and it can't stop tailgating. But I wonder why Betty Stanton was here so early? She told me she'd come at noon, so I made sure I was back from the supermarket by then."

"I thought I overheard the arrangement as being at ten o'clock. Did you know her, before yesterday?"

"I'd never had the pleasure. She inveigled me into speaking at her Women's Institute meeting, then we all became caught up with the frightful hunt for those kids, and I didn't have the chance to say anything else. Anyway, come into the wheelhouse. Hold on to the handrail."

We stepped over a sill and entered his boat. Windows at chest height surrounded the square room, under which seats with long cushions bordered the walls. A wooden and brass steering wheel around three feet in circumference was mounted facing the bow of the vessel, where I presumed the captain would stand to navigate the barge. To its left, steep steps led down to lower decks. Circular, highly polished, brass instruments surrounded the wheel, each with a needle pointing to a numbered dial. I inspected them and realised these were the old-fashioned versions of the electronic system we had on the rescue boat, as they showed speed in knots, temperature and other readings related to the engines.

"What d'you think?" asked Captain Salisbury. "Bit of jolly fun, what?"

"I love it," I said. "This would be a perfect spot to grab a coffee and read or write." I turned and took in the all-round view.

"Is this where you eat?" asked Emily.

"No, that's below, in the converted hold. Shall we take a look?" He pointed down the steep steps. "After you."

I paused before I headed down the steps, and pointed to an inscription above them, on a rectangular brass plate. "What's this? I don't recognise the language."

"It's Dutch. Remember, this barge lived in Holland when she was a working boat. She would've carried coal or other goods, until she became superseded by those marvellous, modern, larger vessels."

"Wow," said Emily. "I'd love to visit Holland to see the canals and windmills. So what does the inscription on that plate mean?"

"It says, 'If we hadn't bought a boat, we'd be millionaires.'"

"Is that the case, Harry?" I asked.

"They're expensive to run, yes. Money's always tight. But I reckon people who buy barge conversions obtain waterside homes much more cheaply than if they bought an apartment. Anyway, shall we? Mind your head."

He pointed down the steps again, and I ducked to climb down them into a narrow passageway with a closed door to my right. Emily followed, and Harry tailed us.

"Go ahead. That leads to my cabin; the original living space for the bargekeeper's family. They lived, ate, and slept in there." He opened the door, and we peeked into an area with a double bed, a fitted wardrobe, and another door at the end, which I guessed led to an en-suite bathroom.

"It's so cosy," said Emily, peering around me. "But it wasn't very big for an entire family to live in."

"Rather," said Harry. "I have a little more space than they did. Have a look further down the passage."

We continued along the wood-lined corridor and entered a luxury kitchen with windows in both sides. Beside the worktop stood a dining table with four chairs and, beyond them, a living room which might've come from the centre pages of *Red Carpet Superstars* magazine.

"Take a seat here in the galley," said Harry, pointing to a row of stools the opposite side of the counter. "Tea?"

"Yes, please," said Emily. "I need one to calm my nerves."

"Me too," I said.

Harry upended one of the supermarket carrier bags onto the worktop, and a loaf of bread, a packet of ham and salad items tipped out. The second bag seemed bulkier and remained closed. A rectangle of paper fluttered out of the one he'd inverted.

Harry picked it up and squinted at it. He handed it to Emily. "Could you check the time on this receipt for me? I've mislaid my glasses, which is a bind."

"Sure." She frowned and scanned up and down the receipt. "10:57 a.m."

"That sounds spot on, what? I was out for two hours from 9:45." He switched off the kettle as it boiled. "Milk and sugar?"

"Just milk, thanks," I said. "For both of us."

"This is so luxurious," I said. "D'you live by yourself?"

"Yes, since my divorce. My wife suffered, as many navy wives do, from the ghastly long periods of separation, and our marriage ended many years ago. We didn't have children." He laughed once. "I call my wife 'The Housekeeper'. She kept the house. And that's why I ended up living here. All I could afford to buy once her lawyer finished with me was one unconverted barge. I lived in the original barge captain's room while I worked on her. You're standing in the hold, which would've been crammed full of goods when she was in service. It took me two years to convert this one, and now she's a showhome, which is why I keep her immaculate. I've sold eight since then, and the two alongside will be next. I'm becoming quicker at finishing them, but each one takes a year, so I have to go cap in hand for progress payments. Money's frightfully short; I never have enough cash to buy supplies."

"What an amazing lifestyle," I said. "And a unique business. I was attracted to the little canal boats you see on the waterways in London when I used to walk through the area called Little Venice, but I always thought how cramped they must be. This is much bigger; many London apartments aren't this large."

"I wouldn't live anywhere else," said Harry. "Plus, it's a marvellous talking point whenever I meet anyone new. Like you two. Did you come to see me for any reason in particular?"

"I have a confession," I said. "Emily suggested a day out, and I wanted to be nosey and see what it was like to live on your boat. And we were going to ask if you'd like to join us for a pub lunch. But finding a body's put a stop to that."

Emily clasped her head in her hands. "I can't believe that Betty woman's dead. We only saw her yesterday. Shocking."

"Quite understandable. Frightful thing to have happened. Let's talk about something more pleasant, shall we? So, living on boat is like this." He swept his arm around the cabin in a dramatic gesture. "On warm, sunny days, when the water glistens and the seagulls are calling, it's paradise. Here, let me give you each one of my business cards, in case you meet anyone who'd enjoy a life on the ocean wave." He opened a drawer and handed us both a white rectangle with gold embossing stating 'Captain Harry Salisbury RN (Rtd): Supplier of exquisite on-water homes to the discerning purchaser.'

"Any downsides?" asked Emily. "Does it get cold?"

"The finished barges come with modern heating, so no. I suppose if there were an entire family living here it might be a squash. By myself, I have all the space I need. Golly, I don't even own a car; I have a rowing boat I paddle around in."

He spread the groceries out on the galley counter. "Are you sure I can't tempt you to a ham and salad sandwich?"

"Okay," I said. "I'll see if I can eat one, after what just happened."

"May I try one too?" asked Emily. "You own a well-equipped kitchen bigger than mine at home."

"Galley? Yes. Last night I cooked dinner for a lady friend."

I felt a tiny, completely unreasonable, pang of envy.

"We feasted on steak with dauphin potatoes and French beans. Followed by home-made Dorset apple cake and cream."

"I do like a man who knows how to cook," I said, hoping that wasn't too forward a statement. I mean, with my culinary prowess, there wasn't any chance of me pulling off a quick *coq au vin*.

"I enjoy it," said Harry. "Though, living by myself, I don't always finish packets and tins before their best before dates." He pulled a jar of pickle from the fridge, turned it around in front of his face and examined it. "Jolly good. This doesn't go off until the end of next month. Would you like some in your sandwiches?"

"Yes, please," I said. Emily nodded. Harry spread the pickle, added the other ingredients and passed us a plate each.

THUMP THUMP THUMP

Three bangs sounded on the boat's roof.

"What-ho," said Harry. "We are having a lot of visitors today. Do excuse me." He nipped up the steps towards the wheelhouse door.

I glanced at Emily and raised my eyebrows.

"Something's not right here," she whispered. "I'll tell you later."

CHAPTER THIRTEEN

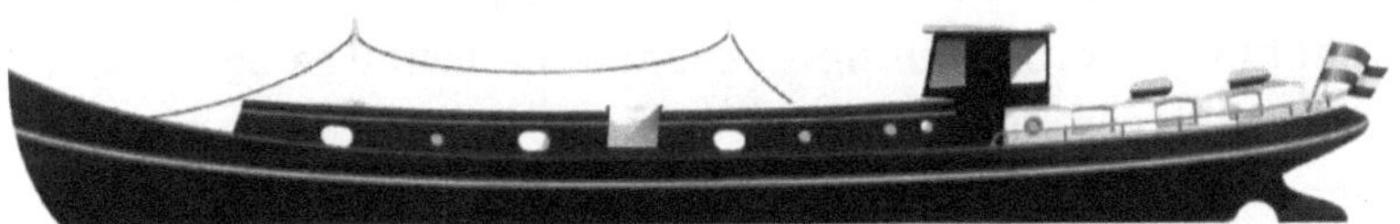

Harry reappeared tailed by a man in his thirties with a short, brown beard. The man removed his cap and laid it on the counter next to our plates.

"Afternoon, all. Detective Inspector Martin Buchanan from Brighthaven police. Sorry to interrupt your lunch. This is nothing to worry about, just routine."

"How can we help?" asked Harry. "I presume this is about the beastly accident we discovered. The poor person who drowned between my barges."

"Yes. Tell me what happened, please. Which one of you found her first?"

"Me." I raised my palm.

"Your name, please?"

"Shiraz Jones."

"And the other lady…?" he said glancing at Emily and smiling.

"Emily Philpot," she replied.

"And I'm Captain Harry Salisbury," said Harry. "This is my barge you're aboard."

"Quite. Ms Jones, how did you come to find the body?"

"Emily and I had arrived to visit Captain Salisbury, as we'd met him yesterday during an event at Redcliff vicarage, and we wanted to see what it was like living on a barge. We, um, decided to be nosey."

"You decided to be nosey," said Emily, rolling her eyes at the policeman.

"Anyway, we knocked on his barge door, but he wasn't in. As we were discussing whether we should wait for him to return, I glanced down in the water and saw what looked like an old coat. I realised it was someone who'd fallen in the water, and Emily and I tried to pull them out, but we couldn't do it by ourselves. Luckily, Captain Salisbury came home at that moment and, between the three of us, we heaved the body onto the dock."

Inspector Buchanan wrote notes. "Was the deceased known to you?"

"None of us knew her well. Harry and I only met her yesterday, at All Saints Redcliff Easter egg hunt. Emily, did you know her before?"

"I recognised her. I mean, Redcliff's a small town, but I'm not a member of the Women's Institute or a churchgoer, so I hadn't met her properly."

Inspector Buchanan wrote more notes. "Why was she here?" he asked. "Were you expecting a visit from her, Captain Salisbury?"

"Yes, but not until noon. She asked me yesterday if I would speak to her Women's Institute members about life on board a boat, and she said she was meeting a friend in Brighthaven for lunch. I invited her to pop in beforehand."

"Did she know anyone else in the marina?"

"Not to my knowledge, but I did only meet her yesterday. I haven't seen her here before. And it's a mystery how she ended up in the water. Golly, maybe she was a bit blotto after a morning gin and tonic. You know these dames."

"I see. Anything else you can tell me about her? Anything at all, however insignificant?"

"She's very snooty," said Emily. "I can see how she might rub people up the wrong way."

"I'm not sure what you're inferring," said the policeman.

"I mean, her demeanour might've made her some enemies."

"Are you suggesting she was pushed in? You believe someone drowned her because of her attitude?"

"Anything's possible."

"Until evidence reveals otherwise, we can only conclude she slipped into the water. Okay, I think I have all I need. I'll make a note of all your addresses and phone numbers, in case I need to contact you again."

We gave the inspector our details, and he left.

Harry poured himself a glass of whisky. "That was unexpected," he said. "Surely he doesn't believe this is suspicious? Beastly business. Anyway, he can't suspect any of us. None of us were here when she fell in."

Emily left the top down on the Morris Minor as we cruised home. Clouds covered the sun, and the drop in temperature made me wish I'd brought a coat.

"The pub lunch didn't quite go to plan, did it?" she said. "And we never hired a pedal boat. We'll have to tell Murph we put our man, or woman overboard skills to use."

"Yes. You mentioned something wasn't right before that policeman came in. What did you mean?"

"Oh, yes. Harry asked me to read the supermarket receipt to him. Don't you think that's strange?"

"He said he didn't have his glasses. Quite understandable."

"Yes, but he specifically asked me to tell him the time on the receipt. That's the odd part. Why would he do that? Think about it. Have you ever studied the time on a supermarket receipt?"

"I've barely seen a supermarket receipt. In London, our cook used to arrange for our groceries to be delivered."

"Gosh. You did live in a different world. And then, I remember, he read the best before date on the pickle jar without any need for spectacles. Now we've been involved in more than one murder investigation, we're finding clues where they don't really exist."

I laughed. "Detective Emily. And Detective Shiraz. No. Just no."

Emily furrowed her brow. "The supermarket receipt might be of no consequence, but another thing I spotted is stranger. When we popped our heads around his bedroom door, did you notice an object on the chair in the corner?"

"A cushion?"

"Yes, and stuffed beside the cushion?"

I squeezed my eyes closed and tried to recreate the scene in my mind. "Sorry, I give up. What was it?"

"A doll. Exactly the same as Gracie's."

CHAPTER FOURTEEN

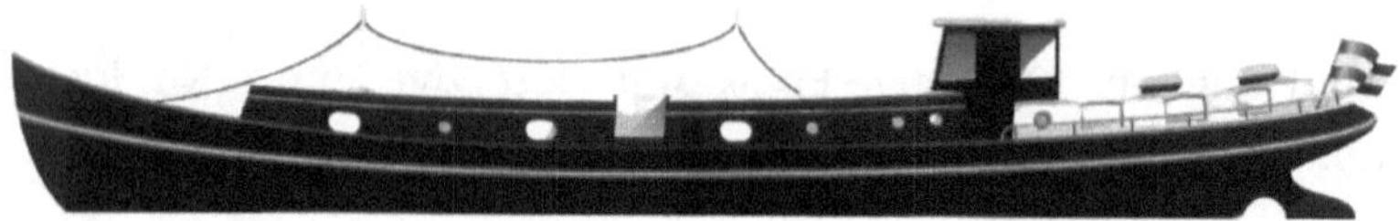

The soldier wasn't accustomed to reflecting on successful executions.

Life was cheap in the battle arena, and this latest kill was one of many.

This operation was no different to previous ones.

Identical to all the rest.

Although, on this occasion, the outcome wouldn't be quite the same.

More constructive.

More beneficial.

More...personal.

The soldier's eyes closed, and a smile formed.

CHAPTER FIFTEEN

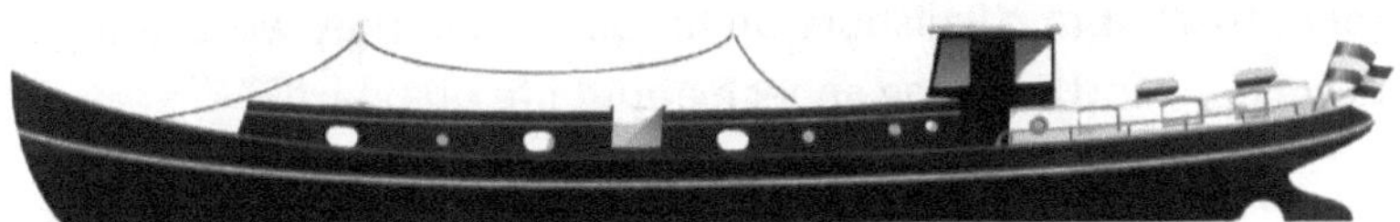

Oscar stared out of the window of our apartment above the Wicked Whelk that evening. The sun had dissolved into a band of cloud before it met the horizon, and tonight's sunset didn't promise to be as spectacular as we'd hoped. Holidaymakers had abandoned Redcliff's beach as afternoon turned into dinner time, and those that hadn't booked self-catering accommodation would soon be heading to the Smuggler's Tavern for a meal and drinks, or to The Plaice To Be for takeaway fish and chips.

"Did you know her well?" I asked him.

"Only through my wife, who's a member of the Women's Institute. Betty Stanton, was, of course, the chair. Despite her diminutive stature, no one dared to be on the wrong side of her. *Une femme formidable*, as the French might say."

"Did she have any family?"

"One son, I remember, although he moved away, and I haven't heard of him for decades." He paused and sipped from the glass of Sauvignon Blanc in his hand.

I stood behind him and gazed over his shoulder while Emily assembled crackers and cheese. As night fell, the lights of fishing trawlers twinkled over the bay in front of us.

Oscar turned to face me. "You mentioned she'd arranged to meet this Captain Salisbury on his boat? And they were going to discuss his forthcoming speech about life on board?"

"Yes. I had the impression she was almost going to dictate it to him."

"Hmm," said Oscar. "She regularly harangued me to speak to the Women's Institute. I did once, many years ago, giving a short talk about how to protect your home from burglary. Some of the older members fell asleep, so I wasn't inclined to repeat the exercise." He laughed. "Betty had become interested in designs of the Middle East and published a book on the subject. Very niche, don't you think?"

"Shall we search for it on Amazon?" I suggested. I unlocked my phone and opened amazon.co.uk, then browsed to the book section and typed 'Middle East designs'. "Here it is. *Uncommon Household Articles of the Middle East*, by Elizabeth Stanton. Published by Author Support Press. Only available in hardback." I showed Oscar the screen.

"That's the one," he said. "Almost fifty pounds. Goodness. I'd be surprised if she'd sold any. Author Support Press are one of those vanity publishers; you pay them, rather than the other way around. They contacted me about writing a book on the history of Redcliff Marine Rescue. I was flattered, until I realised they made their money from me, not readers. Last month, Betty asked me if the Marine Rescue gift shop would stock her book, but I politely informed her we only sold items related to our organisation. She wasn't too impressed. Hatcher's book shop in the High Street might have copies, or Headland Bay Library perhaps. Both of them like to support local authors, of which Redcliff has many."

Oscar turned away from the window and sat down at Emily's table. We joined him, and I sliced a triangle of Brie. As I turned my back, a ginger paw poked above the table and prodded the cheese.

"Boots, off. Goodness. D'you even like Brie?" Emily swatted him away.

"Did you know Betty before yesterday?" Oscar asked Emily.

"I knew who she was, but I didn't 'know' her. When Shiraz and I attended the vicarage Easter egg hunt at the invitation of the two kids we rescued, we enjoyed scones and tea at a table with their mother, and Betty was also sitting at the same table."

"That's where we met Captain Harry Salisbury," I said. "His business is converting decommissioned Dutch barges into floating homes, and I must say the finished product is very attractive. Luxurious, even. He's an ex-navy officer and lives on one of his creations in Brighthaven Marina."

"Did he and Betty know each other?" asked Oscar. "Because if they met yesterday, and today she turned up dead at his home, that's suspicious."

"Harry said he'd never met her before the egg hunt. But here's something odd. I'm sure they arranged to rendezvous at the marina at ten. But Harry thought it was twelve. Their meeting never happened."

"And while she was waiting for him to come home," said Emily, "she paced up and down the jetty, slipped and fell between the barges. She couldn't climb out and drowned. Nothing suspicious about that. Case closed."

"Woah, woah, woah." I grinned at her. "This isn't a case, so we can't close it."

"Good, because, for whatever reason, we've tangled ourselves up in several murders this year, and I don't want to be involved in any more."

"Even so," said Oscar. "Any death in unexplained circumstances raises my hackles. I'd like to know more about this Captain Salisbury. What else did you learn about him?"

"He's a competent cook, apparently, and quite good looking, and probably has a string of female friends."

"The facts, Shiraz." Oscar grinned. "Not whether women find him attractive."

"Sorry. Right. After the undertakers had removed Betty's body, he invited us aboard his barge, which, as I said, is very luxurious. He made sandwiches, and we discussed our finding of Betty Stanton in the water. He hadn't been home when we found her, although he had left his barge door open. He said he often does, as the marina's quite secure. Oh. Then the police came. An Inspector Martin Buchanan."

"I know that name," said Oscar. "When I was in the later stages of my career, he was a constable. I thought he had promise, and I spent some time mentoring him. Gosh, he's become an inspector now? He'd often call me about a case at Brighthaven and ask me what I'd do in his situation. I presume he came to interview you about your find?"

"Correct. But he said his visit was just routine."

Oscar puffed. "All police visits are just routine. Until somebody says something unexpected, and then they aren't anymore."

"Nobody said anything unexpected," said Emily. "He asked us to describe what happened, from the start of our visit to the marina until when we found Betty in the water and called the ambulance. Then he took our names and addresses and departed. There was no intimation he suspected anything but a tragic accident."

I cradled my chin in my hand. "We were suspicious about one or two things, Oscar. I do wish we'd never become involved with those previous cases, as now we don't take anything at face value."

Oscar tipped his head back and laughed. "Oh dear. Welcome to my life. What do you suspect?"

"Two things," said Emily. "The doll. The little girl we rescued had a doll, dressed in an attractive, Arabian-style outfit. We also found a doll exactly like it in the vicarage cellar. Then, when Harry Salisbury showed us around his barge, I noticed an identical doll on a chair in his bedroom."

"You're sure they weren't all the same doll?" asked Oscar.

"No. The little girl was very attached to hers. When we rescued her from the ocean, she wouldn't let it go."

"She named it 'Shiraz'," said Emily. "Isn't that sweet?"

"Maybe a local toy shop had several dolls for sale," said Oscar, "and Harry bought one as a present for a young relative? Most toys are mass produced, aren't they? What was the other thing you found suspicious?"

"He told us he couldn't read without his glasses," I said. "He asked Emily to check a supermarket receipt for him. But then he was able to read a best before date on a jar by himself."

"It was a funny list of items he'd shopped for," said Emily. "As well as food for lunch, the receipt had four bags of flour, three tins of talcum powder and a box of laundry detergent. Why would a man living by himself need four bags of flour or that much talcum powder?"

"You said he cooks?" said Oscar. "Perhaps he bakes too?"

"And," added Emily, "he insisted I read out the time on the bottom of the receipt. That seemed an unusual request."

Oscar frowned and rubbed his chin, then looked up. "What was the time on the receipt?"

"10:57 that morning."

"And what time did you find Betty Stanton in the water?"

"11:30."

Oscar leant on his elbows and tapped his fingers together.

"I may be going completely down the wrong track here, but I think he was giving himself an alibi."

CHAPTER SIXTEEN

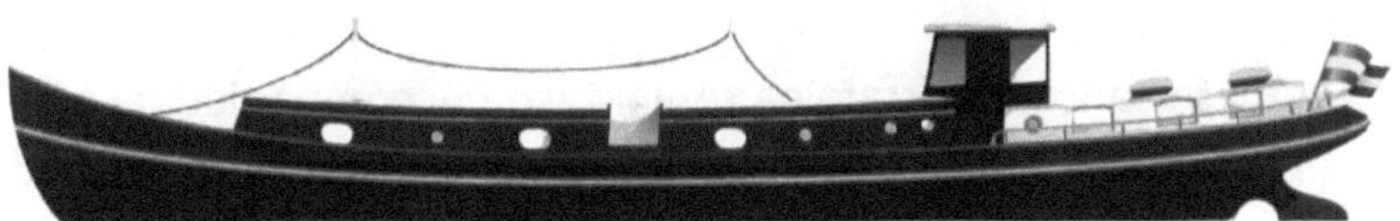

I shrugged. "You think Captain Salisbury was giving himself an alibi? For what?"

"Let me bounce this off you. You found Betty Stanton's body at 11:30. We don't know how long she'd been submerged, but maybe the marina has cameras, and we can find out? Harry Salisbury was very careful to let anyone know he wasn't home in the two hours beforehand. He'd left his barge door open, and you two arrived and knocked. So you could confirm he wasn't in at that point. Then, he asked you to study a supermarket receipt and specifically requested you note the time he was in the shop making his purchases. Again, you could tell anyone asking that you'd seen evidence placing him away from the marina in the hours before Betty Stanton's death. The chances are, he was constructing an alibi to prove he didn't kill Betty."

I sat back in my chair and blew out my cheeks.

Oscar set his lips straight. "Of course, this may be fanciful conjecture. The whole thing may be a coincidence."

I drummed my fingers on the table. "I remember you saying you don't like coincidences."

Oscar nodded. "You're right. I don't."

"Team, for once, our training tonight isn't accompanied by a presentation, so you're excused any delay caused by the stupid computer not working."

Murph stood at the front of the training room and addressed four of us; Emily, me, and two other recruits named Colin and Paul.

"First thing tonight," continued Murph, "we'll practice our knot tying. Can everyone do a bowline, a reef knot, a clove hitch, a sheet bend and a round turn with two half hitches? Those are the primary knots we use every day, and you should all be able to tie them with your eyes closed. Grab a rope each and demonstrate all of them to me."

"Why would we need to do them with our eyes closed?" I asked.

"Simple. Many of our operations take place at night. We can't have white lights on the boat; as you know, they destroy our night vision and make searching less effective. If you can tie a knot with your eyes shut, you can tie it in the dark. You'll be glad you practised one day."

We each picked up one of the long, black ropes lying on the table in front of Murph. I successfully tied a bowline and then tried again with my eyes closed, which resulted in a spaghetti-like muddle on the floor. Emily almost managed it, but then ended up with a slip knot.

Murph shook his head. "Take a rope each with you after training and practise at home. Next time we're on the boat, I expect you all to be perfect. The next item on tonight's agenda is to run step by step through the procedure if anyone's fallen off the boat, or if we discover someone in the water. Some of you've already experienced retrieving people for real, but we can always improve, and I don't think anyone's ready to be signed off on this exercise yet."

Emily and I shared a knowing smile.

"Okay, man overboard. We're motoring along, keeping watch as we always do, nothing too exciting's happening. I'm at the wheel, and you four are all behind me. One of you"—he pointed—"let's say Colin here, steps out on deck because he's feeling unwell. He leans over the side, and before anyone can stop him, he falls in. What's the first thing we do?"

"Call 'Man overboard'," I said.

"Anything else?" asked Murph.

"Say where the person is. So, 'Man overboard, starboard side'," for instance.

"Spot on. And, naturally, make sure the skipper's heard you. Now, what's the most important thing to do next? You cannot get this step wrong."

"Harness up," said Colin.

"Before that."

"Hit the MOB button," said Paul.

"The skipper or navigator should've done that as soon as they heard your call. If you"—he pointed at each of us in turn—"that's you crew on the aft deck, don't do what I'm thinking of, all the harnessing up and hitting buttons will be a waste of time. What is it? Anyone?"

"Point at the person," said Emily.

"Correct," said Murph. "At least one crew member, probably the one who originally called 'Man overboard' must keep their eyes on the casualty at all times and their arm outstretched in their direction. If you have two people available, even better. Right, we're at the point where the skipper's driving the boat towards the person in the water. For the sake of this run through, we'll assume they're conscious and yelling, 'Help! Help!' What's next?"

"Harness up," said Colin again.

"Yes. A crew member, but not the one keeping watch, should unpack the harness and clip it to their colleague. Next?"

"Open the boarding door," I said.

"No," said Murph. "Almost."

"Sorry. Request permission to open the boarding door."

"Right. Then once the skipper's granted permission, open the door and...?"

"Kneel," said Emily.

"Who kneels?"

"The person who's harnessed."

"Why them?"

"Because they'll be the one leaning out over the sea to grab the casualty, and we don't want them falling in the water and becoming a casualty as well."

"Perfect. And one other person helps them grab the person in the water to pull them on board. Is that everything?"

We all glanced at each other. "Pack the deck away, obviously," said Paul. "Close the boarding door, roll up the harness, and so on."

"Look after the casualty," said Emily. "Fetch towels and blankets to dry them and keep them warm."

"All of those," said Murph. "What else?"

Nobody spoke.

"Okay," said Murph. "Let's walk through everything you described. We tidy the deck, wrap the casualty in blankets and take him or her back to Redcliff. We reach the safety of the harbour, and the casualty turns to us and says, 'Where's my friend?' At that point, we realise we only rescued one person, and there's a second in trouble still out there."

Emily and I met eyes. I bit my lip.

"Communication's vital," said Murph. "With your skipper, with your colleagues, with the casualty and with Coastguard Headland Bay. Keep everybody updated all the time. Next time we're out on the boat, we'll run through the exercise again with the rescue dummy. Has everyone understood?"

We all nodded.

"Lastly, tonight," said Murph, "let's discuss giving a safety induction. When members of the public board our vessel, their visit may be either planned or unplanned and, in both cases, we need to ensure they're safe while in our care. Everybody on the vessel from the skipper to the most junior trainee knows more than any visitor about safety on board, and we all need to understand the correct way to share that knowledge."

Emily raised her hand. "Would we give a safety briefing to young children?"

"Depending on their age, children on board might not receive the formal safety briefing an adult would, but they still need to know how to behave and where the dangers are. If they're very young, 'Sit down and don't touch anything,' might suffice. Right. The first question's easy. What's the biggest danger for anyone on board our vessel?"

"Falling in the water," I said.

"Correct. What do we do to stop a visitor to our vessel falling overboard?"

"Ask them to remain sitting in the cabin."

"Excellent. And what would we give them to wear?"

"A life jacket, with a Personal Locater Beacon in it."

"Right. Any other hazards on board? How do we tell them to move around the vessel if they need to?"

"Three points of contact," said Paul.

"Does everyone understand what three points of contact means?" asked Murph. "Two feet and one hand, or two hands and one foot touching the boat at all times. What else?"

"Tell them to mind their heads when entering the cabin, and not to touch anything," I said.

"Yes," said Murph, "and the last thing? The big catch-all?"

I shrugged. Emily pursed her lips. Paul and Colin shook their heads.

"We're in charge," said Murph. "They do what we say. It doesn't matter if you're the newest recruit and the visitor's a naval rear-admiral. They follow our instructions when they're on our vessel. It's for their own safety. All right, everyone. That's all for tonight. We'll practice man overboard and safety briefings next time we're on board. For anyone who's on duty, see you at the weekend."

I was helping Emily bring in the Wicked Whelk signs the following day when Oscar turned up outside the café with Cadbury. Unusually, he appeared older than his seventy years, and his face seemed to slump. Bags had formed under his eyes.

"Good afternoon, ladies," he said. "I was hoping to catch both of you. D'you have a moment?"

"Of course," said Emily. "Pop in for a cup of tea. The customers have gone, so Cadbury can come in too."

"Is everything all right, Oscar?" I asked. "You don't seem your usual lively self."

"Everything is not all right," he said, mysteriously. "I'll tell you when we're all sitting down."

"Earl Grey?" asked Emily once we'd gathered inside.

"Yes, please. And then I'll share my news." Oscar removed Cadbury's lead, and the dog settled in the corner. I sat opposite Oscar and stared at him until I could stand it no longer.

"Spill the beans, Oscar," I said. "You look exhausted. What've you been up to?"

Emily placed mugs of tea and a plate of gooey chocolate cakes between us and sat opposite.

Oscar cleared his throat and glanced at both of us in turn. "Yesterday, after we'd discussed your finding of Betty Stanton's body, and what I believed was Captain Salisbury creating an alibi for himself, I couldn't sleep for turning events over in my mind. You know how problems always magnify themselves at 2:00 a.m. when you're lying awake?"

"Tell me about it," said Emily. "The number of times I've opened the café absolutely exhausted because I've spent half the night worrying I'd left the coffee machine switched on."

I frowned at her. "Why wouldn't you simply walk downstairs and check, so you could go back to sleep?"

"Because Boots sleeps on my bed, and I don't want to disturb him."

"Right. Do go on, Oscar."

"Last night, I tossed and turned, trying to piece everything together. Betty Stanton and Captain Salisbury had only met the previous day at the vicarage egg hunt. She came to see him, and he was out because he'd made a mistake with the arrangements. Then she drowns. How did she enter the water? And why was Captain Salisbury insistent you read the time on the supermarket receipt?"

He paused and sipped his tea.

"I wanted someone to bounce ideas off, like we three do when confronted with something which doesn't make sense, but I couldn't very well knock on your door in the middle of the night, could I?"

I laughed. "Emily might've been awake, worrying about her coffee machine."

"Nope," said Emily. "Last night I slept like a log."

"I didn't," said Oscar. "More like a tree blowing in a gale. I needed to talk to someone before my head overflowed with theories. So I rang Brighthaven police station and, as luck would have it, Martin Buchanan was on duty."

"Did he remember you?" I asked.

Oscar puffed. "Of course he did. He was overjoyed to hear from me again and, once he'd recovered from the surprise of my call in the middle of the night, we spent some time reacquainting ourselves and reminiscing about old times and notable cases we'd worked on. Then I asked him the question which I'd intended to all along. The real reason for my call. I asked if he would tell me anything about the Brighthaven Marina drowning."

I paused with my cup halfway to my lips. "Would he be allowed to divulge anything about that to you?" I asked.

"Strictly, no, but I can be very persuasive. Especially at 2:30 on a quiet Wednesday morning, when the police have nothing else to do."

"What did you find out?"

"He corrected me. He said it wasn't the Brighthaven Marina drowning, because Betty didn't die by drowning."

"Really? But we pulled her out."

"I said she didn't drown. Not that she didn't enter the water."

"Ooh," said Emily. "Are you intimating…?"

"I knew Inspector Buchanan was withholding something. And I also believed he desperately wanted to confide in me; to ask my opinion. So I told him to pretend we were in the old days again, when he used to consult me about any case he was working on. I think by this stage he may have chosen to ignore the fact I'm no longer a serving officer, so I asked him if he suspected foul play. Perhaps he was going to tell me he'd found security camera footage showing she'd been pushed, or similar?"

"You were looking to disprove Captain Salisbury's alibi, weren't you?"

"Yes, although I hadn't yet told Inspector Buchanan about the matter with the receipt. Imagine my surprise when he finally divulged the real cause of her death."

"Which was…?" I prompted.

"Betty didn't drown. She would've been dead by the time she entered the water. Betty died from a severed *medulla oblongata*."

"Speak English, Oscar," said Emily. "What's one of those?"

"The *medulla oblongata* is the connection between the brain and the spinal cord. It's essential for staying alive. Without it, your brain and your body can't communicate. And here's how it became severed."

He paused and leant forward.

"Somebody had stabbed her in the base of her skull."

CHAPTER SEVENTEEN

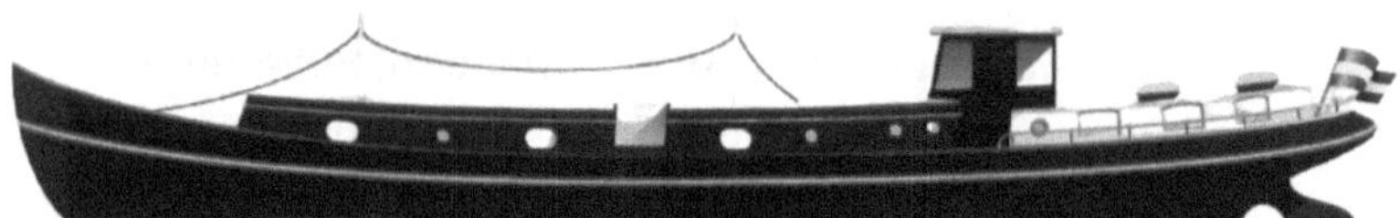

"Betty Stanton was stabbed?" I asked. "We didn't notice any injuries when we pulled her out, did we, Emily?"

"No, but we only saw her from the front." Emily stuttered and her voice cracked. "This is unbelievable. Why would anyone do that to a woman like her? I know she rubbed people up the wrong way, but no one goes around stabbing people because they've been rude. D'you think it might've been a mugging gone wrong?"

"Unlikely," said Oscar. "Victims of knifepoint muggings are usually stabbed in the front, the chest or the stomach for instance. Not in the base of the skull."

"Wow. Did your policeman friend disclose any other details?"

"No. He probably realised he'd told me too much. I mentioned that I knew both of you, and I'd ask you whether you had any other pertinent information. He seemed grateful for the support. His station's understaffed, and I think he's working too many hours. But he wouldn't give anything else away."

"It would've been hard for you to sleep after discovering that."

"Indeed. I lay down and tried to rest, but I was more awake than ever. And something red flagged in my mind. I'm a fan of a military thriller writer called Blair Stryker, an ex-special forces soldier. And I recalled a passage about that method of killing in one of his books. But d'you think I could remember which one? I climbed out of bed again, walked downstairs for the second time and began to search through my library. Blair Stryker wrote a lot of books, and I own them all. I stayed up all night poring through them until my wife came downstairs to make her morning tea at seven o'clock and found me asleep with my head on the dining-room table."

"Goodness. No wonder you look exhausted. But did you find the reference you were looking for?"

"I did, finally. In his book *Kill Patrol*, Blair Stryker describes that type of stabbing as being peculiar to soldiers, specifically special forces operatives. Let me read an extract to you."

Oscar tugged a paperback from his pocket and opened it at a bookmarked page. He ran his finger down the text and read aloud. "Vince sat at the locker room table, and the rookies faced him. 'If you need a silent kill,' he said, 'you creep up from behind and stick your blade in the indent at the base of your enemy's skull where the bone's thinnest. Then you slam upward at a 45-degree angle. You'll scramble his *medulla oblongata* and cut off his motor senses immediately. Dead before he hits the ground, and no one knows.' Vince's cold, dark eyes met those of his students, and none was in any doubt he'd committed this act many times himself."

"He's writing about special forces like the SAS?" I asked.

"Correct. Or the Navy Seals."

"Harry Salisbury was in the navy," said Emily.

"Exactly." Oscar nodded. "I think we may have blown his alibi out of the water, to coin a phrase."

Emily grimaced. "This seems too obvious. Betty Stanton wanted Harry Salisbury to speak at her Women's Institute meeting and pressured him to do so. We heard her, Shiraz. She wasn't going to take 'no' for an answer. The following day, she came to visit him to discuss her desired contents of the speech. He became angry with her forcefulness, stabbed her in the back of the skull using his navy seal training like in Oscar's book and threw her in the water. Then he attempted to construct an alibi with the supermarket receipt which placed him elsewhere at the time. It's all too open-and-shut, as they say in detective novels."

I shook my head. "Really, Emily. She wasn't the most pleasant person, but I can't imagine anyone murdering someone simply because they didn't want to make a speech."

"They might do," said Emily. Her voice hardened. "I'm petrified by the thought of public speaking. It's my biggest fear."

"So will Inspector Buchanan arrest Harry Salisbury?" I asked Oscar.

"I'm sure he'll interview him further. He'll probably want to talk with you again too." He put down his cup. "I don't suppose, Shiraz, you have one of those giant pieces of paper we've used in the past to do mind maps, have you?"

"No. Why? Do you want to help Inspector Buchanan like the old days? This murder doesn't involve Emily and me, right?"

"If you discovered the body, and you're going to be interviewed by the police, you're already involved. We should at least make sure there's nothing we've missed which could help him. And nothing which incriminates you."

I sighed, removed the band around my ponytail, ran my fingers through my hair and tied it up again. "Are we really getting into another investigation?" I asked. "A fourth one?"

"This is becoming ridiculous," said Emily. "Almost normal. I'm struggling to remember a time when we weren't putting our heads together trying to pin evidence on someone, or prevent the wrong person being arrested. Actually, I can remember a time. Last year, before you turned up in Redcliff, Shiraz."

"Hey, it's not me strolling around picking off the local population. D'you want me to return to London? Because I'm not going."

"Don't be silly. I'm just not sure if this is really my thing."

"Regardless of whether it's really your thing," said Oscar, "let's at least do this initial exercise. I wish we had a big piece of paper to make notes."

"What about that roll of paper you use?" I asked Emily. "Butcher's paper, you call it."

Emily huffed and stood. "Okay. I'll fetch it. Could you clear the table?"

While we relocated cups and plates, Emily departed to the rear of the café and returned with a long white tube. She laid it at one end of our table and unrolled it. I repurposed crockery to hold the corners down and, within a minute, we had a beautifully flat, white sheet.

"Now we need something to write with," I said. "A ball-point pen will go straight through. D'you have any black markers, Emily?"

"I have chalk which I use to write the blackboard menu. Is that any good?"

"Better than nothing," said Oscar, rubbing his hands together. "This'll be fun."

I rolled my eyes as his earlier tiredness evaporated. Emily returned with the chalk.

"It's been a while since we've done this," I said, "but I recall we draw a circle in the centre with the deceased person's initials."

"Well remembered," said Oscar. "Emily, would you be scribe?"

Emily drew a circle in purple chalk with the letters 'BS' for Betty Stanton.

"Now we draw more circles around it with the initials of the primary suspects?"

"Correct. Who are our primary suspects?"

"Harry Salisbury," said Emily. "No one else." She drew a circle and wrote 'HS' in it. "Finished. One suspect. One victim. One answer. Case closed."

"Not so fast," said Oscar. "Shiraz, recount what happened at the vicarage? I have a suspicion there may be clues hiding in that little rendezvous. Recap all the way back to when you were invited to the Easter egg hunt."

"Really?"

"Yes. We can dismiss ideas once we've reviewed them."

"Okay. We rescued the two children and returned them to the beach where their mother, Chloe, was waiting with her baby. We left the kids with her and departed in the rescue boat with Murph and our colleague Jules. The following day, Emily, Jules and I went to the vicarage and paid to enter. We collected a cream tea from the volunteers on the refreshments stall, one of whom must've been your wife."

"Yes, although she told me she spent the entire afternoon in the vicarage kitchen washing up. But do go on."

"We sat at a trestle table opposite Chloe Evans. She introduced us to her partner, who was called Lance. He spent most of his time engrossed in his mobile phone and didn't engage with us. In fact, I'm sure he didn't speak to anyone else on the table. Certainly not Betty Stanton. He looks like a soldier, I suppose. He has a military-style moustache and tattoos, for instance, but I can't think of any motive he would have had to kill Betty."

"Write down Lance. We'll give people scores later; that'll be the next part of the process. Go on, Shiraz. Who else was there?"

"Sister Florrie. We heard her before we met her."

"She has a booming voice, hasn't she? Did she give you a hug?"

"She just about crushed the life out of me."

"Do I write her down too?" asked Emily. "It's probably not PC to suspect the vicar."

"Oh, I don't know," said Oscar. "I believe Agatha Christie wrote at least two books where the vicar was among the accused. Add her to the list for now. She knew Betty Stanton well, and I don't think Betty liked her. Mind you, I don't think Betty liked anyone much, and the feelings were mutual. Did you see Sister Marie too?"

"Yes," said Emily, "although she stayed in the background. They're an interesting pair, those two."

"The comedienne and the straight woman," I said. "Add both to your list, Emily. We can't add one vicar without the other."

"I can't believe I'm noting down the names of vicars as murder suspects," said Emily. "Others at the table were far more likely."

"Such as...?" said Oscar, leaning forward.

"The churchwarden, Jack Walter," I said. "All he talked about was money, or the lack of it, and how much the church needed. And Betty said she was leaving money to All Saints in her will."

"I've solved it," said Emily. "The church is desperate for money to repair the boilers. Jack Walter knew Betty Stanton had left All Saints Church a substantial bequest in her will, so he killed her to, as it were, release the funds early. Case closed."

"I know Jack," said Oscar. "Not the most cheerful fellow, but he's been dedicated to All Saints forever. I can't imagine him being a murderer. Anyone else?"

"Not at the table yesterday."

"Okay, now let's ponder further on Betty's background. What do we know about her? I'll start. And this may be a vital lead. She had a somewhat estranged son."

"I think," said Emily, "if I was her son, I'd make myself somewhat estranged too."

"Yes." Oscar laughed. "I can't remember his name. Roger or Roland? Something beginning with 'R'. He moved a long way away from here, probably as soon as he was old enough to escape her clutches."

"Is he with the military?" I asked.

"Possibly. I'm not sure how we'd find out. Write him down, and we'll investigate further."

"What about Betty's husband?"

"He passed away decades ago. Unkind people might say he died with some relief."

"Next item we know about Betty," I said. "She was chair of the Women's Institute."

"I know, the deputy chairperson wanted her job, and killed her so they could step into her shoes?" suggested Emily.

"We're not ruling out anything yet," said Oscar. "Write down 'colleagues at the Women's Institute'. Although the manner of her death doesn't suggest that anyone of their demographic would've killed her. Most are in their eighties. She was also a regular churchgoer. Again, much of the congregation's retired and unlikely to be capable of murder in the manner Inspector Buchanan described. Anything else about Betty?"

"She wrote a book," I said.

"It doesn't sound like a very good book," said Emily. *"Uncommon Household Articles of the Middle East.* How boring. Not a story I'd curl up on the sofa with."

"I suppose something about her book might've caused someone to kill her," said Oscar. "The Middle East's a volatile place. Perhaps she inadvertently insulted a religion, like that writer Salman Rushdie did? Note down 'Middle East connection.' Anything else we know about Betty, or is that all?"

We glanced at each other. I shook my head.

"Let's draw circles now," said Oscar. "Out of everyone on our list, who could be a primary suspect?"

I pointed at the names. "The most likely murderer's still Harry Salisbury, simply because of the location of her death and his military past."

"Yes, but we can't have only one suspect. Put aside your personal opinions about people and look at the facts. Who knew the victim? Who was closest to them at the time of their death? Emily, I think you should draw circles for three primary suspects and three secondary suspects, or sets of suspects."

"Really?" Emily poised with the chalk.

"Yes. Harry Salisbury is definitely a primary suspect. Jack Walter should be too, with your theory about Betty's will. Betty's son as well; he's her only family to my knowledge, and therefore potentially a beneficiary of her estate. Then add secondary circles for colleagues at the WI and one for people at the church, including the vicars. I'll ask my wife if there was anyone there specifically who had a reason to murder her."

He laughed once. "I expect her response will be that everyone did. The final circle should have 'book' in it for now. We'll come back to that."

Emily drew while we watched.

Oscar sat forward and looked at our diagram.

"Most of these suspects seem to have the most tenuous connections to Betty's death," said Emily. "Several of them couldn't have killed her in the way you believe she died. And what about Lance Evans?"

"He'll be an outlier for now. Trust me on this, Emily. Even if the people we're naming aren't viable suspects, their inclusion might help us unravel more concrete clues. Now, continue your recap of what happened at the vicarage, Shiraz."

"Okay. Sister Florrie kicked off the Easter egg hunt, and the shrubbery thronged with kids, including the two we'd rescued, Hunter and Gracie. The eggs were hidden under bushes, in the crooks of tree branches and in the long grass. Sister Florrie gave the under eights a head start, and we began chatting with Chloe Evans. She told me Lance runs an import export business. That's the reason they were in Redcliff."

"Import export business dealings over Easter weekend? Seems odd."

"You're being too suspicious, Oscar. They might've tacked a few days holiday onto their business trip."

"Hmm. I'll give them the benefit of the doubt for now."

"Then Sister Florrie announced the older children could start hunting and, once they'd begun, she marched over to our table and introduced us to the people at the other end of it: Betty Stanton, Harry Salisbury and Jack Walter."

"Can you recall anything else about any of them? Think hard, Shiraz. Recreate the scene in your mind."

I rubbed my temples. "I am thinking. Betty seemed very snooty. She made some comment to Sister Florrie about how she wouldn't know much about fashion, which wasn't very pleasant. Although, she mistook the location of a London store, which pricked my ears up. It's probably nothing."

"I doubt she visited stores in London often," said Oscar. "But she'd have liked everyone to think she did."

I laughed. "Got it. Jack Walter grumbled about money to repair the church. He seems to know a lot about historic buildings; he said the vicarage barn was probably one of the oldest buildings in Redcliff."

"He's not wrong," said Oscar. "Hundreds of years ago, it was a tithe barn."

"Yes," I said. "Jack Walter explained the arrangement; in the old days the vicar took ten per cent of the crop and stored it there."

"The council does the same these days," said Emily. "I'll have to increase my prices again this year; the rates have gone up so much. You're the acting mayor, Oscar. Can't you do something?"

Oscar shook his head once. "That, I think, is a conversation for another day. Back to the Easter egg hunt, please."

"Right. We met Harry Salisbury. He told us about his barge conversion business, and how he lived on one at Brighthaven Marina. He also mentioned his hobby was local maritime history. This was the only conversation between him and Betty which we overheard, though they were talking before we turned up. She invited him to speak to the Women's Institute."

"Invited?" said Emily. "More like demanded."

"Yes. She was very persuasive, forceful even, and she set a date for his speech, next Thursday at 3:00 p.m. She told him she'd be in Brighthaven the following day to meet a magazine editor for lunch, and she'd drop by his barge at 10:00 a.m. to discuss the content of his presentation, but they never spoke. We know that, because Harry was at the supermarket."

Oscar rocked his head from side to side. "Maybe he was; maybe he wasn't. We'll come back to clues later. Add 'Magazine Editor' as an outlier. Did anything else happen?"

"Yes," said Emily. "As I mentioned when I saw you on Sunday, the kids went missing. Captain Salisbury organised us into two search parties."

"Everyone there?"

"Not Betty Stanton or Jack Walter," I said. "They made their excuses and departed. We three marine rescue volunteers, Sister Florrie, some other ladies and Captain Salisbury performed the search. He split us into groups, and Jules and I searched the shrubbery, then the outbuildings. For some reason, Harry dissuaded us from searching in the barn, and Jack Walter had the only key, anyway. Jules poked her head under the doors and shouted, but there was no response. In the middle of the search, Jules' pager went off, and she rushed to the Marine Rescue Station. We were about to give up when I discovered those hidden steps which led to a cellar under the vicarage. The children weren't in there either, although we found the little girl's doll, which was odd. Then Jules rang me from the boat. She said they'd found them on the beach at Smuggler's Cove, below the vicarage."

"Their parents must've been very relieved."

"Yes, and Chloe gave them a good telling off. But I don't think this helps with our murder hunt."

Oscar squeezed his eyes closed, then opened them again. "You mentioned the names of the searchers. What about the kids' parents? Surely they would've been frantically hunting too?"

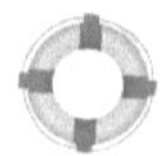

CHAPTER EIGHTEEN

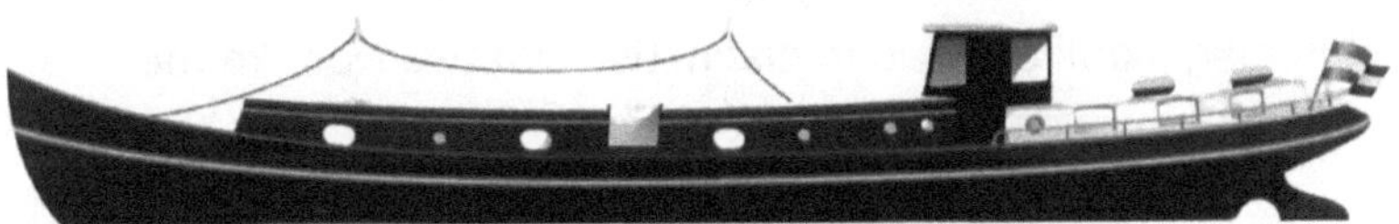

I finished off my drink and cake. "We agreed Chloe Evans would stay at the table where we ate the cream tea. Mainly in case the kids came back, but also because she had the baby to look after."

"A good plan," said Oscar. "Home base is often forgotten when looking for a missing person, and the searchers return to discover they've been at their house all along. And what about her partner? Lance?"

"That's a point," said Emily. "Where was Lance during the search?"

"He wasn't involved," I said. "The next time I saw him was when Murph drove up with the kids in his truck. He approached from the direction of the barn."

"Why would he leave when his kids were missing?" asked Oscar. "Write that down somewhere, Emily. I want to return to that later."

Emily began a list on another part of the paper headed 'clues'. She wrote: 'Lance Evans whereabouts during search'.

"Now we're listing clues," said Emily, "what about the dolls?"

"What dolls?" asked Oscar. "You said the girl had a doll."

"When we rescued the kids," I explained, "the girl was clutching a doll dressed in distinctive clothes. Not like the standard Barbies you buy in toy shops."

"I wouldn't know," said Oscar. "My boys weren't into dolls."

"And, as I mentioned, when we found the cellar under the house, the little girl's doll was lying on the floor. I picked it up thinking the kids must've been in the cellar at some point, and I gave it to her mother. But when Murph turned up with the children, Emily's sure Gracie was clutching her doll then."

"She was," said Emily. "I'm certain."

Oscar rubbed his chin. "And you told me you saw the same type of doll on Captain Salisbury's barge. What's going on with all these dolls?"

"All I can think is, there's a toyshop sale on," I said. "But we're drifting away from the point of our discussion. Dolls won't help us catch Betty's murderer, will they?"

"Probably not," said Oscar. "But Lance Evans needs his own circle. Although we can't see any connection between him and Betty, suspects often give themselves away by doing something unexpected. In this case, disappearing and not joining in with the hunt while his kids were missing."

"He could've simply been looking for them elsewhere," I suggested. "Maybe he was looking in the barn? He's quite slim; perhaps he was able to slither under the doors. The bottoms of them are very rotten."

"Surely he would've told you, or told Harry Salisbury, who you say was organising the search?" Oscar sat up straight and tapped the sheet of paper. "Emily, draw a new primary suspect circle. Put 'LE' in it."

"Are you sure?" I asked. "I don't think he said a word to Betty Stanton, and he only arrived in Redcliff a few days previously, so he didn't know her."

"We'll rule people out later. Include him for now. Okay, let's give everyone a score. First, Harry Salisbury. I say give him a nine out of ten."

"Yes," said Emily. "In my opinion, he's the only viable suspect. I'll give him ten."

"No. Then the case really would be closed," said Oscar. "Ten indicates they're definitely the murderer. I agree, though, he seems to earn the highest score. Next, Jack Walter."

"Five?" I suggested. "Your theory about Betty's will might've been spot on. She intimated she liked to spend money on nice clothes and jewellery and, although she'd left money to the church, there might not have been much of it left by the time she died. But the method of the killing was military. Was Jack in the forces?"

"He might be old enough to have been conscripted, I suppose. National Service in Britain ended in 1963. I'll see if I can discover if he served."

"Five for Jack. Then the son. Roland, you said his name was?"

"Something beginning with R. Call him Roland for now. Presumably he'll make an appearance at the funeral and deal with clearing out Betty's house. I'll make discreet enquiries to find out his background."

Emily wrote 'RS' in a circle. "If you discover he's some kind of army chap," she said, "he'll get nine too."

"Give him five," said Oscar, "until we know more about him. Now for the secondary suspects."

"One for the Women's Institute, the church and the book connection," said Emily. "Even including them on this sheet's ridiculous. How would retired people or a pair of vicars in their sixties enact a special forces-style killing? And we know nothing about her book. I'm not even sure where we'd find a copy."

Oscar tapped the table. "You told me Betty Stanton and Sister Florrie had words at the Easter egg hunt."

"Betty Stanton had words with everyone. If being on the end of her invective makes people suspects, you may as well include half the town."

"We'll give them one," said Oscar. "I agree it's strange adding them, but sometimes, having low-scoring suspects jogs a memory which leads to the real murderer. Finally, Lance Evans. I want to give him a fairly high score. Seven, perhaps. At least until we've cleared up the mystery of his whereabouts while his children were missing."

"Plus he has the air of a military man," I said. "The crewcut hair, the style of moustache, the tattoos. I could imagine him being a fighter pilot. There was an actor in *Top Gun* who resembled him."

Emily wrote '7' next to Lance's circle.

Oscar slit his eyes. "This business he's in Redcliff for; import export? That's a vague term that covers multiple activities. I think there's more to him than meets the eye."

"You're suspicious of everyone, aren't you?"

"If they behave in unusual ways, that definitely raises my hackles. Now, is there anything else you can think of? Anything that didn't seem right? Anything at all?"

"The doll," I said. "I keep going back to it. I found it on the floor in the cellar. Even if there was a sale of dolls going on, why would Gracie's doll have been there?"

"Hunter told us they found a secret staircase and a secret room too," said Emily.

"That boy told a lot of stories. He said there were sea monsters. And that he found a million Easter eggs. And that he has a friend who can do the Rubik's cube in eight seconds. His mum said he exaggerates everything."

Emily pursed her lips. "I think he was talking about the steps you found down to the cellar. The cellar was his secret room. And he also said there was a hole in the floor. Did you see an opening?"

"No. Did he tell you he saw werewolves in there too?"

"Why aren't you taking me seriously? You found the girl's doll in the cellar, down a staircase which was hidden behind a bush. The boy said he found a secret room down a staircase. I think they're one and the same. I think the kids were there, and Gracie dropped her doll."

"That doesn't explain the hole. There was nothing in that cellar; just the bare, whitewashed walls. And you saw her with the doll later."

Oscar wrinkled his lips. "We need more information. I'll contact Inspector Buchanan again and hope he divulges more information. CCTV evidence from the marina, for instance. I'll rack my brains as to who would know about Betty's son and do some digging about Jack Walter. My wife knows him through the church. Would you two have another look at the vicarage?"

"Why? If we're really going to do any investigating, shouldn't we start where the murder happened?"

"Divide and conquer, Shiraz. I believe there are two places where we might narrow down why Betty was killed and by whom. The police will be investigating the first; the murder scene, and I'll provide Inspector Buchanan with, shall we call it, consultancy? The vicarage is the second place, where it seems Betty Stanton and Captain Salisbury met. The catalyst point, if, as we believe, our most likely suspect killed her."

"And how will we find any evidence there?" asked Emily. "Walk up to the vicarage, ring the bell, and when Sister Florrie answers, say, 'Hello, may we sniff around in your outbuildings, because something concealed in there may pertain to a murder fifty miles away in Brighthaven?' We've listed the vicars as suspects. In the unlikely event they're guilty, they'll know we're on to them."

"They're not at home this week, anyway," said Oscar. "Every year, they go on a religious retreat for two weeks directly after Easter. Jack Walter keeps an eye on the vicarage because of the antiques, but he's not there all the time. I wish he were.

Then that burglary would never have happened. You'll have to wait until they return."

"Why, Shiraz, did we have to come here so late in the evening?"

"In case Jack Walter's snooping around, guarding the place."

"We're the ones snooping around. He has every right to be here. We don't. Oscar told us to wait until the vicars came back from their trip next week."

"All we'll do is take a quick look in the cellar, confirm there's nothing in there, check for any holes in the floor, or hidden passages, or anything, then leave. We'll be five minutes, maximum. It's almost dark. We'd better hurry. Come on."

We speed-walked up the vicarage driveway and reached the five-bar gate at the top, which was bolted and locked.

"Are we going to climb over?" asked Emily.

"Yep. I'm glad I wore sensible shoes."

Emily glanced at her feet. "I only own sensible shoes," she said. "Why do I feel like a burglar?"

"We're not burglars, Emily. Burglars steal things. We're only having a look."

"I don't like this. How will we explain ourselves if we see Jack Walter?"

"We can say I dropped an earring at the Easter egg hunt, and we were looking for it in the vicarage garden."

"In the dark?"

"It's not quite dark yet. Let's go."

We jumped down the other side of the gate, and something clinked on the gravel.

"What's that?" I asked. "It fell out of your coat."

Emily picked up the object. "Oh. It's a blade for my food processor. I bought it from the wholesaler's yesterday, but I forgot it was in my pocket." She replaced it inside her jacket.

The gravel crunched as we approached the vicarage.

"If anyone's home, they'll hear us," I said. "Scrunch as quietly as you can."

Emily giggled, and we tiptoed across the front yard. Dusk was well advanced, and the first stars pinpointed the sky above the horizon.

"Here's the bush." I pushed the foliage apart, and we stood poised at the top of the steps.

"We'll break our necks descending these in the dark," said Emily. "I'll shine my phone torch."

"Don't attract attention. Feel your way down."

Emily descended, her left foot then her right foot groping for each stair.

"How many steps are there? I don't know if I'm at the bottom."

"You'll have to keep stepping gingerly. I'll grab your coat hood so you don't fall."

"We'll be arrested for breaking and entering. We should never have come."

"Nobody is going to be arrested. We haven't broken anything."

"We're entering somewhere."

"I'll think of an excuse. You know me; I always do."

"You always get us into trouble. Okay, that's the last step. I counted, and there are twelve. Now what?"

"Pull the door until we can enter the cellars."

A painfully loud scraping sound came from below me.

"Someone will definitely come when they hear that," said Emily. "What if Jack Walter checks the place before dark?"

"No one's here. Give it a good tug."

I clenched my teeth at a longer, louder scraping noise, followed by the sound of Emily panting.

"It's open. Where are you? You'd better be right behind me. Spiders and bats come out after dark."

"Now we're inside, turn on your phone torch and shine it into your palm. Like we were taught on night training. So you don't blind anyone."

"Okay." She fumbled in her pocket for her phone, and the glow of the screen lit up her hand. She exposed a slither of light and shone it around the room.

"At least you can see there are no spiders or bats here. There's nothing in here at all."

"Good." She concealed the light again. "Let's go, before Jack Walter catches us."

"Hang on. Wait." I turned on my own phone torch, and the whitewashed walls reflected the stark, bleached light.

I shone it at the floor.

"Emily, were these footprints here before?"

CHAPTER NINETEEN

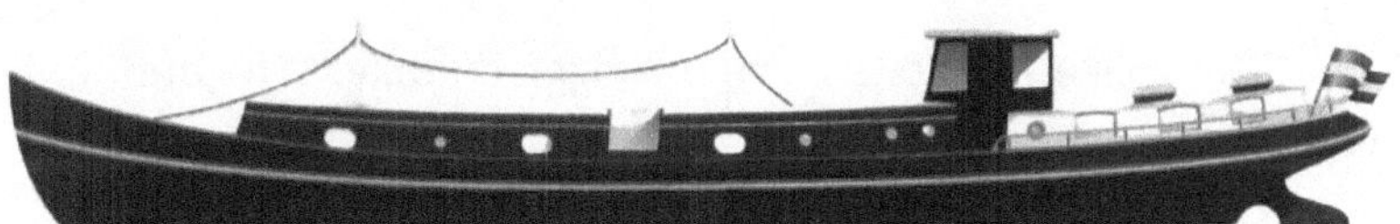

"Emily, look. Footprints, in the dust on the floor."

"Are they? They're very faint." She smacked her forehead. "D'you know whose these are, Shiraz? These are our own footprints from when we were here before. There's nothing else in the room. Let's go, before the spiders come out. And Jack Walter finds us."

"Not so fast." I frowned and studied the patterns on the floor. "What shoes were you wearing on Saturday?"

"Sneakers. Same as now."

"Put your foot next to this print."

She placed her sneaker alongside the faint outline.

I inspected where she stood. "These prints are miles bigger than yours."

"They must be yours, then."

"Cheeky. My feet aren't that large. And I was wearing Gucci shoes with a heel during the egg hunt. These have a distinctive criss-cross pattern, like a hill walking boot, or maybe a boot a workman would wear. Like Timberlands or Caterpillars." I shone the torch around and crouched down to the floor.

"Two people were here. They both wore similar boots, but these two prints have a slightly different pattern."

"This is like *The Lone Ranger*," giggled Emily. "The buffalo went this way."

"Right. Except there were two buffaloes. And there's a patch in the middle of the floor with no footmarks. That's odd."

I swept my hand across the dirt in the torchlight.

"Eek! A bat. Something touched my hair." Emily screamed and her phone dropped in front of me with a hollow clunk.

"There are no bats." I shone my torch at the ceiling. "You're imagining things." I picked up her phone and passed it to her then tapped twice where it had fallen. "The floor sounds hollow here. Hunter said there was a hole in the floor." I rapped on the floor again, and it made a sound like knocking on a wooden wardrobe.

Emily crouched with me and thumped with her fist. "It does sound hollow," she said.

I swept the dust away and uncovered a rectangular shape the size of a manhole. "How are we going to open it?" I asked.

"More to the point, why are we going to open it? You said we'd be in and out quickly."

"Yes, but we promised Oscar we'd make sure there were no clues. And this is a big fat one staring right at us."

"How would a trapdoor in the floor of the vicarage cellar be in any way related to a military-style murder fifty miles away?"

"We won't know until we investigate. Pass me that food processor blade you brought."

"Why?"

"You'll see. I'll buy you another one if we damage it."

She handed me the tool, and I slid it into a thin gap around the edge of the trapdoor. I tried to lever it open, but nothing budged.

"Any ideas, Emily?"

"Give up and go home?"

"Ideas of how to open this trapdoor?"

"Slide the blade around all four sides and see if you can find a weak spot?"

"Okay." I outlined a rectangle with the blade. The trapdoor shifted minutely to the side.

"The blade slips in further here," I said, wiggling it. "I'll use it as a lever. Would you be ready to grab the trapdoor if it opens an inch?"

"Okay. But if we open it, we're looking down it quickly and replacing it. We're not going to climb into the hole or anything. Agreed?"

"Agreed. We'll see what's under this cellar, then replace the trap door and leave. Unless it's crammed full of dead bodies."

"If it's crammed full of dead bodies, we're definitely leaving. And we're telling the police. Understood?"

"Understood." I pressed on the blade. "Although, as we're not supposed to be here…Emily, it's opening. Get ready to stick your fingers in the gap. Here it comes. And… now!"

"Oww. Quick. My fingers are jammed. Help."

I dropped the processor blade and shoved my hand in the gap beside Emily's. The heavy trapdoor shifted open until I could place my palms against its underside. It flipped back with a CRASH, and Emily waved her hand in the air and sucked her fingers.

"*Voila*!" I said. "One hole in the floor, exactly as reported by Hunter."

"Four squashed fingers," said Emily, squeezing her eyes closed and clenching her teeth. "Exactly as reported by me."

"Sorry. Are you okay? Look in here." I shone my torch into a shaft with a metal ladder clamped to one side of it. At the bottom of the ladder, a passageway with rock sides disappeared into the darkness.

"Are you coming?" I asked.

"Shiraz, I told you, there is absolutely no way I'm going down that hole. We don't know what we'll find down there; we'll be stuck forever and there'll be all sorts of creepy-crawlies. If you want to jump down, go ahead. I'm going home. Call me when you need rescuing. No, don't. I won't be entering there to pull you out. Ever."

"What was that?" I said.

"What?"

"It sounded like an engine. Switch off your torch."

We both switched our lights off and crouched silently above the hole in the floor. Tyres crunched across the vicarage driveway above us, and a deep engine rattled. The noise stopped.

"It's Jack Walter," whispered Emily. "Or the vicars have come home early. Now what do we do? We're in so much trouble. I don't want to go to prison."

"Ssh. No one knows we're here. Stay quiet until whoever it is leaves."

We heard indistinct voices. Then we froze as someone rustled the bushes above us, and a light played on the door to the cellar.

"They're coming this way, Shiraz. What do we do?"

"Wait. Ssh."

Footsteps clumped down the steps, and the torchlight found the whitewashed walls of the room.

Emily grabbed my arm. "There's nowhere to hide," she said. "We're done for."

"No, we're not." I swung my legs into the hole, and my feet found the top rung of the ladder. "Down here. Quick. Follow me."

The torchlight paused, and we heard a man's voice, although we couldn't decipher the words.

"Are you coming, or not?" I asked, as I stuffed my phone into my pocket and groped my way down the ladder. The metal felt cold and rough to the touch.

I reached the bottom and shone the phone up. "There are no spiders here. Quick. Do what I did."

I watched the white soles of Emily's sneakers descend the rungs one by one. She joined me at the bottom, while I kept my phone light shaded by my palm.

"Oh, no," she said, glancing upwards. "We left the hatch open."

We both watched as whoever had come down the cellar steps shone their torch directly at the shaft we'd climbed down.

"Come on," I said. "This way."

We stumbled along a low, narrow passageway, where walls had been hewn directly from solid rock. I ducked my head as my torch revealed the uneven roof, with protrusions which could've given a nasty knock. Emily, fortunately, cleared all the obstacles. The tunnel wound on, and I wasn't sure in which direction we were heading.

"We're descending," I said, as we quick-marched. I glanced over my shoulder continually to see if the torchlight of our pursuers followed us.

"Yep," said Emily. "We'll be in the centre of the earth soon. Where are we going? I wish I'd never come out with you tonight."

"This must be an old mine. I've no idea why it's under the vicarage."

"How long will this tunnel go on for? I want to go home."

"We're not turning around, if that's what you mean. I don't know who was back there, but whatever's ahead has to be preferable, right?"

"I suppose so. Can we stop for a minute?"

"Why?"

"Please? I feel faint, and I need to catch my breath."

"Okay. Just for a minute. They might be following us."

We paused at a spot where the tunnel bent. Behind us was the cellar, the trapdoor and whoever owned the torch. To the side, a looming indentation in the rock. In front of us, who knew what?

"D'you hear that?" asked Emily.

"All I can hear is your panting."

"Push your hair away from your ears. Listen. It sounds like waves."

"Waves?"

"Yes. The sea."

"You're right. Come on. I can guess where this ends."

We hurried further down the tunnel. The restricted passageway began to open, and light from my phone no longer illuminated the walls and roof. The sounds of waves increased, and a fresh breeze wafted over us.

"Emily, I can see stars ahead."

"Me too. And the sea sounds really near."

We burst into the open air, and I shone my light back the way we'd come. "It's a cave," I said. "We're on the beach. This is Smuggler's Cove. The children must've found their way into the cellar looking for Easter eggs. Gracie dropped her doll at the entrance, then the trapdoor must've closed somehow, and they were forced to follow the tunnel, like we just did. Hunter was telling the truth all along."

"But why is there a tunnel leading from the vicarage cellar to the beach?" asked Emily.

"I don't know. At least we were able to escape whoever was up there. Now we have to work out how to get home again. Except it must be high tide, and Smuggler's Cove is cut off." I glanced around in the starlight. "There's no obvious way out. Big, black rocks behind us, and the sea in front of us. This is a problem."

Emily pointed up the tunnel. A flicker of torchlight appeared at the rear of the cave. "We've a bigger problem than that," she said. "Those men are coming."

CHAPTER TWENTY

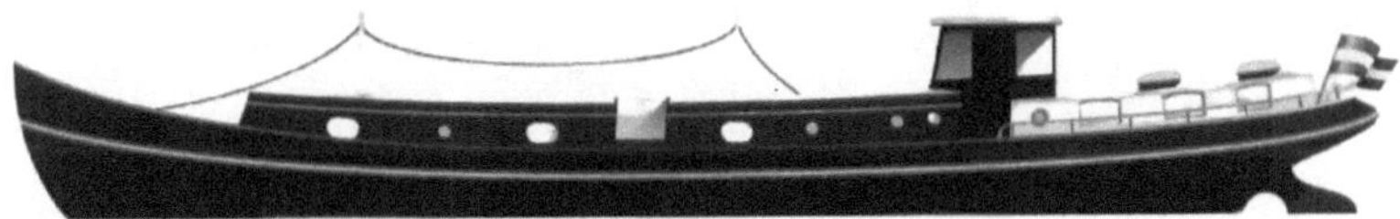

"Hide," I said, as the light from the torch grew brighter, and we heard the crunch of feet on the pebbles. "Quick; behind this rock."

We scrambled over small boulders and secreted ourselves behind a tall, black monolith, smoothed by centuries of waves smashing against it. The torchlight steadied, then bobbed along as whoever shone it walked out from the cave.

"Two men," hissed Emily. "Who is it? Is it Jack Walter?"

"I don't think so." I spoke in a low voice, loud enough to be heard over the waves, quiet enough not to give away our hiding place. "They're dressed in black, so it's hard to see. But the first one's outline looks stockier, and they both move like younger men. Jack limps."

The figures stood on the shore, and one swung their torch in an arc, pointing out to sea.

"What are they doing?" asked Emily. "Are they searching for us? I'm really scared."

"I'd say they're signalling to someone. A boat offshore, maybe? The torch is attached to their hat."

We watched. A short distance over the ocean an answering light described a similar curve.

"I was right. There's somebody on a boat out there. But it has no navigation lights. Murph would have something to say about that."

The figures on the shore switched off their torches and disappeared into the black.

"Where did they go?" whispered Emily.

"They're still there."

"My leg's gone to sleep."

"Change position. Quietly."

She shuffled around and dislodged a pebble which plopped into a rock pool.

"Shh," I whispered. "My eyes have adjusted, and I can see the outlines of the people on the beach. They're sitting on a rock."

"How long are we going to wait for them to do something? It's cold."

"What choice do we have but to sit here? We can hardly jump out and say 'boo,' can we?"

"I wish they'd hurry and do whatever they're going to do."

"Listen. A rowing boat. You can hear the oars creaking."

We watched in the starlight as the black shape of a small boat crunched onto the shingle, and another dark figure jumped out. He unloaded a large box and passed it to one of the men on the shore. A second and third box followed.

The three of them each carried one across the beach into the cave, following the lights of their head torches. We watched until the beams disappeared into the tunnel.

"Who is it?" asked Emily.

"I don't know. They're wearing black. And we haven't heard their voices."

We perched behind our rock, waiting for something else to happen.

Emily fidgeted. "This is boring," she said. "Could we leave now?"

"I reckon all stakeouts are boring. Ask Oscar, or any detective."

"Yes, but we're not detectives, and I didn't come out tonight prepared to squat with my toes in a rock pool. Shall we look in that rowing boat?"

"Ssh. They're coming back."

The three figures exited the cave with their head torches on. One returned to the rowing boat and shoved it away from shore. We heard the creak of the oars, then it was gone. The others switched off their torches and waited in the darkness.

"What d'you think's going on?" I whispered to Emily. "I'd love to take a photo but I daren't in case my flash goes off."

"These two are waiting for the boat to return. Whoever's in it must be fetching more boxes."

The scene repeated; the rowing boat beached, three more cubes were brought ashore, and the men entered the cave.

"We need to look in that boat," I said. "I'll time how long they take to return." I clicked my phone's stopwatch.

Three minutes and seventeen seconds later, the figures reappeared. One of them jumped back in the little boat, and the other two pushed it out to sea, then sat on the beach and waited.

"Next time they enter the cave," I said, poising like a runner on starting blocks, "I have three minutes and seventeen seconds. Three minutes to be on the safe side. Here's what we'll do. You stay here and start a timer for three minutes on your phone. When it gets to two minutes and thirty seconds, make a sound like a seagull. Then I'll know it's time to come back."

"I'm not sure I can do a seagull."

"Any sort of bird then. Doesn't matter. So long as it's not a human noise. Okay, here we go."

The rowing boat crunched on the shingle, and the men unloaded three more cubes.

"Ready," I whispered, as the black figures vanished into the cave entrance. "Three minute timer, starting now."

I leapt from my hiding place behind the rock and stuffed my knuckles in my mouth to prevent me screaming from the pain of pins and needles which shimmied down one leg. The rowing boat's bow was pulled up on the pebbles, and its stern remained in the shallow water. I glanced left and right, then concealed my phone torch in my palm and shone it around inside the boat; a simple rowing craft of the sort I'd hired on the Serpentine Lake in London. It had a bench in the centre, a metal rowlock on each side and two oars which lay in the bottom. Both the inside of the boat and the oars were painted dark grey.

The exterior showed nothing unusual, and I was weighing up whether to wade into the sea to see if there was a name on the stern, when I heard a noise sounding like an animal was in extreme pain. A quick glance behind me revealed the outline of Emily waving and pointing at the cave.

Time to go.

I ran across the shingle and crouched next to her behind the rock.

"What sort of bird was that supposed to be?" I hissed.

"A chicken."

"A chicken? The whole point of the subterfuge was to make a noise like a sea bird. There won't be many chickens wandering around the beaches near Redcliff."

"It worked, didn't it? You're back here, and they didn't see you. What did you find out?"

"Nothing. It's just a rowing boat. Shh. Watch what they do next."

One figure stepped back into the rowing boat, then the others pushed the craft away from the beach. They turned and trudged up the beach into the cave.

"That must be all of tonight's deliveries," I said. "We'll wait a few minutes and then head back into the cave ourselves."

"What, follow those men?"

"How else are we going to escape this beach?"

After ten minutes had passed, I stood and stretched. My legs had pins and needles again.

"Ready?" I said.

Emily stepped from behind the rock. "Should we switch on our phone torches again? The men might see us."

"Shield your torch in your hand like before. There's no hurry. We're not running away from them this time."

We trudged back up the beach in the starlight towards the mouth of the cave. I glanced out to sea, but the little boat had vanished into the darkness.

The return walk up the tunnel didn't seem to take as long and, within two minutes, we came to the foot of the ladder. After making sure no one was shining a torch anywhere above us, I grabbed hold of the metal rungs, climbed and my head struck solid wood.

"Ow," I cried. "The trapdoor's closed."

I shoved the trapdoor, but it didn't move.

"Push harder," said Emily, shining her torch behind me.

"I am, but it's too heavy. Remember it took both of us to lift it? I can't do it by myself."

"And there's no way I can climb up the ladder beside you; it's too narrow. Shiraz, what are we going to do? We'll be trapped down here forever, and one day, someone will find our bones, picked to pieces by sea birds."

"Yes, or chickens. Don't be so dramatic. We'll have to return to Smuggler's Cove and call for help."

"Not again. Murph'll lose his temper if we need rescuing from a beach again. Push harder."

"It won't budge. Perhaps those square packing cases are piled on the other side? Either we get this trapdoor open, or we return to the beach. There's no third option." I shoved until my arm hurt.

"Hang on," said Emily. "Wasn't there another tunnel? The one where I took a break on the way down."

I climbed down the ladder and stood beside her. "That was just a bend in the passage, wasn't it? It didn't go anywhere."

"Let's look. What else can we do?"

I brushed my clothes with my hands, then we followed our phone lights down the passage back towards the beach. Emily's torch suddenly extinguished, and she reached for me.

"Oh, no. My phone's out of battery. It must be from using the light so much. What percentage do you have?"

I studied my screen. "Eight. We'll need to be quick. In a few minutes, we'll be in the dark."

We strode as quickly as we could.

"You're right, Emily." I shone my phone into the darkness. "It's a second tunnel branching off this one. It bends immediately, so I can't see how long it is."

"How many percent do you have now?"

"Six. Come on."

We felt our way along the second tunnel, hewn out of bare rock like the first.

"Look at the ground," I said, pointing my phone downward. "Footprints in the dust. The same boots as the ones we saw in the cellar."

Emily's voice elevated an octave, and her words sped up. "I don't care about footprints. I want to get out of here."

We rounded another corner and found a dead end ahead.

"The tunnel ends here," I said. "It doesn't lead anywhere. We'll have to retrace our steps to the beach."

"We'll never do that before your phone runs out. What percent do you have now?"

"Four. It's not going to increase if you keep asking me. Wait. There's a shaft above the end of the tunnel, like the one leading up to the trapdoor. Maybe there's another ladder. Oh, drat."

Emily screamed as my phone gave up the ghost, and we were plunged into blackness.

CHAPTER TWENTY-ONE

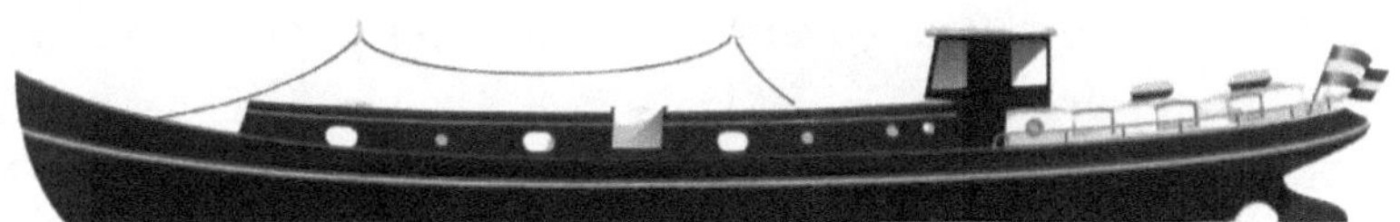

"Emily, stop yelling. Those men might hear if they're still around. Calm. Breath slowly. Deep breaths. Where are you?"

I felt for her in the dark and found her hair, then worked down to her shoulders.

"Stop touching me, Shiraz. Your hands are like spiders." She panted. "I hate this. I've never been in total blackness before. Even on a dark night you can see shadows."

"We're safe for now. In the worst case, we can inch our way back to Smuggler's Cove. That's our backup plan. But we may be able to climb up this shaft."

I glanced upwards, which achieved nothing in the dark.

"Hold my hand, Emily. We don't want to be separated." I inched along with Emily holding my left hand and my right hand stretched out in front of me.

"Stop," I said, as my hand touched rock. "We're at the bottom of the shaft. I'm going to grope around for a ladder." I let go of Emily's hand.

"Don't leave me," she said, scrabbling at my coat.

"I'm not going anywhere. I need both hands. Wait." I ran my fingers around the sides of the shaft, but they were all solid rock with no comforting metal rungs.

Emily wailed. "This is absolutely it, Shiraz. I am never coming on one of your adventures again. Eek! A bat. Something touched my hair."

"Sorry, that was me. There's no ladder. But I don't think the shaft's tall. When you screamed, the sound was very enclosed."

Emily gripped my arm so hard I reckoned I'd have a bruise. "How are we going to reach it, with no ladder?"

"I'll give you a leg up. If you find a trap door, try to push it open and see if you can wriggle through. Then you'll be out of the tunnel."

"But what about you? You'll still be stuck down here."

"You might find a rope to lower down to me? At least let's try that plan and see what happens."

"Okay. How do we do this?"

"I'll stand with my back to the edge of the shaft, and I'll clasp my hands in front of me, like a step. Then you grab my shoulders, put one foot in my hands and push yourself up."

"What if there are bats up there?"

"There are no bats. I think those men came this way from the footprints we saw. Okay. I'm against the wall, and I have my hands clasped. Are you ready?"

"I suppose so. This exercise would be hard enough when it's light, let alone in the pitch black."

"Grab my shoulders. Either side of my voice. That's it. Now put your foot in my hands. Wait, I've got your leg. Here. Found them? There. Now shove yourself up on my shoulders and I'll push your foot. One, two, three, here we go."

BANG

"Ow," said Emily, above me.

"What happened?"

"I bumped my head on something. Don't let me fall. This is terrifying."

"I've got you," I said, in what I hoped was a reassuring voice.

"It's wooden," said Emily. "Another trapdoor."

"Can you push it?"

"Yes. It's moving."

"If you shove with your hands, and I push your foot up, will that help?" Emily wobbled above me.

"We could try. It's definitely shifting."

"Ready? One, two, three, push."

CRASH

"Owwww." Emily landed at my feet. "My back. I think I've broken it."

I reached down to pull her up, and felt a flat, wooden object. "You did it. We're free. The trapdoor fell on top of you." I groped at the object and pulled it away. "Come on, let's get you off the floor."

I tugged her arms, and she leant against me.

"I'm in such pain," she said. "Give me a minute to recover. I'll be covered in bruises. Don't let go of me. I'm shaking."

We glanced upward and saw a slightly lighter-grey rectangle than the surrounding darkness. Fresh air from the opening wafted down.

"Look," I said. "It's open. But we'll have to repeat that exercise. You'll need to stand on my hands again."

"Why don't we change places this time?" asked Emily.

"Because if I escape through that hatch, you'll be down here by yourself. Will you be okay with that?"

"Definitely not."

We repeated the lifting process, and Emily's foot left my cupped hands. She wiggled herself through the hatch above me.

"Okay," I yelled. "You're free. Now get me out of here."

"How?"

"Can you find a rope? Anything?"

"It's dark. I can't see anything. I...oww. Ow, ow, ow."

"What happened?" I called. "Are you okay?"

"I tripped on something. Hold on. Oh. It's a ladder."

"Great. Drop it down the hole."

"Give me a minute. My entire body's bruised and broken. Okay, stand out of the way."

I backed into the passageway and heard the scrape of metal on rock. The ladder clonked in front of me. It felt smooth and light, like the stepladder Emily owned to reach the top cupboards in the Wicked Whelk. I grabbed the sides of it, found the bottom rung and climbed up to join her.

"We're inside somewhere," I said. "I can hear the wind, but I'm not feeling it."

"It's a big space, from the way our voices echo," said Emily. "I reckon we're in the barn. Let's get out of here and go home. I need a hot bath and to put my pyjamas on. We've had far too many adventures for one night."

"Hang on. The Marine Rescue Christmas barn dance takes place in here, right?"

"Yes. Every December. Why?"

"At the dance, d'you have lights?"

"Of course. Loads of beautiful Christmas lights, strung all around. And lanterns, dangling from the rafters. And a big electric star of Bethlehem hanging in the middle."

"Great. Then the barn has electricity. We're supposed to be searching for clues, remember? Oscar told us to look for anything unusual. Where's the light switch?"

"Oscar said we should wait until the vicars came back from holiday. We're breaking and entering."

"No, we're not. We haven't forced any locks or smashed any windows."

"Trespassing, then."

"Whatever. If this solves a murder, our actions are justified."

"I still can't see how anything in here is linked to Betty's death."

"Me neither. But something's not right. People don't land small boats and transport little packing cases through secret tunnels after dark if they're engaged in honest activities, do they? I want to discover what those men were up to."

I walked towards a sliver of lighter grey which betrayed the barn's huge double doors and ran my hands across the walls on both sides.

CLICK

Emily and I threw our arms over our eyes as one stark, bare lightbulb illuminated the barn.

I removed my arm slowly and blinked. Emily opened one eye.

"Gosh, that's bright," she said. "After being in the pitch black for so long, it's like a spotlight in a movie where a suspect's tied to a chair being interrogated."

"Let's hope that doesn't happen to us. We can't be too long, in case Jack Walter sees the glint of the barn light and becomes suspicious." I looked at her. "Oh, Emily, I'm so sorry. You've ripped your trousers and your coat. I'll take you shopping and buy you new clothes."

She rubbed at the tear. "I think I grazed my elbow. It stings. I'll have a look when I hop into a bath."

"The barn's empty, apart from these tarpaulins and whatever's under them."

"It's where we store the decorations and equipment for the Christmas dance." Emily pulled up a corner of the covering. "Chairs and tables here. What's under the next one?"

I lifted one side of the second tarpaulin. "Large hexagonal boxes painted black." I tapped one, and it responded with a hollow sound, like a drum. "What on earth are these for?"

Emily peeked under. "That's the stage for the musicians at the barn dance. The hexagons bolt together somehow. When we're preparing for the event, Jack Walter assembles it in the centre of the room."

"Got it. One more tarpaulin." I tugged the corner of the last cover, which was a heavy canvas and seemed as large as a circus tent. "Wooden cubes." I lifted the tarpaulin and ducked under. "Loads of them. This isn't another stage, is it?"

Emily looked. "We only have one stage. These must be whatever those men were carrying."

I rocked one. "They're heavier than I thought. Those men must be strong to carry them through the tunnel and pass them up the ladder." I ran my fingers around the lid. "They're packing crates. Something's stencilled on the side."

We rotated the box until the stencil marks were on the top.

"P—O—P—P—E—N." I spelt out the word. "What does '*Poppen*' mean?"

"I don't know. I would ask Siri, but our phones are flat."

"Yes. We can't even take a photo of the writing. D'you have a pen?"

"No. Nothing."

"Can we remember it between us, and we'll look it up when we have the Internet again?"

"Okay. *Poppen.* Pop, then pen. I'll remember that. Now, let's get out of here before someone comes."

"Wait, I want to open a packing case."

"Are you crazy? We're not supposed to be here, and now you want to open somebody else's box?"

"They're up to no good; we know that. The cases could have anything in them. D'you have that piece of your food processor we used to lever the trapdoor in the cellar?"

"Here. It's bent now. I'll have to replace it. Again."

I slipped the blade into the gap where the lid of the packing case met the edge and began to lever. The sound of a nail squeaking rewarded my efforts. Moving the tool to another side did the same. Then the third side. Then the fourth.

"It's coming," I said.

We watched, fascinated, as the blade prized the lid off one side, and we glimpsed the contents.

I turned the packing case towards the light.

"What on earth?" said Emily. "It's full of dolls."

CHAPTER TWENTY-TWO

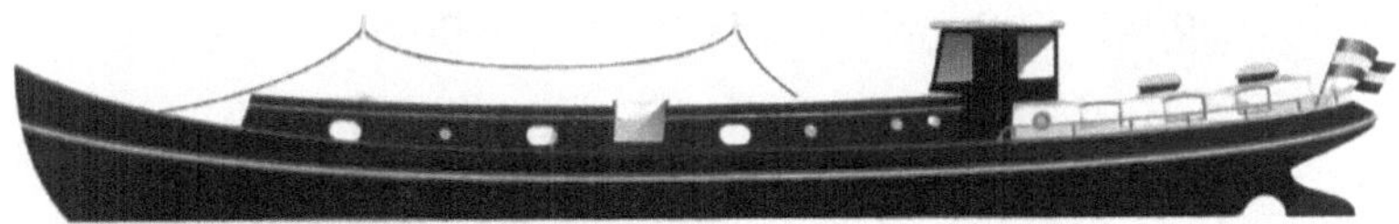

"Put the lid back on the packing case, Shiraz. We need to get out of here."

"Hold your horses. I want to inspect the dolls. Let's take one with us."

"That's stealing. We really will be done for breaking and entering if anyone catches you with the doll. I've never seen anything like them in the shops around here, so it'll be obvious where you stole it from."

"With at least a hundred dolls in each packing case, and possibly a hundred cases, they're not going to miss one." I lifted a doll, pulled back the card which separated the layers, tugged the toy beneath it out and replaced the top layer. "There. Now we'll bang the lid back on."

I fitted the lid, so the nails lined up with the holes they'd come from and thumped it until it sat flush on the packing case.

"Now, please, let's get out of here," said Emily. "Oh. We'd better pull the ladder back up and shut the trapdoor. We need to leave the barn exactly as we found it."

"Minus one doll."

"Yes. You and your pilfering." She picked up the doll from the ground and held it in front of her. "You know what's odd about these dolls?"

"Apart from the fact they've arrived on a deserted beach at night by boat, then been smuggled up a tunnel into a barn?"

"Apart from that. When did you last buy a doll from a shop?"

"Gosh, it must be thirty years ago. With my birthday money. A Barbie."

"I bought one at Christmas for my cousin's daughter. It came in a box with a transparent window in the front. The box protected the toy, but you could still see what it looked like before you bought it. All the dolls I've seen come like that. Except these. These have their clothes but no boxes."

"If they're being imported wholesale, are the boxes added later?"

"Maybe. Just a thought. Right, we'll replace the ladder, shut the trapdoor, put the packing case back with the others, switch out the light and… oh. The barn doors are locked, aren't they? And the trapdoor's still where it fell on me, down the shaft."

"Yep. Can't be helped. Either we go back down the passageway, or we scrape the dirt away and wriggle under the doors. There are no other options."

Emily sighed. "My clothes are ruined. Yours will be too."

Oscar sat at Emily's table cradling a mug of tea while she lay on the sofa. Boots stretched out on top of her, purring at top volume. I relocated a pile of books and wondered for the seventh time whether this flat was really big enough for two people and a cat, and whether it was time to find my own place.

"I don't approve of your actions," said Oscar, finally. "It's all very well trying to work out who killed Betty, and I know I suggested returning to the vicarage because Betty and Captain Salisbury met there, but I didn't mean for you to sneak in while the vicars are away. You were lucky Jack Walter didn't catch you. Don't do that again, please. Or if you do, don't tell me."

He paused, while I stared into my lap like a naughty schoolchild.

"However,"—he looked up and brightened—"your discoveries are very interesting. Very interesting indeed. There have always been tales of smuggler's tunnels under Redcliff, but my understanding was they'd all collapsed or been blocked up centuries ago. Your investigations suggest someone's unblocked them."

"Captain Salisbury," said Emily. "That's who. Our number one-rated suspect. He should be our only suspect. The crates coming off that boat last night contained hundreds of those dolls, and he has an identical doll on his barge. In my opinion, case closed."

"You may as well arrest Gracie then," I said. "On the same evidence."

"She's five years old."

"Yes, but she has a doll."

Oscar pursed his lips. "D'you think one of the men you witnessed unloading the crates was Harry Salisbury?"

"We couldn't tell in the dark," I said. "All we saw were two men appear from the tunnel and signal to someone offshore by sweeping a torch back and forth. Then the same signal was returned by a boat out to sea, and a few minutes later the rowing boat arrived with the boxes. The man in the boat helped carry them, but they were all dressed head to toe in black. It might've been anyone."

"At least this explains the mysterious lights off Redcliff at night. But although this importation of dolls seems odd, I can't see anything illegal in it. There's no law to say you can't deliver packing cases full of dolls to a beach at night, carry them through a disused smuggler's tunnel and store them in a barn. Nothing criminal occurs in that chain of events. And how does any of it relate to Betty's murder?"

"You're right," said Emily. "Unless the vicars weren't aware. Because isn't it their barn? We'll have to ask them."

"We can't do that," I said. "How did we know about the boxes of dolls? We weren't supposed to be in the barn."

"Oh, yes. Now what do we do?"

"Park that thought for now," said Oscar. "At the moment it's enough to know that the dolls, the tunnels and the mysterious boats and people exist. We should note all these new discoveries. D'you have that piece of paper, Emily?"

"It's downstairs in the café. I'll fetch it. Sorry, Boots. Time to get off." She sat up and the cat scrabbled onto the floor. He licked one paw in disgust while Emily clumped downstairs.

Oscar and I sat silently, waiting for her to return before we discussed the case further.

"How long have you lived in Redcliff now, Shiraz?" he asked.

"This is my fourth month. I left London on New Year's Day, after that disastrous New Year's Eve party at my house when I caught my husband in bed with his boyfriend. That was the worst day of my life. Made even worse by my so-called best friend telling me she'd always known about their affair. Why didn't she tell me, for goodness' sake?" I thumped the table, and Boots nipped under the couch, twisted around and stared at me wide-eyed.

"Quite," said Oscar, dipping his chin. "Terrible. So, err, you're enjoying living here with Emily?"

"Ye-es, but it was only supposed to be a temporary arrangement, a stop gap. We're great friends, but this isn't a large apartment, and I'm worried our friendship will be strained by living on top of each other." I puffed and shook my head. "Oscar, I need to find a new home. Gosh, that's the first time I've said that aloud."

Oscar wrinkled his brow. "But you are staying in Redcliff, aren't you?"

"Of course. I love it here. The town feels like home now, and there's no way I'd abandon Redcliff Marine Rescue. But I need my own space."

"Of course. And now it's after Easter and heading into the warmer weather, accommodation will be harder to find as the summer holidaymakers and retirees from the cities begin their annual migrations."

We heard the front door close.

"Shh," I said. "Don't say anything to Emily about that, please."

Oscar winked and tapped the side of his nose twice.

"Sorry I took so long," said Emily. "I'd rolled it up and put it carefully on the top shelf in the pantry, then when I stood on the kitchen steps to pull it down it unravelled all over me. And then I forgot the chalk. Anyway, here I am. Where shall we put it?"

"Your dining table's not as big as the tables in the café," I said. "I think we'll have to work on the rug."

"But Boots has settled on the rug."

"Then Boots will have to move off the rug." I scooped up the cat and deposited him back on the sofa, an action he objected to by fastening his teeth around the end of my hand.

"Ow." I sucked my finger and waved it in the air. "Why do we keep such a savage beast?"

"He's only a savage beast when you do something he doesn't like. Poor Boots." She tickled the cat's head, and he began to purr. "You just wanted a quiet afternoon without all these investigations, didn't you, Boots?" Emily unrolled the paper and lifted four paperback books off a side table to weigh down the corners.

"What should we do now, Oscar?" I asked, looking at the unrolled sheet of paper. "I don't think anything which happened yesterday increases or decreases the scores of any suspect. We don't know who the men carrying the boxes of dolls were, for instance."

"We need to write down your findings. The tunnels, the men on the beach, the boat, the packing cases, the dolls. Everything. Add them to the list in the corner headed 'clues'. At the moment, I can't see any connection between these events and Betty's death, but people don't unload packing cases from rowing boats after dark unless they're up to something, criminal or not."

Emily chose a piece of green chalk and listed our discoveries, then paused at the word 'dolls'. "Shiraz," she said, "fetch the doll you pinched. Show it to Oscar."

"Good idea." I nipped to my bedroom, returned with the toy and handed it to him.

Oscar held it uncomfortably by its arm. Not like a child would hold a doll around the waist or cradled against their body.

"This looks like a normal child's doll." He twisted it upside down. "The clothing is quite distinctive, an Arabic design. Shiraz, you're of Muslim heritage. D'you recognise this style?"

"No. I'm not *very* Muslim. I couldn't tell you whether this fashion was Arabic or African. Or neither."

"Do all the dolls look like this?" asked Oscar.

"Yes," said Emily. "All the ones in the packing case were dressed identically, with the same brown, wavy hair and the same brown eyes. So was Gracie's. And, although we only caught a glimpse of it, I'm sure the one on Harry Salisbury's boat was too."

"Mass produced," said Oscar, holding the doll up. "Like all toys these days." He handed it back to me.

"Now what do we do?" I asked. "We've reached a dead end."

"Quite the opposite," said Oscar. "Your experiences have created several questions. We now need to figure out the answers. And you haven't asked me how my side of the investigation's progressing."

"Oh, yes. Gosh, I was so caught up relating the extraordinary events of last night, I forgot about dividing and conquering. Did you find an excuse to call Inspector Buchanan again?"

Oscar grinned. "I didn't need to. He rang me."

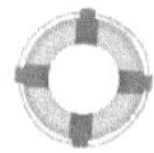

CHAPTER TWENTY-THREE

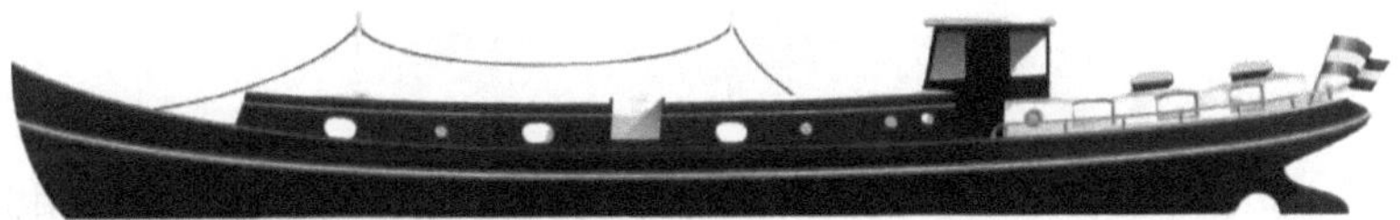

"Inspector Buchanan called you?" I asked Oscar. "What did he want?"

"Actually, he wanted to talk with you both."

"Why didn't he call us, then?"

"He said he did, last night. But neither of you were answering."

"Oh, yes," said Emily. "Our phones were flat after using the torches in the tunnels."

Oscar smiled. "He'd like both of you to view CCTV footage from last weekend."

"From the marina entry gate, I presume?" I said.

"The gate doesn't have a camera on it. But some of the more expensive yachts have cameras to protect them, and the police have secured the recordings. They're apparently not from the best angles, but they'd like our help anyway. Let me know when you're free to visit Brighthaven police station, and I'll call him back."

"Our help? You're coming too?"

Oscar rubbed his hands together. "Of course I am. This is going to be fun."

"Oscar. What a pleasure to see you again. You're looking fit and well. How's the family?"

Inspector Buchanan gripped Oscar's hand and shook it so hard I thought he'd pull it off.

"Everyone's well, thanks, Martin. I'm busy enjoying retirement. Gardening, walking the dog and volunteering at the Marine Rescue gift shop. And my position as a town councillor keeps me out of trouble, too. As does the Rotary club. And the Redcliff Icebergers. I've no idea how I ever had time for work."

"Same old Oscar," said the inspector. "Always on the go." He turned to us. "Thank you for coming in, Ladies. This won't take long. Would anyone like a drink?"

We all declined, and Martin showed us into a room with six office chairs around a table with a laptop on it. A television was mounted on the wall behind. We each took a seat.

Martin stood with a remote control in one hand. "The video I'm about to show you," he said, pointing the remote at the laptop, "came from cameras mounted on vessels in Brighthaven Marina. The cameras are naturally intended to provide security for their own yachts, so many of last weekend's events are out of shot, but we do have some footage of interest. Is everybody ready?"

I raised my hand slightly. "Just one question."

"Of course."

"Has anyone else apart from us seen these pictures?"

"Not yet," said Inspector Buchanan. "But we do have people in mind we'd like to show them to. Let's begin, shall we?"

He pressed the remote control, and an image appeared on the screen. As soon as he clicked the 'play' symbol, the picture began to move.

"It's Easter Monday," said Martin. "This camera gives us a view of the jetty between the marina entrance gate and the moorings. It doesn't show us the gate itself or the place where Elizabeth Stanton entered the water. Okay, it's 9:05 a.m. The first person we see is a man who owns a sailing boat moored in the marina. We now know his name to be Douglas Horsley."

"That must be the man who let us in," said Emily.

"Yep," I said. "I recognise his jacket."

Inspector Buchanan continued. "Douglas Horsley enters and exits several times. We've spoken to him, and he's told us he was carrying tools and supplies between his car and his boat. I'll speed this bit up."

Doug walked at double speed back and forth along the gangplank as if he were in a Charlie Chaplin movie. I stifled a giggle. The video slowed down again.

"The next point of interest is now, at 9:35. Harry Salisbury exits the marina. Would you agree that's him?" He pointed at the screen, where the figure of Captain Salisbury could clearly be seen marching down the jetty.

"He must be heading for the supermarket," said Emily. "He showed me a receipt timed 10:57."

"Watch," said Martin. "This part is important." The camera showed the empty jetty, then Harry Salisbury returned, accompanied by a shorter figure. Harry's frame prevented a good view of this person, and he glanced directly at the camera as they walked together.

Inspector Buchanan pressed pause. "Who's behind Captain Salisbury? Do you know them?"

"It's not a clear picture," I said. "Is there any way to zoom in?"

"Yes, but I don't think it'll help you." He held down a button on the laptop, and the view of Harry and the mystery person enlarged.

"You're right. It's almost as if he were trying to conceal them," said Emily. "And their face is turned away from us."

"Was Harry Salisbury aware of the cameras?" asked Oscar.

"Probably. They're not hidden. You definitely can't identify this second person?"

I shrugged. "All I can tell is, they're a few inches shorter than Harry."

"It's not Betty Stanton, is it?" asked Emily.

"No," I said. "She's tiny; considerably smaller than Harry. This person is taller than her."

"And," said Martin, "she pops up later. We're getting ahead of ourselves. Shall we continue?" He clicked the 'play' button, and we watched Harry Salisbury and the mystery figure disappear out of shot.

Nothing happened, and Martin fast forwarded. "It's now 9:48," he said, returning the recording to regular speed. "Harry Salisbury leaves the marina alone, same as last time."

"Ooh," said Emily. "The mystery person stayed on board his boat?"

"Either that," said Martin, "or on the jetty, or on another boat. There's only one route in and out. Now several things happen. At 9:56, Douglas Horsley leaves the marina on one of his trips to fetch possessions from his car. On the dot of 10:00, he re-enters the marina, tailed by Elizabeth Stanton. It seems he gave her access."

We watched Doug peel off towards his boat, and the clear figure of Betty continue along the jetty leading to Harry's barge. Both disappeared out of shot. The walkway was empty for a few minutes, then Doug returned empty handed, heading out of the marina.

Oscar raised his hand. "Stop the recording, please. Recap. At this point in time, the mystery person and Betty Stanton are both on the jetty where Harry Salisbury keeps his barges. Harry isn't there, because he's left the marina. And Doug has too."

"Correct," said Martin. "I always remember the way you go back over details, leaving nothing to memory."

"Harry should really be home at 10:00," said Emily, "because that's when Betty Stanton told him to expect her."

"He mixed up the time," I said. "Unless he was deliberately avoiding her."

"Okay to restart?" asked Inspector Buchanan. "I'll fast forward, because nothing happens for over an hour. Then Doug returns, and two new actors enter the scene."

"Gosh, it's us," said Emily. "Oh. Is that what I look like from the back?"

I laughed. "It must be shortly before 11:30 now. I remember Emily suggesting we go for lunch when we found Captain Salisbury wasn't home, and I said it was only 11:30 and too early."

"Right," said Martin. "It's 11:25. Then you both disappear out of shot. Ten minutes later, at 11:35, Harry Salisbury returns alone. He strides towards his boat."

"This was when we saw Betty Stanton in the water. We tried to pull her out ourselves, then Harry arrived and helped us."

Oscar raised a hand again. "Pause while we recap," he said.

Martin pressed the pause button.

Oscar cleared his throat. "At this point, there are five people on the jetty by Harry's barges." He ticked off on his fingers. "Betty Stanton, deceased, Shiraz and Emily, Harry Salisbury and the mystery person. You didn't see anyone else, did you?"

"We weren't looking for anyone. We were too busy trying to deal with Betty."

"Understood," said Martin. "Keep watching while I restart the video. Twelve minutes later, two paramedics arrive. You can identify them from their uniforms and equipment. Then two of my constables and the undertakers."

"That was the most horrible part for me," said Emily. "I felt as if we were under suspicion."

"At that point," said Martin, "nobody was under suspicion as we didn't realise this was anything more than an an unfortunate tumble into the water. I'll fast forward, and you can watch them leave with Betty's body on the stretcher. Then I arrive, having been alerted to the incident."

We watched the figure of Inspector Buchanan walk from left to right across the screen.

"And twenty minutes later, I depart. Shortly after that, you two leave. I won't bore you with the rest of the video, because apart from Doug's comings and goings, nobody else of interest appears."

"Which leaves us with a loose end," said Oscar. "At this point, two people still remain down the jetty where Harry Salisbury lives. Harry himself and this mysterious slightly shorter companion of his. Have you asked him who it was?"

"We have, and he maintains it was simply someone he let in through the gate."

"I don't believe that," I said. "He told us he was annoyed at Doug for allowing us to tailgate. And if we look at that part of the recording again, he's walking next to them, like they know each other."

Martin Buchanan rewound, and we again watched Harry Salisbury with the mysterious figure.

"I think it's one of the men we saw the other night," said Emily. "It's the same way they move."

"Really?" I asked. "Are you sure?"

"Not one hundred percent, but I'm wondering if it's Lance Evans."

"Who's Lance Evans?" asked Inspector Buchanan.

"He may be a person of interest," said Oscar.

"Yes. There was the matter of his behaviour while his kids were missing," I said.

"Missing kids?" said Martin. "We haven't received any report of missing kids."

"It happened in Redcliff. During the vicarage Easter egg hunt last weekend, two children went missing. We searched everywhere; in fact, Harry Salisbury led the search effort, but we couldn't find them. Then, just as we were about to call Redcliff police, they turned up."

"Got it. And Lance Evans was their father?"

"Yes. But he didn't seem concerned they were missing. He didn't join in the search, and he vanished while we were trying to find them. If I had kids, and they'd disappeared, I'd be frantic."

"That is odd behaviour," said Martin. "But what leads you to make a connection between him and this incident we've been reviewing?"

"We've been discussing who might've murdered Betty," said Emily. "His name came up."

Oscar turned to Martin. "D'you have any more video? Of any other days following Easter Monday?"

"We don't. Why?"

"If this mystery person didn't return through the marina gate on the Monday, there are three things that might've happened. One: They're still on a boat somewhere. Two: They've departed by water. Or three…"

He cleared his throat, and we leant in to hear his third option.

"Three: Whoever killed Betty, killed them too."

CHAPTER TWENTY-FOUR

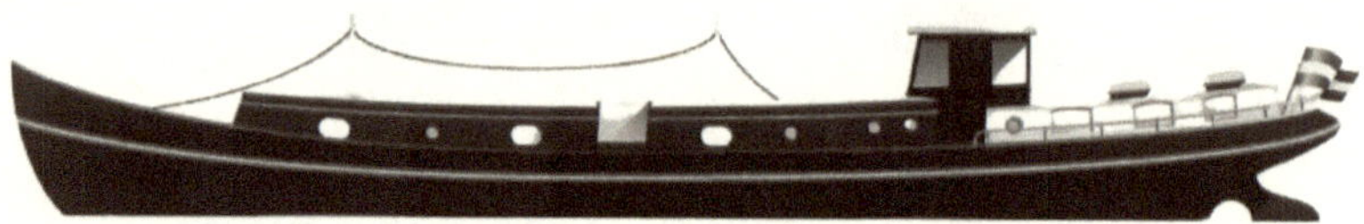

The soldier sipped tea from a china cup and nibbled at home-made rations.

Everything was going to plan very nicely.

Everyone was playing their parts well.

At least, those who still had a part to play.

But one particular member of the platoon was no longer needed.

The traitor.

And the soldier wasn't yet sure when they would finish their part.

But they had to go. They were next.

The soldier rubbed the outline of the knife in its sheath.

Would this need to be used again, or was there another way?

CHAPTER TWENTY-FIVE

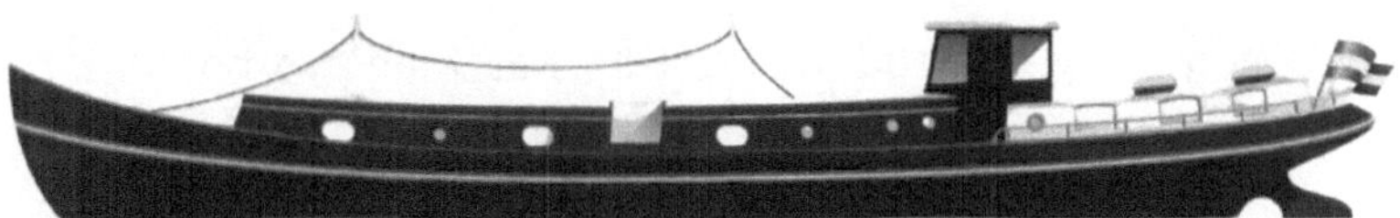

Sunday in Emily's apartment above the café. The picture of perfect domesticity. Emily had made us coffee and breakfast and I'd studied the news in the local paper. Boots had stolen half a sausage from my plate, and I'd bitten the bullet and deleted hundreds of pictures from my Facebook and Instagram accounts, as the photos with Monty at parties and film premieres didn't relate in any way to my life in Redcliff-upon-Sea. Now I was engaging in meaningful activities, saving lives. Last week, I'd saved two. Children, no less. The knowledge I was responsible for them being alive today was more exhilarating than any red carpet appearance. Greater than any magazine interview. Greater than any photograph of me in a designer, single-use, expensive dress.

I couldn't wait to crew the boat again.

"Emily, we're both rostered on this afternoon's shift, aren't we?"

"Yep. Have you revised your man overboard procedure?"

"Shall we run through it together now and really impress Murph? Would you test me from the book?"

"Great idea." She picked up the *Marine Rescue Workbook* and opened it near the centre. "Start from the point where we see someone in the water. What's the first thing we do?"

"Call 'Man overboard'."

"Don't forget to add the location. So: 'Man overboard, starboard side', or 'Man overboard, dead ahead', or, 'Man overboard, thirty degrees to port'."

"Of course. This is for a missing person in the water, right? They're not strictly overboard. They didn't fall off the rescue boat."

"Don't overthink it, Shiraz. Like Murph said, the key thing is to be quick. One syllable might be the difference between life and death. Look how close those kids were to sinking with their deflated whale."

"Sure. Although, if I become a skipper, I'm going to rephrase it to 'Girl overboard'. That's the same number of syllables."

"Murph wouldn't approve. We're all supposed to be following the same procedure. Okay, so we've called 'Man Overboard', and we've included the location. What's next?"

"At least one crew member stands with their arm outstretched, pointing directly at the person in the water, and never takes their eyes off them."

"Very good. If you stop looking even for a moment, you'll lose sight of them. Anything else?"

"Harness up."

"One more thing before that. Something the person pointing at the casualty can't do."

"Drive the boat closer?"

"Nope. Think of the instruments. What do we press?"

"Oh, yes. The man overboard button. It marks the boat's current position on the electronics."

"Correct. And why can't the person pointing do that?"

"Because they'd take their eyes off the casualty."

"Right. You're doing great, Shiraz. Murph will definitely sign both of us off on this today. What next?"

"Harness up. The person pointing gets harnessed up by another member of the crew, so they don't lose sight of the person we're rescuing."

"Yep. This afternoon it'll be me and you swapping roles. Who's the qualified crew today?"

"I haven't looked at the roster. It might be Jules again, or Frances, or David. Shall we continue? At this point, I'm clipped to the boat so I don't fall in the water while I'm pulling the person out."

"Yep. We don't want to become casualties ourselves. What d'you do next?"

"Open the boarding door."

"Before that?"

"Fetch blankets and towels?"

"Someone else can do that. What do you do? What haven't you done yet in your process?"

I shrugged.

"Murph's going to be upset if you forget this. I can hear him now: 'Hysterical harbourmasters, Shiraz. Communicate with the skipper'."

"Of course. Give the skipper constant updates about what you can see. And before we open the boarding door, we have to ask permission, and it has to be granted. The back deck's a dangerous place with it open."

"Aft deck, Shiraz."

I puffed. "There's so much to remember. I've told the skipper what I can see. The position of the person in the water relative to us, for instance. And I've asked permission to open the boarding door when we're close to the casualty, and the skipper's granted it. I open the door and kneel on the deck to lower my centre of gravity."

"Brilliant. And you keep communicating as we approach. By this time, we'll be travelling really slowly, so as not to drive over the top of the casualty. What would you say?"

"Casualty five feet off the bow, casualty alongside and so on."

"Yep. And the condition of the casualty; if they're swimming, if they're calling for help, if they're unconscious. I hope we don't find someone in that situation. The pressure would be on us then."

"Indeed. Let's say the casualty's swimming and yelling. I grab hold of them by whatever I can. Under their arms is best. We don't want to pull their head off."

"No. That would be unfortunate; if they survived immersion in the water and then Redcliff Marine Rescue decapitated them."

I giggled, then stopped myself. "We shouldn't laugh about that scenario. Right, a minimum of two people to pull them out. Unless they're a child, like last week."

"Yep. Two to be safe. Once they're out, what's the first thing you do?"

"Dry them and wrap them in a blanket."

"Before that?"

"Check their response? Ask how they're feeling?"

"All of those, but you've forgotten to tell the skipper you've retrieved them and that they're alive and breathing. Don't do that this afternoon. Murph'll throw you overboard with the rescue dummy."

"It's so easy to forget. Communicate with the skipper all the time. And ask permission to close the boarding door."

"Two other things to do with communication?"

"Is there something else I tell Murph?"

"Not Murph. Two other parties."

"Oh, yes. The first one's the person we just pulled out. Ask their name. Ask why they're in the water. And most importantly, ask if there was anyone else with them."

"Excellent. Top marks. It'd be tragic if we got them safely back to shore and, when we arrived, they asked what happened to the other person on their sunken boat. One other communication that has to happen, although the skipper or qualified crew would probably take care of this. Think of someone not on the boat with us."

I grinned. "You gave me too big a clue. Radio Coastguard Headland Bay and give them an update on the situation."

"Perfect." Emily clapped. "Just remember about communicating with the skipper, and Murph will sign your workbook. One more step towards becoming qualified crew. Another coffee?"

"I'd love one, thanks, after all that brain effort."

Emily headed for the kitchen area. I sat back and smiled. Times like this were precious, chatting with Emily about our shared interests. I just wished the flat was bigger. It only had one shower and one basin, for instance, which was great for a single person or maybe a couple; not so great for me. I needed an entire bathroom for my collection of Chanel and Decorté beauty products. Emily had become annoyed with me this week when I'd spent an hour in there, and she'd had to pop downstairs to the Wicked Whelk to use the lavatory.

But how would I broach the subject of moving out? I'd need to find new digs nearby. Close enough to see Emily socially as regularly as now. Not so close that we collided in our domestic arrangements.

I picked up this week's *Headland Bay Times* and subtly turned to the 'Houses for rent' page.

I threw the newspaper down and stood as three thumps sounded at Emily's door.

"That must be Oscar," I said. "I'll get it."

"Where's Boots?"

"Asleep on the couch."

"Okay. Ask Oscar to tie Cadbury up outside the Wicked Whelk, please. Boots would take his nose off."

I clumped down the stairs and found Oscar dressed in an open-necked shirt and old trousers.

"Morning, Shiraz," he said. "Don't worry, I've left Cadbury at home. D'you mind if I pop up?"

"Please do. Emily's making hot drinks."

I followed him up the stairs.

"Hello, Oscar," said Emily. "Would you like an Earl Grey?"

"I'd love one, thanks. I've been gardening while my wife's at church, and this warm weather's making me sweat."

"What brings you here today?" I asked. "D'you have any news for us?"

Oscar accepted the mug of tea and sat at the little kitchen table. "I do. And it adds to our investigation. After we'd viewed the CCTV, I began my tasks to find out about Betty's son and Jack Walter's backgrounds, specifically whether either was ever in the military. I couldn't work out how I'd do this without drawing attention to my motives. If Jack was Betty's murderer, and I began asking if he'd ever been a soldier, the game would be up, wouldn't it?

"Yes. Or if he was involved in any way, he might become suspicious."

"Right. I had to be subtle. First, the son. My wife remembered his name was Rodney, so we were almost right. I Googled 'Rodney Stanton' and found seventeen potential people on a website called LinkedIn. I had to sign up and create a profile, which I didn't really want to do, but I had no other way to see these people's details. Once I'd done that, I studied the website and was able to discount several Rodney Stantons instantly as they lived overseas or were too old to be Betty's son.

"He moved a long way away," said Emily. "Maybe he emigrated?"

"I hadn't ruled out that possibility. I also accepted that the Rodney Stanton we were looking for might not have a presence on that website. But then I found a man I knew to be him as, under his educational details, it said he'd attended Redcliff-upon-Sea Secondary College. He's 44 years old, married, lives in Scotland, and…"

"And he's in the Scottish Highland Elite Army Squadron?" I asked.

"Sorry, Shiraz. Much more mundane. He runs a gift shop in Edinburgh."

My shoulders slumped. "Not him, then. Let's reduce his score to two or three. What about Jack Walter?"

"As I told you, my wife knows him through the church, but I wasn't sure how well. So I asked her, and it turns out she's friendly with Jack's wife, Rose, who I only know vaguely. I made up a story on the spot. I said the council were considering compiling a list of retired servicemen and women who lived in Redcliff for this year's Remembrance Day celebration, and we wanted to ensure everybody who qualified was on it."

"Gosh, Oscar, you'll get into trouble."

"Not at all. Don't forget, I'm currently acting mayor, and if anyone questions this, I can bring it up as a potential project at the next council meeting. I said a colleague of mine had mentioned Jack Walter as being ex-forces, but I thought they were mistaken. And my wife said she'd ask Rose about Jack's past service. As luck would have it, she was going to church last night to arrange flowers for this morning's communion. She mentioned Rose would be there, and she thought Jack might be too. Obviously, I didn't want Jack to know about the question, so I had to think quickly. I told her to be subtle; it had to be a secret, as they were considering giving out awards, and Jack might be nominated."

"Sorry to interrupt, but I had a thought," said Emily. "If you really could make that scheme happen and compile a complete list of all ex-servicemen and women in Redcliff, it would give us a register of suspects."

"It would," said Oscar, "but there'd be hundreds of names on it. We wouldn't know where to start. Anyway, as soon as my wife came home from the church last night, I asked her. She was rather suspicious about why I needed to know immediately, but she said she'd asked Rose, and Jack Walter did have a military past."

"Yes!" I said. "We can increase his score to nine, same as Captain Salisbury's."

"I knew it," said Emily. "Jack Walter's an ex-commando, isn't he? It wasn't Lance Evans on CCTV; it was him."

Oscar sighed. "Not so fast. Jack Walter was in the army. Fifty years ago, in his twenties. He was a cook."

CHAPTER TWENTY-SIX

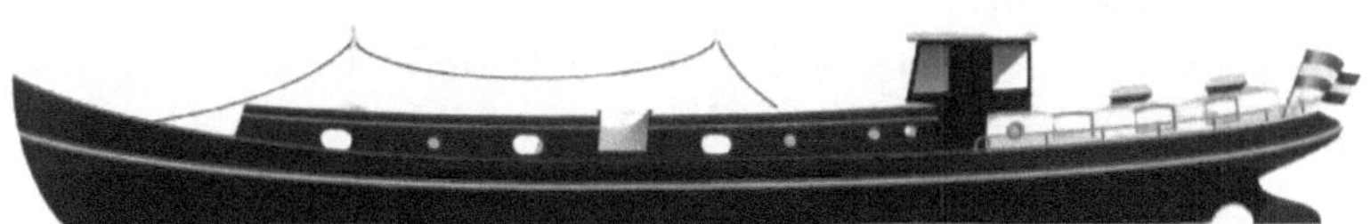

"Oh. Jack Walter was a cook," I repeated. "A cook wouldn't be taught unarmed combat, would they?"

"Unlikely," said Oscar. "And he was only in the army for four years. I think Jack's score can be reduced. Maybe to three."

"I'll pull the paper out again," said Emily.

I grimaced. "Yes, but this time, could we put it away afterwards? There's not much room in the flat and having to negotiate a gigantic white crime board makes things very crowded."

Emily threw her arms in the air. "Where else d'you expect me to keep it? I don't really even want it here."

"Sorry; it's your flat, not mine. You do what you like."

I really need to find somewhere else to live, before we fall out.

Emily spread the paper and knelt beside it with pink chalk in her hand. She summarised. "Jack Walter's score changes to three. He can't have killed Betty, because Betty died from a knife to the skull which we suspect was done by someone who had special forces skills, and Jack was an army cook, who probably had never fought." She rubbed out the '5' next to Jack's name and replaced it with '3'. "Where does that leave us? Everything still points to Harry Salisbury. He's our number one suspect and always has been. Ex-military, met with Betty only the previous day, and she drowned between his barges. I can't see it could be anyone else."

"How d'you explain the CCTV?" I asked. "Regardless of the time on the supermarket receipt, the cameras show he wasn't in the marina when Betty entered the water. But someone else was."

"I don't know," said Emily. "I'm just convinced he killed her. There are too many coincidences, and we don't like coincidences, right, Oscar?"

Oscar nodded. "I agree he's still the prime suspect. As is this Lance Evans. Let's recap Lance now."

"Okay," I said. "He's in his late thirties or early forties with three kids aged six months, five and eight. He runs an import export business in London, which brought him to Redcliff where he has dealings with persons unknown."

"Persons unknown?" Oscar laughed. "I'm struggling to believe you're a reluctant detective. You're using the lingo."

"Dealings with people we don't know about, then. Here's more about Lance. He's antisocial and spends his entire time staring at his phone. He doesn't join in with conversation, doesn't engage with anyone, including Chloe and the kids and didn't seem concerned when his children had gone missing."

"Didn't seem concerned or didn't actively join in the hunt?" countered Emily. "I mean, he didn't sit there and play on his phone while we were all searching the shrubbery, did he? He vanished and returned once the children had been found."

"There's something not right about him," I said. "I can't put my finger on it."

"It sounds like he needs further investigation," said Oscar. "As does Harry Salisbury. Divide and conquer again. Who'd like to speak with Harry?"

"I will," I said. "I'll visit him on the pretense of being interested in purchasing one of his barges."

"I think you find him attractive," said Emily.

"He's a good-looking chap; I'll admit. But I certainly don't want a romantic interlude with someone trained to kill."

"That takes care of him," said Oscar. "Would you be able to investigate Lance, Emily?"

"Me?" She pointed at her chest. "How? I don't even know where he's staying. And I couldn't simply walk up to a complete stranger and ask for directions, let alone inquire about their background." She turned red in the face. "Sorry. I won't do it."

I held her arm. "Would you, if I was present?"

She shrugged. "I suppose so."

I stood. "Oscar, I'll take the train to Brighthaven tomorrow to visit Captain Salisbury while Emily's running the café. On Tuesday afternoon, we'll track down Lance Evans and see what we can discover about him. I don't know exactly where they're staying, but Chloe mentioned it was a bed and breakfast in Redcliff beside the river."

"Hmm," said Emily. "There are at least two establishments which fit that description. Riverside Bed and Breakfast and Water's Edge Guest House. We'll try both."

"And I'll inquire about Betty's contacts at the Women's Institute and the church," said Oscar. "I was going to say, I'll find out if she had any enemies, but Betty made so many enemies, it's hard to see the wood for the trees."

We all laughed.

"Thanks for the tea," said Oscar. "I'll see myself out."

"And you and I," said Emily, turning to me, "need to prepare for marine rescue training in two hours. Communication with your skipper, remember?"

"David, would you take the wheel?" asked Murph, shortly after the rescue boat had departed from Redcliff Harbour. "Steer us to the east of Blakey's Island. Emily and Shiraz, stay in the cabin and keep watch. I need to, um, check something on the aft deck." He handed the controls to David and stepped out of the cabin door.

David, the qualified crew for this shift, eased himself into the skipper's position, adjusted the height of the seat to take into account his smaller-than-Murph frame and pushed the throttles forward. "Going up," he said. "Hold on."

"Holding on," we both replied.

"Are you training to be a skipper?" I asked him, as the vessel reached cruising speed and headed towards the horizon.

"I've started the course. There's a lot of academic study as well as practical work on the boat. I already have the required number of sea hours, which is a start. Is it something you'd be interested in doing?"

"We need to finish our qualified crew certificates first," said Emily.

"Yes," I said. "I looked at my workbook today, and we're not even half…"

"Man overboard, port side," yelled Murph's voice from behind us.

I jumped, and Emily glanced around. She poised one finger over the navigator's controls as David pulled the throttles back and swung the boat through 180 degrees.

"Shiraz," hissed Emily. "Where's the man overboard button gone?"

"It's the symbol of the person with their arms waving. Above the number '1' on the keypad. Push and hold number one."

"Penny-pinching pursers," yelled Murph. "Why is nobody out here pointing at the casualty?"

"Sorry," I shouted. "Coming." I stepped out and swept my eyes around the ocean for the rescue dummy, which I knew he'd thrown into the sea. "There." I held my arm out straight as the boat turned.

"Tell your skipper you have visual," instructed Murph.

"I have visual," I shouted to David. "Starboard side; fifty feet away."

I kept my eyes firmly on Ruth Lee, the bright-orange mannequin whose weight and build was intended to replicate a human. A reassuring tug on my lifejacket told me Emily had clipped the safety harness on.

"Twenty feet," I yelled, keeping my arm horizontal. "Ten, coming up on the starboard bow. Permission to open boarding door?"

"Open boarding door," called David.

I swung open the section of the boat's side, and the dark-green water appeared directly beneath me. The deck of the boat felt hard against my knees.

"Five feet. Preparing to retrieve."

Emily leant over me and, between the two of us, we grabbed Ruth Lee and heaved her on board. The dummy folded onto the deck, and I pretended to assess her.

"Casualty is conscious and breathing. Let's wrap her in blankets."

Murph raised his eyebrows and pointed at the boarding door.

"Oh, yes," I said. "Permission to close boarding door."

"Close boarding door," called David.

"Stop," said Murph. "Exercise over. David, please join us on the deck. Debrief. What went well?"

"We retrieved the casualty quickly," I said. "I don't think we could've done it any faster." I felt Emily at my back unclipping the safety harness.

"I'd agree," said Murph, "although the fact that Ruth Lee's a bright-orange dummy certainly makes her easy to spot. We did take too much time exiting onto the aft deck and pointing at the person in the water. If we'd lost sight of them, we might've spent valuable minutes or even hours searching."

"Sorry," said Emily. "I forgot where the man overboard button was."

"That's why we practise," said Murph. "Anything else to improve on?"

"Communication," I said, grimacing. "I didn't communicate enough with David about the boarding door and the position of the dummy."

"Over-communicate if you need to," said Murph. "More is better. Anything else? David?"

"We completely forgot something," he said. "My fault. We didn't radio Coastguard Headland Bay."

"Right," said Murph. "And what other communication did we forget?"

My mind cast back to the walkthrough Emily and I had performed that morning. "Oh. We forgot to ask the casualty their name, how they felt and whether there was anyone else with them."

"Exactly," said Murph. "Even if the shout from Coastguard says we're looking for one person, they might've received misinformation. But, as I said, this is why we practise, practise, practise so our actions become automatic. Let's do it again. This time, Emily, you can be harnessed up, and Shiraz can help. And remember—lots of communication. Ready?"

The radio crackled. "Marine Rescue Redcliff, Marine Rescue Redcliff, this is Coastguard Headland Bay. Come in, please. Over."

David swivelled and stepped into the cabin. He grabbed a pen and paper, then spoke into the handset. "Coastguard Headland Bay. This is Marine Rescue Redcliff receiving. Go ahead. Over."

"Marine Rescue Redcliff, are you available to search for a missing sea swimmer? He entered the water at Redcliff Harbour two hours ago, heading west around the coast. His partner's reported him late. Over."

"Received. We will commence a search for a sea swimmer heading west from Redcliff. Do you have any other details? Over."

"Yes. The casualty is called Robert, 35 years old, wearing a black wetsuit and black swim cap. We understand he's physically fit, and an experienced sea swimmer. Over."

"Received. Searching for a 35-year-old male named Robert, wearing a black wetsuit. We'll update you when we reach the search area. Over."

"Coastguard Headland Bay out."

"Everybody holding on?" asked David.

"Holding on," we replied, as he pushed the throttles forward, and we passed Blakey's Island, heading towards Redcliff Harbour.

CHAPTER TWENTY-SEVEN

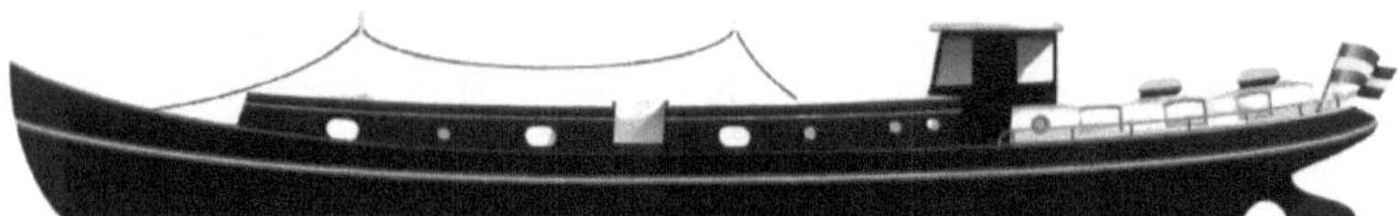

"This may be a difficult search," said Murph, pressing buttons on the navigator's screen while David drove the boat. "A human in the water is hard enough to see, but when they're dressed in black like some kind of navy seal, it becomes nearly impossible. Flickering furnaces; why can't wetsuits be made bright-orange, or candy-pink?"

Emily giggled. "Can you imagine frogmen in movies swimming under the water in candy-pink wetsuits, like something out of *Barbie*?"

"You know what I mean," said Murph. "Why does this chap have to be dressed in black?"

"Entering search area," said David, as we rounded Redcliff Harbour and swept into West Cove.

"Eyes on the water, crew," said Murph. "David, a sea swimmer should be no more than five hundred feet offshore. Take up station off West Cove beach and follow the shoreline three hundred feet out, roughly in the centre of where we expect to find him. Maintain a maximum speed of seven knots; we don't want to run him over. Emily, Shiraz, I want you two on the aft deck. One searches port, the other starboard. David and

I will search forward. That way, we'll cover the entire search area. How far does a swimmer travel in two hours?"

I swiped my phone and entered 'Sea swimmer speed' into Google. "It says here open water swimmers travel at around two miles per hour."

"In that case," said Murph, "we should come across him in four miles, maximum. That takes us all the way past Church Point and into the area off Smuggler's Cove." He plucked the radio handset from its mount. "Coastguard Headland Bay, this is Marine Rescue Redcliff. Come in, please. Over."

"Marine Rescue Redcliff, this is Coastguard Headland Bay. Go ahead. Over."

"We are west of Redcliff Harbour and commencing a search along the coast, remaining three to five hundred feet offshore. Over."

"Received. We'll contact you if we receive an update on the casualty's position. Coastguard Headland Bay out.

"Ready?" said Murph. "Take us up, David."

Emily and I stood on the aft deck, gazing in opposite directions. Emily stared towards the horizon, and I studied the area between the boat and the shoreline.

"Crew," called Murph.

"Yes," I shouted.

"Don't forget to keep an eye on the beach. If he's hurt himself, or he's exhausted, he might've swum in for a rest."

"Got it," I yelled back.

I was surprised how fast seven knots felt when we were searching. I knew it was only around eight miles per hour, very slow for a car, but staring at the waves roll past repeatedly, it felt like we'd miss anything in the water.

"Object off the port side," yelled Emily.

David brought the boat to a halt, and we all turned to see Emily with her arm outstretched, pointing to the horizon. The vessel swung as we navigated towards it.

"Do you still see it?" called Murph. "I can't see anything."

"One hundred feet off the bow."

"Shiraz, harness Emily up. She must keep her eyes on the casualty."

I grabbed the safety harness from the locker, unravelled it and clipped it to the metal ring on Emily's lifejacket.

"Fifty feet," called Emily. I stood behind her and shaded my eyes.

"It's a log," I said.

"We'll make certain before we continue," said Murph.

David drifted up to the item in the water, and we saw the slimy-green trunk of a tree, smoothed by the waves.

"I need to get better at searching," said Emily. "Sorry, that was a waste of time."

"Better to call it out than not," said Murph. "Shiraz, take the harness off her and we'll continue."

"Don't feel silly," I said. "No one else saw it, and it was about the same size as a person. Shall we swap sides, so you're looking at the shore?"

"Okay."

We took up station again as David powered up the throttles, and we regained our search speed.

"We're at Church Point," said David. "The swimmer shouldn't be on shore here. There's no beach, and he'd be dashed on the rocks."

We passed the black promontory jutting into the sea.

"Now we're in Smuggler's Cove," said David. "The furthest point we estimated the swimmer would reach in two hours. If we don't find him here, either we've missed him, or..."

"He's drowned," said Murph. "Sorry to be blunt, but that's the reality."

"Object off the starboard side," called Emily.

"Not another log?" I asked.

"That's not funny, Shiraz." She stood with her arm outstretched. "Logs don't wave."

We all stared at the sight of an arm extending from the water.

"He's going under," called Murph. "Shiraz, harness Emily up. Now."

I grabbed the harness again and clipped it to Emily. "Permission to open boarding door?"

"Granted," yelled David. He powered the boat towards the swimmer. "I have visual," he said.

"Twenty feet," called Emily, kneeling by the boarding door. I stood behind her. "Ten, nine, eight, slow down, four…"

We came alongside and Emily grabbed one of the swimmer's arms. I grasped the other, but we couldn't lift him in that fashion. I felt Murph's bulk between us; then he reached over and slipped his hands under the swimmers' armpits. Between the three of us, we pulled him on board, coughing and spluttering.

"Casualty is conscious and breathing," shouted Emily.

I heard David radioing the coastguard.

"What's your name?" I asked the man, who Murph had rolled into the recovery position.

"Robert. And I'm so sorry about this."

"There's no need to be sorry, Robert. Here, I'll dry you with this towel and throw this blanket over you. When you feel able, tell me what happened."

His explanation was punctuated by coughs and splutters. "I swim this distance regularly. But today I had extreme cramp in my right calf, and I couldn't kick that leg anymore. Did my wife ring you? I'm really sorry to have put you to all this trouble."

"It's fine. This is what we're here for. Is anyone else with you?" I glanced up at Murph to make sure he noted I'd remembered this question.

"No," said Robert. "Just me."

Emily pointed with her outstretched arm. "If he's by himself, who's that?"

"What?" said Murph. "Is it another log? We need to get this chap back to base and have the paramedics assess him. Close the boarding door, Shiraz. We'll quickly check out what Emily's seen." He stared in the direction she pointed. "David," he called. "Pass me the binoculars."

David grabbed them from the locker beside him and handed them to Murph.

Murph lifted them to his eyes. "David, drive over to the object Emily spotted. I don't think it's a log."

Emily kept her arm out straight. "One hundred feet off the port bow. Fifty feet. Oh. It's a person."

"You were definitely by yourself?" I asked Robert. He nodded, flaked out on his side and coughed. I was torn between caring for him and desperately wanting to see what Emily had spied.

"David," said Murph. "Permission to open the boarding door."

"Go ahead," said David, from the wheel.

I noted this role-reversal and realised that even though Murph was in charge, as David was acting as skipper, he was the one who granted permission to Murph.

"Emily," said Murph. "You still have the harness on. Kneel down. Same as before."

"Thirty feet," said Emily.

"They're face down in the water," said Murph. "We're not supposed to retrieve bodies, but we're going to have to. We can't leave it here, and if we wait for the coastguard to turn up, we risk Robert's safety. He needs urgent medical attention. Here, I'll do the lifting. A dead body will be a dead weight, obviously. They can't help themselves into the boat."

"Ten feet," called Emily. "Five. Here we are."

Emily grabbed an arm, and Murph held the person around the chest. They pulled, while I helped Robert shift himself out of the way. A human shape appeared, as floppy and helpless as the rescue dummy.

Murph turned the casualty over, and Emily and I both gasped.

"Emily," I said. "It's Jack Walter."

CHAPTER TWENTY-EIGHT

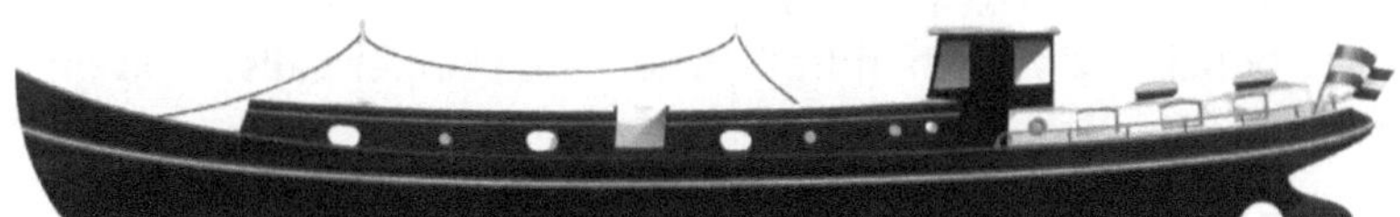

"David," called Murph. "Get on the radio to the coastguard and tell them we've recovered a body. Make sure they understand it's nothing to do with the swimmer, who's conscious, breathing and needs assessment by the paramedics immediately."

"Will do, Murph."

"Shiraz, cover him with something. I'm not accustomed to having a dead body on the boat."

I grabbed a blanket and threw it over Jack Walter.

Emily sidled up to me. "This is awful. How on earth could he have drowned? I feel sick. We saw him alive only a week ago."

"If he was one of the men on the beach, more recently still."

David stepped out of the wheelhouse. "Coastguard Headland Bay request we immediately return to Redcliff Harbour, where we'll be met by paramedics. And the police and undertaker, I suppose, given this turn of events."

"Take the wheel, David," said Murph. "Everybody inside the cabin while we're travelling at speed, please."

"Robert," I asked the rescued swimmer. "D'you feel well enough to stand?"

"I think so." He pushed himself up. "Yep."

I held onto him and helped him balance. "Take a seat on the rear bench. Grip the handrail. When the skipper calls 'Hold on', we all reply, 'Holding on'. Mind your head as you step inside. Stay on the seat and follow crew's instructions at all times."

"Great safety briefing," said Emily, keeping her eyes looking away from the body on the deck. "You'll be qualified crew in no time."

"You too, I reckon."

We sat Robert in the cabin. Murph occupied the navigator's position, and Emily and I gripped overhead rails.

"Everybody ready?" called David. "Going up. Hold on."

"Holding on," we all responded, as the engine noise increased, and the bow of the vessel rose to meet the oncoming waves.

A disco of blue, white and red flashing lights decorated the dock outside Redcliff Marine Rescue as we powered around the outside of the harbour wall and entered the mouth.

"Slow down," said Murph to David. "Keep our speed under five knots. There's a crowd watching, and we need to look professional."

"Got it, Murph." David pulled the throttles back, and the boat settled into a slow cruise.

"Shiraz, Emily," called David. "Ready with lines and fenders, please. Starboard side."

The two of us left the cabin and joined the body of Jack Walter on the deck.

"It's a good job we dragged him to the port side," said Emily. "Otherwise I'd have to stand on top of him to tie the lines on." She grimaced.

I raised my eyes at her. "We must catch up with Oscar when duty's finished and tell him one of our suspects now has a score of zero."

"No, they don't. Just because Jack Walter's dead doesn't mean he didn't kill Betty Stanton."

"True, but it's looking less likely." I shouted into the cabin, "Fenders secured."

"Thanks," came the answer.

We motored slowly up to the dock, which was lined with four paramedics, two policemen, a van with 'Redcliff Undertaking Services' written on the side and a multitude of locals and holidaymakers. Many had their mobile phones pointing at us.

"What a welcoming party," I said. "We'd better not mess up securing the boat. I'll climb up to the bow."

"Permission to go forward," I called into the cabin.

"Granted."

I stood with a black rope in my hands, ready to throw it over a bollard on the dock. Although I'd practised multiple times, this was the first time I'd done this in front of dozens of cameras and six emergency service employees.

Colleagues. Fellow emergency service workers. This is me, living my new life. Shiraz, do not stuff this up.

The gap between the rescue boat and the dock closed to two feet, and I threw the rope—line, I corrected myself—with both hands in an outward motion, as I'd been shown.

And missed.

No! Take two.

The vessel's forward motion halted, which meant Emily had successfully secured the stern line. At least we weren't going to drift away.

I recoiled the rope and threw it again. This time, it found its mark, and I secured it back to the boat's bow with a swift, practised movement. Nobody had noticed my slip-up. They were all too busy studying the object on the deck.

Emily helped Robert step up onto the harbour wall, and he departed with two of the paramedics, which left the other two, the undertakers and the policemen, both of whom I'd met before.

Sergeant Will Bishopstone from Redcliff police was the first to speak.

"Good afternoon, Redcliff Marine Rescue," he said to Emily. "Where is the deceased, please?"

"Under this blanket," said Emily, pointing.

"Step aside," said Will. "We'll take this from here." He turned to his left. "Constable Lachlan, please ask the public to take three steps back. Keep them well away."

"Right away, Sarge," said Lachlan. He turned, gestured with both arms wide and yelled, "Please keep well clear. This is a police emergency."

Sergeant Will turned to his right. "Paramedics and undertakers, please accompany me onto the boat. We'll remove the body to a more appropriate place for examination, away from these onlookers."

Murph stepped out of the cabin and planted his hands on his hips. "Officer, I'm the coxswain of this vessel. And no one boards without my permission."

I watched, fascinated, at these two alpha males facing off as if we were watching a David Attenborough documentary about Grizzly Bears.

"Very well, Coxswain. Please give us your permission to board your vessel and remove the deceased. Which is, in fact, a police matter."

"Not until you've completed a safety induction. The last thing we want is any of you injuring yourselves, or worse." He turned and glanced up at me, still standing on the bow. "Shiraz, please run through a safety briefing with the visitors."

"Me?" I shrugged.

"Obstinate outboards; there's only one Shiraz on the boat, isn't there? Yes, you."

"Gosh. Err, okay."

I stepped around the cabin onto the rear deck. A combination of pride that Murph had entrusted me with this task and nervousness that I'd mess it up washed over me, as I began to recite the lines I'd been taught in training. Sergeant Will crossed his arms and fidgeted while a mere trainee gave him instructions, but this was our domain, not his. I reminded myself there was no way he'd allow me to step into his patrol car without permission.

"And finally," I said, "always follow our directions. Especially the skipper's. If he gives you an instruction, don't question it." I glanced at Murph, then stared directly in Sergeant Will's eyes. "Is that all understood?"

"Yes, yes," said Will, raising his voice and adopting a challenging tone. "Have you finished? May we come aboard now?"

"You may," said Murph. "My crew will assist you if needed." He gave me two subtle thumbs-ups, and I grinned.

I held out my hand for Sergeant Will to take but he brushed it away and stepped down. "I'm Sergeant Will Bishopstone, for anyone who doesn't know me."

"Darcy and Michael," said the young, female paramedic, indicating her colleague.

"Hi, Darcy," I said. "I'm Shiraz, and this is Emily and Murph, and David's the chap in the cabin. We met before, last month."

"Did we? Sorry, I see so many people."

I observed Sergeant Will's annoyance at our familiarity, and I smiled to myself.

Sergeant Will crouched beside the body and flipped the towel off its face, showed it to Darcy and covered it again. "We're all in agreement, I think, that this person is dead."

"Yes," said Darcy. "By the looks of them, for several hours. Shiraz, where did you find them? Were they in the water, or washed up on a beach?"

"In the water, near Smuggler's Cove. I knew this person, actually."

"I'm so sorry," said Darcy. "Were you close?"

"No. We'd only met once, last week."

"Name?" asked Sergeant Will.

"Shiraz Jones."

"Not your name; the deceased."

"Oh. Jack Walter. He was a churchwarden at All Saints, Redcliff."

Sergeant Will beckoned Constable Lachlan, who abandoned his crowd control and stood on the dock by the rescue boat.

"Constable," said Will, quietly, "who was the man reported missing last night?"

"Walter. Either the first name or the surname was Walter."

"I reckon we've found him. I'll ask the undertakers to remove the body for pathology, and could the marine rescue crew please accompany me to the police station?"

"We'll attend the station once we've packed our kit away and the boat's back in the shed, Sergeant," said Murph.

"How long does that take?"

"Around an hour, and we're not going to be rushed. My crew have had a nasty experience this afternoon, and I'd like them to grab a cup of tea before they attend your premises."

"I'll see you in an hour then." He sighed. "Quicker, if possible."

I smiled at the power plays between Will and Murph. But I also realised something for the first time. Something I probably should have realised from the start of my marine rescue career, if it wasn't for his gruff nature.

Murph had my back. Despite his frustrations at me forgetting instructions, turning up to training without having revised the subject matter and messing up the drills, Murph put his crew's wellbeing ahead of anyone else's demands. Goosebumps formed on my arms.

I'm part of the team. Part of Team Redcliff Marine Rescue.

And I nodded and set my jaw in confirmation that my decision to leave London, with its empty, vapid, meaningless lifestyle to move here was the right one. I glanced at Murph and smiled, but he turned away and began coiling a rope.

The undertakers fetched a stretcher from their van and lifted Jack Walter's body onto it. They covered him with something more official than a blanket and carried him off the boat. Constable Lachlan could keep the crowd back, but he couldn't prevent all the mobile phones from clicking.

Once the police had departed, David backed the tractor down the boat ramp and pulled the boat out of the water. While Emily and I packed up ropes and stowed fenders, Murph grabbed a bucket of water with disinfectant and swabbed the deck with a mop. I was impressed that no job was beneath him. The crowd dispersed as our routine clean up no longer provided entertainment, and David drove the tractor and trailer with the boat on it into the shed. The roller doors clattered closed, and we stripped off our overalls.

"Gather round, everyone," said Murph. "Who wants a tea?"

"I'll make them," said Emily, probably more out of her mistrust of Murph's tea-making skills than anything. She plopped teabags into mugs and boiled the kettle.

"Is everybody okay?" asked Murph. "It's almost unheard of for us to retrieve a body. Can anyone tell me what we would've done if we hadn't had the swimmer on board?"

"Yes," I said. "We would've marked the body with something which floats, such as a fender, and stood by until the coastguard arrived."

"Correct," said Murph. "They're the paid professionals. We're still professional; I'd never use the word 'amateur' about our organisation, but volunteers aren't trained in body recovery. Shiraz and Emily, I have no hesitation in signing off both of you for your man overboard skills. I'm not aware of any other recruits, certainly not in my time, who've retrieved a body and rescued a conscious swimmer in the same duty.

Pass me your workbooks for my moniker. Then, once we've finished our tea, we'll all go to see what Sergeant Will wants. We'd better not keep him waiting too long." He winked at me and opened the fridge to find the milk.

Murph drove us in his glazier's van. After giving Sergeant Will our statements describing the circumstances of finding the body, Emily and I began the walk home. As we left the police station, her phone rang. She missed the call, then mine began its ringtone, and I pressed the green button.

"Hi, Oscar," I said. "Is everything okay?"

"No. Rose Walter's going frantic. Jack went out to check on the vicarage last night after she returned from flower arranging at the church. He never came home. Rose rang the police last night, and they told her they'd look for him, but I wouldn't be surprised if they hadn't yet. Most so-called missing people turn up within a few hours with a perfectly normal explanation. Still, it's unlike..."

"He's dead."

"Sorry?"

"Jack Walter. He's dead. We pulled his body out of the water this afternoon. We're just leaving the police station."

"What?"

"Tell him to come over," said Emily.

"Oscar, Emily says come over. We'll meet you at the flat."

CHAPTER TWENTY-NINE

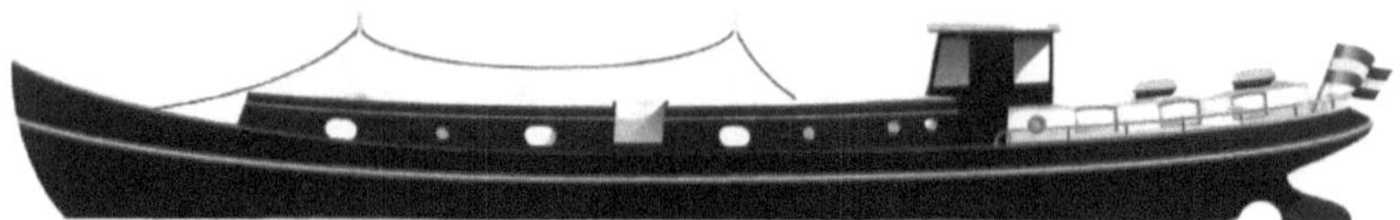

Camouflage clothes were neatly folded, as the soldier checked and rechecked equipment.

The frontline of the battle arena was about to advance, and it was time for the patrol to relocate to their new station.

Forward communications had been established, and evidence of the patrol's last position would be eliminated.

All the phases of this operation had gone completely to plan.

It was time.

Time to begin phase four.

The final phase.

As leader of the patrol, the soldier took the responsibility.

And, very shortly, the soldier would take the glory.

CHAPTER THIRTY

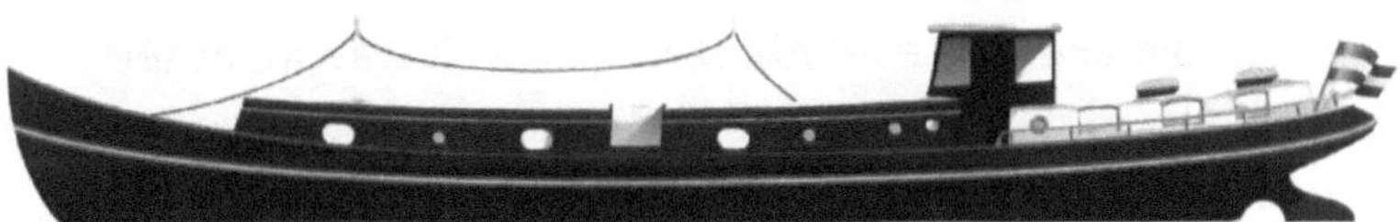

"This is extraordinary," said Oscar. He clutched a glass of red wine and leant on his arms at Emily's table. Cadbury lay in the corner of the living room, having been banished from the floor where our investigation paper was spread out. Boots was absent, presumed out for an evening rendezvous with the incoming fishing fleet.

"Jack Walter," continued Oscar, "had no interest in boats or the sea. I've heard he couldn't even swim. What on earth would he be doing in the water off Smuggler's Cove?"

I shrugged. "He'd been in the sea for a long time when we found him, according to the paramedics."

"How far offshore was he?"

"Three hundred feet. We'd rescued a man who'd swum from Redcliff Harbour to Smuggler's Cove when Emily saw the body floating nearby. If it wasn't for the shout to that swimmer, we might never have found him."

"D'you think he entered the water the previous night?" said Emily. "He left home to check on the vicarage and hadn't returned, and his wife expected him back that evening."

"Let's work on that basis until proved otherwise," said Oscar. "Play it out. Jack Walter visited the vicarage to check on it before bed. He lived on the same side of town, and knowing Jack, he would've walked. I can't imagine him driving up there. So Jack strolled up to the vicarage, and he shone his torch around to make sure everything looked as it was supposed to. How did he end up in the sea? The building has a walled garden; it's not possible to drop over the edge of the rocks."

"He might've entered the tunnels to Smuggler's Cove?" suggested Emily.

"Did he even know about the tunnels?" asked Oscar. "And didn't you say there were ladders which were hard to negotiate?"

"Perhaps Jack was one of the mysterious figures unloading the crates from the boat?" I suggested.

"I don't think so," said Emily. "Although we didn't see their faces, those men moved like younger people. Not someone in their seventies."

"Ahem," said Oscar. "I could carry a crate full of dolls."

"I'm sure. I just don't think either of those figures was Jack. He limped."

"We should return to the vicarage," I said. "Maybe we missed something."

"No," said Oscar. "Not until the vicars return. I don't approve of snooping around while they're away."

"We're not going to snoop around," I said. "Let's offer to keep an eye on the place in Jack Walter's absence."

"Hmm," said Oscar. "I have been curious about these tunnels you mentioned. And I'd like to inspect the packing cases you saw being carried into the barn. Here's what we'll do. I'll ask my wife to contact Sister Florrie. She must know about Jack; someone will have told her. My wife can say I've offered to look after the vicarage now Jack can't. I'll suggest that in a way that doesn't rouse anyone's suspicions."

"Perfect. Shall we go tomorrow?"

"The café's open tomorrow," said Emily, "so it'll have to be later on."

"Of course, and I'm travelling to Brighthaven to check out Harry Salisbury during the day. We'll go in the evening. That's when Jack used to do his final check for the night, didn't he?"

"Apparently so. Let's meet at seven o'clock," said Oscar. "Oh, Cadbury. What have you got there?"

Cadbury glanced up at us with a guilty look. He held something between his paws.

Oscar stood and approached him. The dog grabbed the object and chewed it.

"Cadbury! Put it down. Now. Give it to me." Oscar wrestled the object from Cadbury's mouth. "Sorry, Shiraz. It's that doll you showed me. Cadbury has a thing for plastic toys."

I took the doll from Oscar, and it came apart in two pieces.

"He pulled the head off," said Emily.

Cadbury hid his eyes with his paws.

"He always does that when he's in trouble," said Oscar. "He thinks we can't see him."

I held the two halves of the doll up to each other and rotated one. "There," I said. "The head screws back on. It's designed to be removed." I unscrewed it again and showed Oscar and Emily. "And it's hollow inside." I twisted the doll back together. "No harm done, Cadbury. You're not in the doghouse."

"What-ho, you liked the look of my barge the other day, and now you're interested in buying one?" said Harry. "There's a deucedly long waiting list, but if you give me a deposit now, your home should be ready by the end of next year."

"I'm in no hurry," I said.

We sat in the living room of the barge which he inhabited, his showbarge, as he called it. Just like a showhome, except…a barge. Outside, grey clouds scudded past the distinctive, half-moon-shaped windows, seven cut in each side.

"Where we are now was the original hold," he explained. This entire section of barge"—he waved his arm in a movement which encompassed the kitchen, the living area, a bedroom beyond and a bathroom—"was where the goods were stored to be transported up and down the river in Holland. The roof"—he pointed upward—"came off in sections, and cranes would unload the cargo at the wharves.

"It's a fantastic space. And in this configuration it has two bedrooms?"

"Cabins, I prefer to call them. I find buyers, whether they have a nautical connection or not, like me to use marine terminology. It makes the entire experience quirkier for them. So, for instance, the kitchen is always referred to as the galley. Take a look."

We stood and wandered into the kitchen—sorry—galley.

Harry opened cupboards, a dishwasher and a full-size fridge. "As you can see, this marvellous space is as well equipped as any central London apartment. Probably better. You wouldn't want for anything."

"People in the London film industry would love this lifestyle," I said, idly studying a Post-it note stuck to his fridge. "They'd cover the walls with ships in bottles and original paintings of harbours to pretend they were experts on all things nautical."

Harry laughed. "They sound like some of my clients. Let's discuss your requirements, and I'll note down your details. Would you want this layout, with two cabins and two ensuites; or do you need three, perhaps for overnight visitors?"

"I haven't decided."

"No problem. The barge next door has a three-cabin configuration. I'm building it for a London film director to use as a second base." He lowered his voice. "My suspicion is, it's a love nest. I've seen magazine photos of him being a little too cosy with a ravishing blonde, and I suspect he and his wife may be separating. He's asked for a pair of cabins in the bow for his children."

"You may well be right. I have some experience in errant husbands."

"Golly. And you're not attached now?"

"No. Happily separated."

"Could I note down your phone number? As a potential client?"

"Of course. It's 07700 900119. May we look at the barge next door now?"

"Rather. It's a construction site, so we'll need to be careful. Grab your coat; it's cold outside."

Harry led me out of his barge onto the dock. The weather had begun to drizzle, and I hugged myself. Brighthaven Marina appeared deserted, devoid of human presence.

Desolate.

Eerie.

Harry produced a bunch of keys and opened the door to the next barge. The wheelhouse was almost identical to the boat he lived in, except everything was covered in a layer of dust. The wheel itself had been concealed by a white sheet, and the brass fittings were green and discoloured.

"As you can see," said Harry, "this is a work in progress. I always refurbish the wheelhouse last, as I'm constantly traipsing in and out with tools, supplies and dirty boots. Come below."

He switched on a light, led me down a steep ladder, and we arrived at the bargekeeper's accommodation under the wheelhouse. Instead of the plush carpet and expensive furniture I'd seen on Harry's barge, this room had a bare floor and contained a portable workbench and two sawhorses. A piece of timber rested across them.

An electric saw was on the floor with a power cable trailing from it, and sawdust covered every surface.

"I use this handy little area as my workshop when I'm doing a barge conversion," he said. "It's jolly marvellous for the purpose, with power and everything. This will eventually become the main cabin and the bathroom for my client's bolthole." He grinned.

"I'm sure it'll be lovely when it's finished," I said.

Harry flicked another switch, and a stark, white light illuminated the hold area. Bare partition walls betrayed the layout of the conversion, and sawdust again covered the floor.

"The first job is always to seal the hold and ensure structural integrity. Then I reinforce the roof so no beastly rain gets in, punch a door so the hold can be accessed from the original living area and cut the windows in the sides. Only then do I begin the fit out. You can get a feel for the layout, but you'll observe all the fittings are missing."

Our footsteps echoed on the bare floor as I followed him.

"This area will be the galley. It's in the same position as on my boat, but the client's requested a different configuration with the kitchen sink in the centre, and the oven over here. Then the dining room and lounge will be beyond that, but they'll be more squashed than on my boat owing to the extra cabin in the bow."

He led me into the area at the far end of the hold where he'd run a dividing wall, and two rooms mirrored each other. Dim light entered through the side windows.

I peeked into the rooms, and decided I'd prefer a two-bedroom barge. Or a one-bedroom one. Just for me. But what was I thinking? I needed somewhere to live now, not in two years' time, or whenever Harry could fit me into his schedule. And the point of my visit was to try to find information confirming Harry's guilt of Betty's murder, not to go house shopping.

"There's nothing else to see," he said. "Do you want to order a barge today, or think about it?"

"I'd like to think about it, please. But thanks for showing me around."

We climbed up the companionway and stepped out onto the jetty. Harry locked the door behind him.

I turned towards the third barge, moored at the end of the dock. "What about this one? May I see that?"

Harry's demeanour changed. "Definitely not. It's completely unconverted. I only sailed it from Holland three weeks ago."

"But it might be useful for me to see inside the hold? Then I could visualise what a single-cabin configuration would be like? I might want the main cabin in the bow and keep the original bargekeeper's accommodation as a bathroom-cum-dressing room, for instance."

"Nobody's allowed on that barge. It's too dangerous. And there are no lights."

"Oh. Shame. Would it be possible to have a quick look around the outside?"

"What's the point? It's identical to the other two." He looked at his watch. "Now, if you don't mind, I have an appointment to meet a friend for a late lunch in town. I'll lock up my barge and see you out."

"No problem. And thank you for showing me your barges. I'll let you know."

Harry nipped inside his barge, switched out his lights, locked up and escorted me through the marina gate.

"Don't forget," he said, "if you'd like to order one, please give me a call."

He clanged the gate shut, and I watched him march away towards the centre of Brighthaven.

I stood with my hands in my pockets. The drizzle intensified, and I knew I should walk to the station and head back to Redcliff. The café would've closed by now, and Emily and I needed to prepare for this evening's foray to the vicarage. Goodness knows what we'd find there, but at least this time we wouldn't have to worry about Jack Walter catching us.

I was about to leave, when the marina gate opened from the inside, and Doug stepped out.

"Afternoon, again," he said, touching his beanie hat deferentially. "Are you here to visit the barge chap?"

"Yes. Harry Salisbury."

"I remember you," said Doug. "You came to see him before. Here, let me hold the gate for you."

And in two seconds, I was back inside the marina.

The gate clanged behind Doug, and I glanced around. No one else stirred on this dreary afternoon. Boat owners were at home keeping warm and dry, and their vessels lay unloved at their moorings waiting for the next sunny day, when the fair-weather sailors would resurface.

I marched back down Harry's jetty. I knew the cameras would be able to see me, but I counted on no one monitoring the footage unless something happened which needed investigating. Like a murder.

Why was Harry so insistent I shouldn't see the third barge? If, as he'd said, it was an empty shell, where was the harm? And where had the doll on Harry's chair gone? I suppose he could've given it to whoever it was intended for. But my instincts told me something wasn't right, and I was determined to find out what.

I passed Harry's barge and glanced in the window, although I knew he was out. The black water between the barges where we'd discovered Betty's body still looked as ominous today.

I hesitated before approaching the third barge. What would I find there? Without Oscar or Emily with me, if I discovered something I didn't like the look of, I'd be on my own. I gritted my teeth, glanced over my shoulder, stepped onto barge three's deck and rattled the wheelhouse door handle. Locked. Maybe the other side was open? I climbed around the stern to the opposite side of the wheelhouse and tried the door there, but it was locked too.

I shaded my eyes with my hands and peered into the windows. The third barge appeared the same as the other two, with the wheel surrounded by brass instruments. But they were uncovered and devoid of sawdust. I turned away and was about to step off the barge when something caught my eye. Something in the water tied to barge three.

A grey, timber rowing boat.

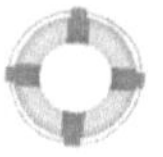

CHAPTER THIRTY-ONE

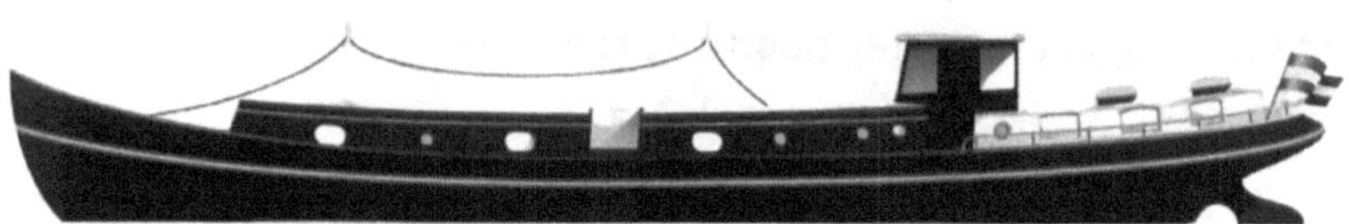

"Where've you been, Shiraz? It's six-thirty. We're meeting Oscar at seven."

"Sorry, I missed the train I intended to take and had to wait an hour for the next one. Then there was a points failure or something, and we were stationary for twenty minutes. I'm here now, and I've got some interesting information."

"Ooh, do tell. What did Harry have to say?"

"Harry didn't give away anything. We talked about boats and barges, and he gave me a tour of the one he lives on and the one next door which is being converted. I did a fantastic job of pretending to be a potential customer."

"That's great, but did you uncover any clues?"

"Two. First, he didn't want me to look in the third barge. He said it's dangerous, and there aren't any lights."

"That's not a clue. He would've been telling the truth. There are probably insurance reasons members of the public can't enter construction sites."

"He showed me around the second one, which had bits of timber and power tools scattered everywhere. So I'm not sure about that. Let's see you try to pour cold water on this clue, then. I returned to the marina after Harry had left, courtesy of Doug, the least security-minded person on the planet. And I climbed on board the third barge; the one Harry wouldn't let me on."

"I'm glad I wasn't with you. What would you have done if he'd returned, or if it was as dangerous as he said it was, and you injured yourself?"

"We'll never discover anything without taking a few risks. I clambered up and peeked through the wheelhouse windows. The barge was locked, so I couldn't get in, but, get this, d'you remember the craft which transported the packing cases to the beach at Smuggler's Cove?"

"Of course. You said it was a grey, wooden rowing boat. Nothing out of the ordinary."

"Correct. The same boat's tied to Harry's third barge."

"So one of the people on the beach probably was him? But all your discovery intimates is that he was involved in bringing the boxes of dolls ashore. As Oscar said, although that activity was definitely suspicious, it wasn't criminal. No crime was committed. None of that means he murdered Betty."

"What about Jack Walter's murder?"

"Was that murder? Nobody suggested that. You're over thinking this. Are you ready? We need to leave to meet Oscar."

Despite the light drizzle, Emily drove her vintage Morris Minor out of the garage with the convertible top down.

"Honestly," she said, "it's so much effort to raise and lower the roof, I prefer to leave it down all the time. Unless it's pouring with rain."

We headed out of town past the turning to Redcliff Manor then, before we reached Alnchurch, we veered left along a narrow, hedge-lined road, following the direction of a fingerpost indicating 'All Saints Church and Vicarage.' At the end of the lane, the road became a rough track bordered by dry-stone walls. A left fork led to the church, and a right one to the barred vicarage driveway. We found Oscar leaning against the gatepost with Cadbury lying at his feet. Both jumped up at our approach.

"Where will you leave the car in this rain?" I asked. "It'll get soaked."

"Under this sycamore tree. The ground's dry under it."

I rolled my eyes at her and smiled. "Hi, Oscar. Hello, Cadbury."

"Good afternoon, Ladies. Cadbury and I enjoyed a lovely walk along the cliffs past West Cove, didn't we, boy? Although it was sludgy underfoot. I'm glad I brought my raincoat."

Cadbury shook himself violently and sprayed a cloud of fine mist over us.

"Shall we?" said Oscar, and he opened the gate.

"No breaking and entering for us tonight," I said to Emily.

"No," said Oscar, holding up a large key. "I collected the barn key from Jack Walter's house. Poor Rose is beside herself. She can't understand what Jack would've been doing going anywhere near the sea, and she imagines he'll walk back in the front door at any moment."

We crunched up the vicarage driveway. Oscar held a long, black sturdy torch in his hand. By 7:15 this evening, the sun had begun to dip towards the horizon, but there was still over half an hour of daylight. I assumed he'd brought it with him to search the cellars or the barn.

"I've been here many times before," said Oscar. "My wife drags me to various church functions. I keep protesting it's her thing and not mine, but to no avail. At least they usually feed me."

We laughed.

I pointed. "Here's the bush. Push these branches apart, and on the other side you can see the steps down to the cellar."

"I'm scared," said Emily. "What if those men come back?"

Oscar held up his torch. "This may come in handy. On several occasions in my time as a serving policeman, I used a torch identical to this as a deterrent. In self-defence only, you understand. Lead on, Shiraz."

I switched on my phone light and descended the steps. Emily followed, and Oscar brought up the rear. The strong beam of his torch lit up the entrance in front of me.

"This is where we found the doll we thought was Gracie's," I said, "and the trapdoor's here." I jumped up and down to demonstrate where it was. "Look at these nail heads. Someone's sealed it closed. Emily, d'you have your food processor blade?"

"No. I threw it away; it was so broken. Now I'll have to buy a third one."

"Do we need to open it?" asked Oscar, flashing his torch around the walls and ceiling. "From what I understand, the important tunnel's the one that comes up in the barn." He swivelled on his heels and marched back up the stairs. Emily and I followed.

The barn opened with a twist of the gigantic key, and I found the light switch and clicked it.

"This looks so different than at the Marine Rescue dance, doesn't it?" said Oscar. "I must've attended twenty or more of those. All very enjoyable occasions. Where's the trapdoor?"

"Over there," said Emily, pointing.

We strode to the opposite side of the barn. I bent down and ran my fingers over the hatch. "Someone's nailed this shut too."

"You're right," said Oscar. "The only way to crack it open would be with a crowbar. Where are the packing cases with the dolls in them?"

"They're under this tarpaulin," I said, lifting a corner and peeking beneath it.

My eyes didn't deceive me, but I flapped the tarpaulin to make sure.

The packing cases had gone.

CHAPTER THIRTY-TWO

"It's like I dreamt those packing cases were ever there," I said, after we'd locked the barn door. "Honestly, Oscar, there were over a hundred. All full of those dolls."

"And a shaft down to a tunnel," said Emily. "My bruises from last week confirm its existence."

"I believe you," said Oscar. "But they're not in the barn now. And, as I said, bringing packing cases full of dolls from a boat via a tunnel and storing them in a barn isn't illegal."

"What if they're related to Jack Walter's death?" I asked. "What if he stumbled across the packing cases, and whoever was storing them killed him because he'd seen them?"

"Didn't he have the only key?" asked Oscar, holding it up. "Even though you managed to wriggle under the door, there's no way anyone could've removed packing cases without opening it."

"Ooh," said Emily. "Jack Walter was part of the scheme."

"Let's wait until we gather all the evidence about our primary suspects before jumping to conclusions," said Oscar, as we reached the gate. "You've visited Harry today, Shiraz, and you're both going to track Lance down tomorrow. Then we'll put our heads together again. Something's not right about any of this."

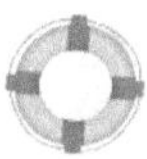

"I know the people who run Riverside Bed and Breakfast," said Emily, as she locked up the Wicked Whelk the following afternoon. "They're called Marion and Vic. He's a retired builder, and she used to work at the bank. A lovely couple."

"That's good," I said. "Hopefully, Lance and Chloe and the kids are still staying there."

We strolled along the sea front, past the deckchair and boat hire kiosks whose trade had fallen away to nothing following the Easter rush. A few families with pre-school-aged children remained in town, but almost all the Easter holidaymakers had departed, and the beach was taking a breather before the onset of summer.

Emily rang the bell at the bed and breakfast, and a woman in her seventies answered the door.

"Good afternoon," she said. "Are you wanting accommodation?"

"Marion, it's Emily."

"Emily, sorry. I didn't recognise you." She pushed her spectacles up her nose. "You've done something with your hair. Come in, come in."

"I haven't done anything with my hair since she last saw me," whispered Emily as we followed Marion into a kitchen with a central circular table. A wide window gave a view onto a garden full of spring flowers, and we caught sight of a man wearing gardening clothes, digging with a spade. Behind him, the little brook which pierced Redcliff's town centre bordered a lawn. An outdoor table and chairs stood on the riverbank, and three white swans floated backwards and forwards. The comforting smell of home baking filled the space, as Marion grabbed a plastic container and a knife.

"Gingerbread," she said. "May I offer you a cup of tea and a slice?"

"Lovely," said Emily. "Marion, this is my friend, Shiraz."

"Shirley?"

"Shiraz."

"Got it. Hello," said Marion, in a tone which indicated she was never going to remember my name.

"Pleased to meet you, Marion," I said. "It's a lovely place you have here."

"Thank you. I'm sorry I didn't recognise you, Emily. We see so many people coming and going with the bed and breakfast business. Milk? Sugar?"

"Just milk, thanks," we both said.

Marion handed me my hot drink. "Here you are, Sharon," she said.

I decided not to correct her.

"Marion, it's lovely to see you," said Emily. "But this isn't just a social call."

"Oh?"

"We wanted to ask you about a couple staying with you. Lance and Chloe Evans."

"There's no one staying at the moment. The last people checked out on Sunday. They said they were heading along the coast to Brighthaven. When were your friends here?"

"They weren't friends, as such," Emily began, and I made a subtle zipping motion across my lips.

"They were holidaymakers here," I said, "and we'd met them during their stay. We planned to call around and ask for their details so we could stay in touch once they returned to London."

"Those weren't the names of the last people," said Marion. "Let me fetch my guest book."

She pushed herself up, walked over to a dresser at the side of the room and tugged a hardback book from the top drawer. "Here we are." She opened it in front of us. "The people who checked out last week were Mr and Mrs Brown. From Norfolk."

I inspected the scrawly writing. "How long did the Browns stay? Our friends were in town over Easter weekend."

"Ten days, I suppose."

"I'm sorry; I think we've wasted your time. They told us they were staying at a bed and breakfast by the river, and we thought it must've been yours."

"There is one other guest house by the river, Water's Edge, further up the town. Maybe try there?"

"We will, thank you. This cake is delicious. How long have you lived here now, Marion?"

"Forty-one years. Vic built the place himself. We brought up three daughters in this house, and now between them they have seven children."

"I'll bet your grandchildren love this place, with the lawn to play on, and the swans to feed."

"They do, and it's a real attraction for guests with youngsters. Those people, the Browns, they had three. A boy of eight, a five-year-old girl and a baby. The boy was always making up stories about pirates and sea monsters. He'd stand by the river and pretend to be a ship's captain. The poor swans; I had to ask him politely not to try to strike them with pieces of bread while he was feeding them. He'd stand there and yell 'fire!' and 'direct hit', every time a crust collided with one."

"What was his name?" I asked, pursing my lips.

She rubbed her forehead. "Ooh, let's see if I can remember. Some modern name. I want to call him Hudson, or Hubbard. And the girl might've been Greta. She always carried a doll and sucked her thumb. I can't remember what the baby was called. I would mind them many evenings while their parents were out; I even put those kids to bed." She lowered her voice. "They said they were in Redcliff on business, but what kind of business keeps people out until almost midnight; that's what I'd like to know? I suspect they were enjoying themselves at the pub, availing themselves of my babysitting services."

I frowned and studied the guest book again. "Are you sure these people were called Brown? Not Evans?"

"Evans? No, I'm sure it was Brown. Larry and Charlotte Brown. That's what's written in there."

"Oh, our friends were called Evans. We'll check at the other bed and breakfast further up the town. We must've been mistaken about them staying here. Thank you for the cake. It was delicious."

"Two deaths," said Oscar that evening, "with multiple mysteries, and nothing seems to connect."

"Yes," I said, glancing over at our investigation sheet covering Emily's carpet. "I feel like scrumpling up that sheet of paper and throwing it in the bin. I can't see how it helps at all. The secret night-time shipments through the tunnels, the grey rowing boat, the dolls, the packing cases, Harry's mysterious third barge; and the fact that Lance and Chloe appear to have given false names at the bed and breakfast; none of that relates to Betty and Jack's deaths."

"Marion might've simply been mistaken," said Emily. "She doesn't have a great memory for names."

"No, the guest book contained entries by each guest, with a one-line review. And the last line definitely said Larry and Charlotte Brown. Marion's recollections of the kids' names were similar to their actual names. And their ages were identical. I'm sure we're talking about the same people."

"What do the police say, Oscar?" asked Emily.

"Jack's death isn't being treated as suspicious. Redcliff police believe the poor chap was suffering from memory loss, and he wandered over the edge of the rocks into the sea. That may well be possible. In my time as a serving police officer, I was involved with more than one search for an elderly person who'd done exactly that. It's not an unlikely scenario."

"And what about Betty Stanton?"

"Betty's death is a different matter. It has Martin Buchanan stumped. He's never had a special forces-type killing on his patch, and he's complaining his investigation's more like a spy novel. Although there are ex-military people of all ages around Brighthaven, he hasn't identified anyone who was in the special forces, or who meets the description of the unknown person on the CCTV. And Harry Salisbury hasn't been forthcoming. He says he's provided all the information he can, and there's nothing else to tell."

"It couldn't have been him," said Emily, "because of the supermarket receipt and because of the CCTV. Unless…"

"Yes…?" I said.

"Unless he exited the marina, fetched his rowing boat which he'd secreted elsewhere, rowed to the end of the jetty where the barges are tied up, killed Betty, then jumped back in the rowing boat and returned via the gate later. Arriving by sea, he would've been out of sight of the cameras the entire time."

"Gosh," I said. "That might very well be what happened. But who was the mystery person on the CCTV?"

"We need to put our incident sheet to use again," said Oscar. "We're theorising without jotting things down. Very risky. Let's study our list of suspects and update it, as well as noting down these new clues. Emily, d'you have the chalk?"

"I do. Where should we start?"

"Lance Evans," I said. "Or Larry Brown. Whichever was his real name. I'm inclined to give him the same score as Harry Salisbury. Nine. How would we find out if he had a military background? He looks like a soldier, with the crewcut hairstyle, neat moustache and tattoos."

"I'll ask Inspector Buchanan to check him out," said Oscar. "He was compiling the list of members and ex-members of the forces so he must have access to military records or know someone who does. I'll ask him to check out Lance Evans and Larry Brown. Whichever alias he uses, he's aged around forty, correct?"

"Yes. And I think we'll reduce Harry's score to eight. Still high, but lower than Lance's. I'm convinced Lance was the mysterious person on the CCTV. And the footage showed Harry was almost certainly not in the marina when Betty died. Unless Emily's scenario with the rowing boat is correct."

"I agree," said Oscar. "And I'd reduce Jack Walter's score. As well as being deceased, he didn't have any kind of special forces training. Make him a two. And put a cross by his name, to indicate he's passed away."

Emily chalked the updates. "That leaves the Women's Institute people, the church congregation, including Sister Florrie and Sister Marie, and book contacts. Who we haven't narrowed down yet. Plus the son who lives in Scotland."

"Out of all of those," said Oscar, "the son, Rodney's the most likely. But he left Redcliff over twenty years ago, presumably as soon as he was allowed to make his own decisions and doesn't seem to have returned much. He married a Scottish lady and lives near her family in Edinburgh."

"Hopefully her family's nice to him. Goodness knows what it must've been like having Betty as a mother," said Emily. "Should I update his score from three?"

"I don't think so. He's been off the scene so long and doesn't have a military past."

"Maybe bitterness and resentment about the way Betty raised him welled up for twenty years. Finally, one day, he snapped, drove five hundred miles south to Redcliff and murdered her. Case closed."

"She was murdered in Brighthaven," I said. "Her son wouldn't have gone looking for her on Harry's barge."

"The son might've been one of the men on the beach?" said Emily. "There were three. Perhaps it was Harry, Lance and this Rodney chap?"

"Guesswork," said Oscar. "We don't have any evidence to suggest he's involved in any way, whereas Harry Salisbury's directly connected to Betty's murder via the location. Lance, or Larry; I'm not so sure about. He needs further investigation. Especially considering he appears to have an alias." He cleared his throat. "I believe the chances of the Women's Institute or the church harbouring a special forces operative are minimal. I've checked with my wife, and, apart from Jack Walter and his service in the catering corps, the only person she knows of with a military background at the church is a Major Jenks, and he's 91 years old and in a wheelchair. The book may be a possibility; we theorised Betty upset someone with her content, although I have to say I think it's unlikely. I do have a plan, though, as to how we could investigate all those avenues more closely. But I'll come back to that once we've recapped what we know about the clues."

"You're being mysterious," I said. "Okay. Let's look at clues related to the man who's become our top suspect. The man who might have been the only person present when Betty was killed. Lance Evans, also known as Larry Brown."

"That's suspicious enough in itself," said Emily. "Why would Chloe tell us their name was Evans, but give the names Charlotte and Larry Brown to their accommodation host?"

"Play it out," said Oscar. "Let's say Lance Evans was the murderer. Assume he was the man accompanying Harry Salisbury into the marina, the man who killed Betty and one of the men you saw on the beach at night. What motive could he have?"

Emily shrugged. I formed a straight line with my lips and shook my head.

"Okay," said Oscar. "Come back to him. Harry Salisbury. Our number two suspect."

"Again, we don't have anything concrete," I said.

"Recap your visit to his barge," said Oscar. "Close your eyes and visualise the scene. Was there anything that looked wrong?"

"Inside his barge, no. I mean, I noticed the doll had gone, but that tells us nothing."

"Oh, I don't know," said Oscar. "Sometimes the absence of evidence is as important as the presence."

"His barge still looked stunning inside, like a showhome, a place where a neat and tidy person would live." I squeezed my eyes closed and attempted to relive my visit. "There was a bowl of fruit and a chopping board on the kitchen counter, two wine glasses, a note pinned to the fridge…"

"What did the note say?" asked Emily.

"Nothing important. Something about solder."

"Solder?" asked Oscar. "As in the material used to weld electrical joints?"

"Was it 'soldier'?" asked Emily. "Could this be the military connection between Harry and Betty's death? Was the note to remind Harry to meet with a soldier? I've got it. Harry was so afraid of speaking to the Women's Institute, he decided to murder Betty so he wouldn't have to and paid a mercenary to perform a special forces killing. Case closed."

"If it wasn't for the manner of Betty's death," said Oscar, "I'd say your theory was very fanciful. But who knows?"

"And," I said, "why wouldn't he let me see the third barge? That is very suspicious."

"As I said before," said Oscar, "it may be a very simple explanation."

"What if it's not? Whatever's in it might hold the key to the entire mystery."

"Without a search warrant, we'll struggle to find out. And unless there's reasonable suspicion, the police can't get a search warrant."

"Could you ask Inspector Buchanan? Tell him I think there's something in that third barge which may pertain to Betty's death. Or, at the very least, something secret in there."

"I can suggest he may like to investigate Harry Salisbury more closely. I'd be surprised if he's not doing that already."

"Those are our two main suspects," I said. "You mentioned you might have a way to confirm whether there was any connection with the Women's Institute and the church?"

"Indeed," said Oscar. "I may be clutching at straws, but, honestly, we don't have much to go on at the moment. Betty's funeral's being held tomorrow. I'm going to attend, and I think you should as well. I remember a case early in my career where the killer attended the funeral of his victim. He was a family member, so it would've been odd if he hadn't. But a chance remark he made to the vicar formed a connection between him and the location where the body was found. And that's how we solved the case."

"Gosh," said Emily. "Are you thinking Betty's murderer will attend tomorrow? I feel like bringing our investigation sheet, pinning it up beside the coffin and ticking people off as they pass by."

"That might not be the best idea. But let's keep our eyes and ears open for anything at all which doesn't seem right. At the very least, we'll get a cup of tea and a sandwich afterwards."

CHAPTER THIRTY-THREE

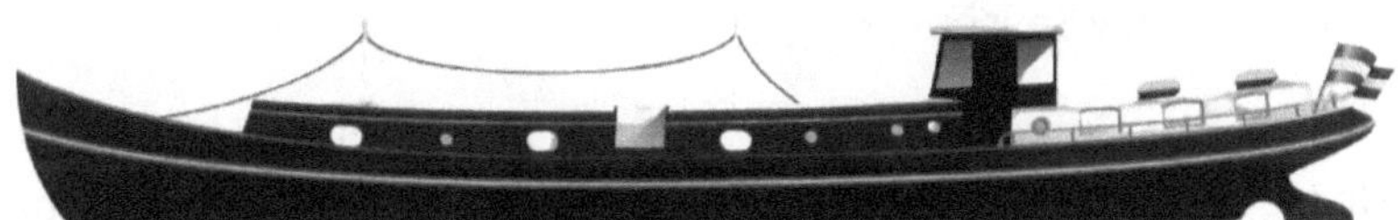

RING RING

"Hello? Troy speaking."

"Is that Troy Mortlake? Troy, it's Shiraz."

"Shiraz? Shiraz Jones? Darling, goodness me, where've you vanished to? We missed you at the Easter function this year, dazzling us with your beauty. The party simply wasn't the same without you. Your ex attended, of course. He was polite enough not to mention the breakup. So, how are you?"

"I'm fine, Troy. Living out of town for now, to recover."

"Ah, yes. A few weeks at a good friend's country estate can work wonders."

"I'm sure. Troy, tell me something. You still live on that Dutch barge in Chelsea, right?"

"Of course. I wouldn't live anywhere else. Perfect postcode, and life on the water's simply marvellous, darling."

"How long ago did you buy it? I'm, err, thinking of buying one myself."

"Almost ten years ago. You won't regret it. Your home becomes a curiosity, a conversation point. And a unique place to entertain, as you'd know."

"Who did you purchase it from? Was it a chap called Captain Harry Salisbury?"

"Yes. He imported it from Holland, decommissioned decades previously. I told him exactly how I wanted the interior to be arranged, and he fitted it out for me."

"I'm going to test your memory now, Troy. Harry has a barge I'm interested in. It's like yours was; a bare, unconverted shell. I'm desperate to see inside it, but Harry's lost the key, and he's not being very quick at finding it. I simply must glimpse the interior of the hold; I'm bursting with design ideas."

"I know that feeling. You want to visualise it; see the space available to you. When Harry first showed me my boat, he opened the wheelhouse, and we inspected it and the original bargekeeper's accommodation underneath. But even with the key, we couldn't get from there to the hold because Harry hadn't yet cut a hatch between them."

"Oh, what am I going to do, Troy? I absolutely have to see my new home before I burst with ideas."

"Easy. If this one you're thinking of buying's completely unconverted, there'll be three or four wooden hatches directly in front of the wheelhouse. One of them will lift off, and you can climb down into the hold that way. I'm surprised Harry didn't show you that. Ask him when you see him. And say hello from me. Good chap, Harry. Ex-navy. Made of the right stuff."

"I will. Thank you so much, Troy. You've been an absolute darling. Goodbye."

"Bye, Shiraz. Come back and see me when you yearn for the city lights again."

"I have never, in the many funerals I've attended, seen so many service sheets left untouched at the end," said Oscar. "I know Betty made enemies in her life, but I didn't expect us to be almost the only mourners. Just her son and daughter-in-law, and one other person; the deputy chair of the Women's Institute, and they're not staying for the wake. However, this has given us an opportunity. We can subtly interview Betty's son without fear of being interrupted by anyone."

We left the main entrance of All Saints Church and entered the hall next door. Sister Florrie greeted us, dressed in a long, white cloak with a simple rope as a belt. She hugged us all so tightly I wondered if she'd given me bruises.

"What a terrible business," she said. "Betty, and now Jack. Sister Marie and I returned early from our retreat to support the families."

"Yes," I said. "Dreadful. I thought there would be more people here, with Betty being the chair of the Women's Institute and involved with the church."

"We all loved our Betty," said Sister Florrie. "Some more than others. But the Lord adores all his children unconditionally." She leant forward, clutched my arm and whispered conspiratorially, "At least there'll be plenty of food and drink to go around."

"Let's grab a glass of sherry and talk with Betty's family," said Oscar.

We each plucked a small glass of golden liquid from a table.

"Mr Stanton," said Oscar, shaking the hand of a plump, balding man who wore a v-necked jumper and brown trousers. "I'm so sorry for your loss."

"Call me Rodney. This is my wife, Gloria."

Oscar introduced Emily and me, and we all shook hands.

Rodney appeared to have consumed almost all the glasses of sherry which had been provided for the guests. He continued to swig them like lemonade. "I," he said, jabbing himself in the stomach so we were in no doubt who he was referring to, "I always knew someone she'd upset would throttle her in the end. She was a very difficult woman, and I'm not sorry to say I haven't seen much of her over the past twenty years."

I wasn't sure what gestures or facial expressions should be employed in response to this statement, so I glanced at the floor.

"Rodney, that's your mother you're talking about," said Gloria in a soft, Scottish accent. "She may not have been the easiest person to get on with, but we mustn't speak ill of the dead."

"Not the easiest?" exploded Rodney. "Not the easiest? Have you forgotten how, ten years ago, we drove all the way from home to collect her, at her request no less, because she felt she was too important to take the train, then she expressed distaste at our Ford Mondeo and suggested we should've hired something more fitting for a lady of her standing? And how she refused point blank to eat lunch at the motorway service station and made us drive into Stratford-upon-Avon as she wanted to try a Michelin-starred restaurant she'd heard about. And then she made me pay. She never carries cash, apparently, like the King. And"—he tipped back his glass of sherry—"when we finally reached home, she turned her nose up at the sight of our house and demanded I book her into the Balmoral Hotel. At a cost of six hundred pounds per night, no less. Guess who ended up paying for that? Excuse me. I'll just grab another drink."

He tottered to the refreshments table.

"I'm sorry," said Gloria. "Betty was a unique character." She brightened. "Have you had a chance to look at her book? It's on display on the table over there."

"We haven't, have we, Emily?" I said. "Shall we take a peek at this publication we've heard so much about?"

"Hmph. Don't know why you'd bother with that," said Rodney, reappearing with another glass of sherry. "It's not exactly a New York Times Bestseller. She paid to publish it with a vanity press. Eight thousand pounds, and all she has to show for it is twenty-five boxes of books in her garage." He laughed and tipped his drink down his throat. "I didn't even buy a copy myself."

Betty's book had been propped open at a centre page on a small table. A thick, hardback volume, the pages had colour photographs and beautifully formatted text.

"This must've cost a fortune to produce," said Emily, flipping the pages and stroking the colour images. "I'm not surprised it's priced at fifty pounds; it's beautiful. Look at this dress from Jordan. The colours; I can't imagine anyone in

England wearing this. And on the next page, a jug from Iraq. We always associate Iraq with Saddam Hussein and the Gulf War, don't we? But this pottery is stunning. Who'd have known?"

I nodded. "Where my father's family live, in Egypt, the bazaars stock items you'd never be able to find here. I haven't visited since I was a child, but the memories of the colours and the sounds stay with me. And the smells. Completely unique. I'll see if there are any pictures from Egypt."

I turned the page, and a vivid photo immediately stood out.

My eyes blinked, and I did a double-take.

On page 34, Betty's book showed a picture of Gracie's doll.

CHAPTER THIRTY-FOUR

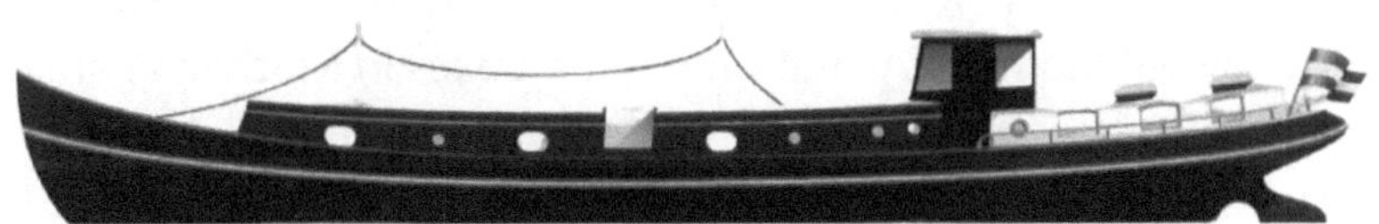

"Gosh, it's one of those dolls," said Emily. "The costume's slightly different, but it's definitely the same face and hair. What does it say about it?"

I read from the description next to the photo. "A child's doll, originating from Helmand province, Afghanistan. These dolls were manufactured in a modern form of a tradition stretching back over two hundred years. No longer fashioned by hand, the dolls have had the same purpose since the 1800s. Their unique property, and what makes them such a curiosity, is that the heads unscrew, but the join is well crafted and almost invisible. For decades, western scholars puzzled over the reason for this. However, in the 1970s, a researcher based at the Sorbonne University in Paris surmised the dolls might be employed in the opium trade, specifically the smuggling of opioids across borders. Because which customs agent would suspect narcotics to be stored inside what appears to be nothing more than a child's toy?"

Emily's jaw dropped, and she stared at me. Oscar reached around me and flicked the page over, but the following one only contained a picture of a colourful carpet.

"I think," I said, "we may have discovered the key to our mystery. I'll snap a quick photo."

I removed my phone from my pocket and held it up.

"I don't know why you're bothering with that," slurred Rodney behind me. "All but one of the boxes in Mother's garage containing her books are still sealed. Deluded, that's what she was. Utterly and completely deluded."

"This changes everything," I said, sweeping Emily's table clear of cups, saucers and a rather annoyed Boots, who swiped his paw at me before I deposited him on the carpet.

"Where's the investigation sheet?" I demanded. "We can finally fill in some gaps."

"I'll roll it out," said Emily. "That picture of the doll was the missing link between Betty and everything else. Somebody was importing those dolls from Afghanistan, bringing them via boat to the beach at Smuggler's Cove, carrying them through the tunnels and storing them in the barn. They must've seen the photo in Betty's book, and decided she knew too much to be allowed to live."

"Hang on," said Oscar, raising one hand in a 'stop' gesture. "We can't conclude that. It's guesswork. Yes, I agree, there's a connection between Betty and the smugglers, whoever they may be, in that she knew of the existence of the type of dolls and the purpose behind their design, but why would that have resulted in her death? She may not have known cases of these very dolls were right under her nose in Redcliff and, even so, with Betty dead, the book still exists. Someone else could still see the picture and make the link."

"Uh-uh." I shook my head. "You heard Betty's son. She paid some vanity publisher to print the books, and they were all still in boxes in her garage. He didn't even buy a copy. Didn't even buy his own mother's book. That's how much regard he had for her publication. And her, by all accounts."

"I think," said Emily, "the killer somehow saw Betty's book, discovered she had hundreds of copies in her garage and killed her to prevent them being distributed. I'm not going to say, 'case closed' for once, but you'll agree that's a very possible scenario."

"Let's say it was," said Oscar. "It's the best lead we've got at the moment. Who is this mysterious assassin?"

"We were all present at the Easter egg hunt when Betty was talking about it," I said. "All the people on our investigation sheet. It doesn't narrow our list down at all. We've found a potential motive, but we're no closer to identifying the killer. We need more clues. Where's that doll which Cadbury had hold of?"

"There," said Emily. "On the mantelpiece, out of his reach." She stood and collected it.

The doll lay on the table between us. We all glanced at each other and hesitated to be the first to touch it.

"Go on," said Emily. "Unscrew the head."

I picked it up and turned it over. It had gained several Labrador tooth marks since its manufacture, but, as Betty's book described, the join was completely invisible. I grabbed the head in one hand and the body in the other. This seemed an unnatural action, but I twisted them. Though the movement was stiff, the doll began to unscrew. After three spooky rotations of the doll's head, it came off, and we looked inside the cavity.

I held it up to my nose and sniffed.

"What are you smelling it for?" asked Emily.

"Drugs. Most of them have no smell, but some, such as cannabis, do. Remember, even though it wasn't my thing, I witnessed drug taking on a daily basis among the London circles I moved in."

"Of course. And can you smell anything?"

"No. Just plastic. I'm not sure this particular doll ever had narcotics inside it."

Oscar peeked in the doll. "And that doll came from the packing cases, didn't it?"

"Yes. I took it from the second layer so as not to be too obvious."

"Hmm," he said. "Are we wrong about the drug connection?"

"I don't think so. If the packing cases were an innocent importation of children's toys, why were they brought ashore after dark through an old tunnel and stored in a vicarage barn. No above-board import export company would go to those lengths."

"Import export?" said Emily. "That's the business Lance Evans is in. Let me play this out, to use Oscar's terminology. Lance was importing drugs, he may've been a special forces soldier, and he killed Betty because her book revealed the dolls were used to store narcotics. I also think he killed Jack Walter, because Jack had the key to the barn, and he saw the packing cases. Maybe he opened one and found the drugs inside a doll, then threatened to tell the police?"

"I'm waiting for a call back from Inspector Buchanan about Lance Evans," said Oscar. "If he was in the special forces, he'd definitely be the most likely suspect. But we still need more evidence."

"And I think I know how we're going to get it." I stood and threw on my coat. "How d'you fancy a trip to Brighthaven, Oscar? Emily, would you drive us?"

"Now? Why? It's almost eight o'clock at night, and it'll be pitch black by the time we arrive there."

"Exactly. What we're about to do needs the cover of darkness. Oscar, fetch your long policeman's torch from home, please. It's time for an adventure."

CHAPTER THIRTY-FIVE

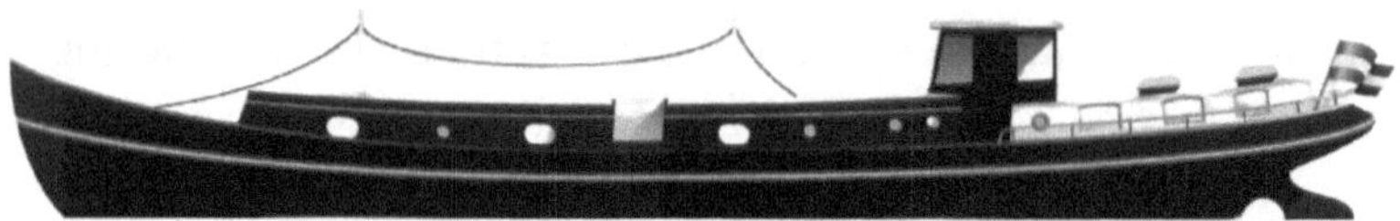

"I can't be out all night," said Emily, above the noise of wind whistling past our ears. "I have to open the café at six tomorrow morning, and I'm usually in bed by nine."

She pressed the indicator stalk, and we swung right out of Alnchurch along the road towards Headland Bay and Brighthaven.

"I'm sure we won't be out the entire night," I said, "but the evidence we discovered in the vicarage barn has already vanished, and I'm desperate not to lose anything else."

"What makes you so sure something's in the third barge?" asked Oscar. "It might be completely empty, and then we'd have a wasted evening."

"I don't want a wasted evening," said Emily. "I was hoping to finish my book before I went to sleep. That's not going to happen now."

In the absence of seatbelts in Emily's vintage Morris Minor, I was able to lean between the front seats and speak to both of them.

"I'm convinced Lance Evans is the key to this. I'm going to stick my neck out and say he's the ex-forces chap who killed Betty. He looks like a soldier. And we know he's definitely involved, otherwise why would Gracie have owned one of those dolls?"

"Perhaps Harry Salisbury gave her one," said Emily. "He's connected to the dolls in the barn, because he has, or had, a doll on his barge."

"Harry and Lance must be in this together. D'you remember when we were hunting for the kids in the shrubbery? Harry Salisbury was very keen for Jules and me not to investigate the barn. Now we know why. He didn't want us anywhere near the barn as it was stacked with the packing cases full of dolls. And potentially, the dolls contained narcotics."

Emily swerved suddenly, and I was thrown across the back seat.

"Sorry," she yelled. "I had to dodge a badger."

"We've got no evidence whatsoever that Betty's death was connected with drugs," said Oscar. "Seeing a photo in a book of a similar doll doesn't prove anything."

"Regardless, Harry didn't want us to find the dolls. I think they were full of drugs. Why else would they be importing them in such a clandestine manner? So he warned us to stay away from the barn. And, later, in the same tone of voice, he told me the third barge was too dangerous for me to go on."

"But maybe it is?" said Oscar. "If it's under construction, it might be very dangerous."

"He had no hesitation in showing me around barge two, which definitely was a construction site. It was full of timber offcuts, trailing power leads and very dangerous-looking cutting tools. No, I think there's something in barge three he doesn't want us to see. And I mean to discover what it is tonight."

"You're going to look through the windows and see what's in there? Is that why you need my torch?"

"No. The windows are all blacked out. That's something else suspicious, because they're not on the second one. We'll need to gain access to the third barge to have a good look."

"No breaking and entering, Shiraz. You've already entered the vicarage cellar and barn without permission, although I admit your little evening foray down the smuggler's tunnels paid off."

"Yes," said Emily. "Don't ask me to do anything like that tonight. My back still hurts from falling down the shaft while opening the trapdoor. But if we'd never ventured down there, we'd be none the wiser about these dolls and the connection to Betty's murder. We'd have attended her funeral, looked at the picture in the book and turned the page."

"I'm not going to break anything, Oscar," I said. "I might do some entering, though."

"If you're determined to access private property without permission, I'll wait in the car. Don't forget, I'm an ex-policeman and currently the acting mayor of Redcliff council. Imagine what a field day the local paper would have if I was caught inside someone else's property without their knowledge."

The sound of AC/DC's 'Thunderstruck' boomed from Oscar's pocket.

"I still haven't fixed that ringtone," he said. "Oscar Wainwright speaking. Ah, hello, Martin. Thanks for calling back. Excuse me shouting, it's a bit windy where I am. Any news on your hunt for a special forces operative among the local populace? No? How about that chap Lance Evans I mentioned to you? Or his alias Larry Brown? It's probably nothing, but I thought he might be worth checking out. Right. I see. Back to the drawing board. I'll call you if I think of anything else. Not at all, Martin, Great to be working with you again. Bye."

Oscar pressed 'end'. "That was Inspector Buchanan. Lance Evans was never a soldier. He didn't have anything to do with the forces. He's a long-distance truck driver, which may explain the import export business."

I thumped the back of the seat, which prompted Emily to swivel her head and give me a dirty look. "Drat," I said. "I was convinced it was him who'd delivered the fatal blow. We need a rethink. Maybe there's a suspect we haven't considered at all?"

"We're arriving in Brighthaven," said Emily. "Where d'you want me to park? By the marina entrance?"

"No. Even if Doug was around to let us in, I don't want us to be obvious. We, Emily, are entering via the back door."

"Entering via the back door? What does that mean?"

"I'll show you. Pull in here."

We parked in the pay-and-display car park next to Brighthaven beach. On any sunny Saturday, finding a space would've been tricky, but on a cool Wednesday evening in April, nobody else occupied the spots. We left Oscar in the car reviewing his notes about the case and stepped onto the sand as dusk turned to night.

"What's your plan, Shiraz? I'm not swimming, if that's what you have in mind."

"Nothing so cold, Emily. We're going to pedal."

"Pedal? D'you mean...?"

"Yep. Tonight we need to pedal silently without making any splashes."

"Gosh. This is all very *Swallows and Amazons*, isn't it? There's even a houseboat."

"The difference is, in *Swallows and Amazons*, nobody was murdered. We have to be considerably more secretive. D'you remember I told you I had time to kill when I visited Harry on Monday because I missed my train back to Redcliff? I strolled down to this beach and found the kiosk where the pedal boats are hired. I can't imagine they'd rented a single boat that day as it was grey and windy, and they were packing the boats away early. And I noticed that they tie the boats together."

"And?"

"That's their security to prevent the pedal boats being stolen. They tie them together. They don't lock them with anything. Tonight, we're going to untie one of the boats, and enter the marina via the back door."

"Ooh. D'you mean we're stealing a boat and pedalling it into the marina?"

"Not stealing, Emily. Borrowing. Although it's a shame the boats are painted bright yellow. It'll be hard to be covert. But you can see the end of the marina where the barges are from here." I pointed. "Ten minutes pedalling, at most."

I tugged at the coarse rope lashing the boats together, upturned on the sand. I needn't have worried about the knots being hard to undo, the twine that secured them was so old and frayed it parted with my final tug.

"Ready, Emily? You grab that end, and we'll pull the pedal boat down to the water."

The boat left a groove in the sand as we dragged it to the sea. It was more awkward than heavy, and we correctly assumed it was made from hollow plastic. Once in the shallows, we flipped it over and hopped in. I gave Oscar a quick wave as he sat in Emily's passenger seat under a streetlight, shaking his head.

"Thank goodness I'm wearing a skirt," I said. "I wouldn't want to get my trousers wet. Here, catch my shoes."

I threw the Gucci wedges into the boat and flopped in ungracefully.

"Ready?" said Emily, as we drifted away from the shore.

"Yep. Start pedalling."

We both pedalled hard. The splashing we made could probably have been heard from Redcliff, and the boat span on the spot.

"If anyone's on that barge, they'll be able to hear us from miles away," said Emily. "And we're going around in circles. Are you pedalling backwards?"

"No, you are. See?" I demonstrated my solo pedalling, and we performed another pirouette.

"We need a skipper," said Emily. "I'll call the directions. Okay, pedal hard now."

We headed away from the beach into the darkness. Several hundred feet away, we saw the lights illuminating the jetties and the outline of the boats in the marina.

"Stop," called Emily. I ceased pedalling, and she continued, resulting in a turn to port.

"Now both pedal," she said.

We recommenced and, in this fashion, we weaved across the sea towards the marina.

"We'll have to be quieter as we approach the jetty," I said. "These pedal boats splash too much. Let's paddle the last part with our hands."

All we heard was the rippling of the waves and the cry of an occasional night bird. We swept our hands through the water and soon fetched up against the gangway where the third barge was moored.

"How will we tie up?" whispered Emily.

"Stay there. I'll find a rope."

I pulled myself onto the jetty and paused. There were no lights on board either the third or the second barges, but light peeked around the blinds on Harry's houseboat. I grabbed a rope and tied the pedal boat to the end of the walkway.

"Emily," I whispered. "Be as quiet as you can. Harry's at home."

We climbed onto the third barge and stood next to the wheelhouse.

"How are you going to enter?" asked Emily. "Have you pinched a key as well as a pedal boat?"

"No. A friend of mine who lives on a barge in London told me how you can break into the hold. See these three hatches in front of the wheelhouse? He said one of them will lift off, and then we can climb down."

I tried the first one. It wobbled but wouldn't move.

"Uh-oh," I said. "This may not be as easy as I'd been led to believe."

The second one similarly wouldn't budge. I pulled the third. And pulled. And dug my fingers under the lip and tugged with all my might.

CRASH

I fell on my back with the hatch on top of me.

Emily crouched down and glanced in all directions. "If anyone was listening out for our arrival," she whispered, "they'll know we're here now. Stay still until we're sure no one's coming."

"Give me a moment to recover." I pushed myself up from the deck, knelt and looked through the hatch. "Drat. Oscar's big torch is with him in the car. I was counting on him accompanying us tonight."

"Turn on your phone light."

"I will, but we need to enter the hold first. I can't see anything from here. No one's around, and it's pitch black. Are you coming?"

I grabbed both sides of the hatch and swung my feet down. They connected with the rungs of a ladder, and I edged down into the darkness.

"This is giving me smuggler's passage vibes," said Emily, as she joined me. Even though we were whispering, our voices echoed around the bare metal interior.

"Okay. Let's both switch on our phone torches."

We rotated gradually to light up the inside of the barge and found the conversion at its initial stage. A passageway had been cut leading towards the wheelhouse, and I saw the dim outline of a ladder at the end of it. Along one side of the hold, a metal workbench was fixed to the wall. A pile of tongue and groove timber offcuts cluttered one corner mixed with discarded containers. I shone the torch on them and read: "Flour, talcum powder, baby formula, laundry detergent." Weighing scales, spoons and other utensils had been scattered over the workbench. And on the floor, under it, two discarded dolls' heads.

"What's all this stuff for?" asked Emily.

"It's a drugs lab." I said. "The empty containers contained products used to cut cocaine or heroin. They're powders that have a similar appearance and texture to the drugs."

"Cut? What does that mean?"

"Drugs are cut, or mixed, with cheaper products to make them go further, and increase the profits for the drug dealers. Among my friends in London, there was always discussion about which dealer had the purest cocaine."

"This is a world I know nothing about, Shiraz. Snap some photos for the police and let's escape back on the pedal boat. I'm scared the drug dealers will return and murder us too."

"I agree. We won't achieve anything else, now we know what's in here. Shine your torch while I take the pictures."

Emily illuminated the workbench. As I raised my phone to take the picture, we froze.

The clump of heavy boots sounded from the deck above us.

"Hide," hissed Emily.

"Where?" I said, sweeping my phone around the hold. "This is one big open space."

The boots clomped towards the hatch where we'd entered.

"We're done for," said Emily. "Goodbye, Shiraz. I won't say it's been fun."

A torch beam illuminated the steps leading up to the wheelhouse, then an overhead lightbulb came on in the barge's hold, and I threw my arm across my eyes.

"Well, well, well," said a voice from the top of the steps. "Isn't this nice? We have visitors."

The heavy boots descended towards us and reached the bottom rung.

Their owner spoke. "This is a long way from Redcliff Marine Rescue, isn't it? What brings you two here?"

I broke out in a cold sweat and completely failed to show bravado. Emily gripped my shoulder and whimpered as the figure advanced towards us holding a long-bladed knife. They wore camouflaged army fatigues, and their face was smeared with dark grease.

"There's no need for this," I stammered. "We can work this out without violence."

"Violence is my middle name," said the soldier.

I gritted my teeth and spoke slowly.

"Put the knife down. Chloe, please, put down the knife."

CHAPTER THIRTY-SIX

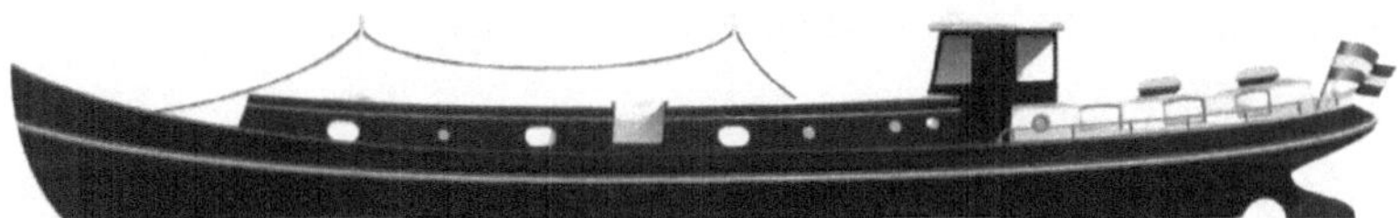

Chloe Evans stepped menacingly towards us with an evil smile on her face. She traced the blade down the side of my face, and I felt a warm trickle of blood. Emily yelped.

"Chloe," I said. My voice shook. "We rescued your children from drowning. Surely that counts for something?"

She grabbed my ponytail, pulled it back and held the knife to my throat.

"Shut up," she said, "or I'll finish you, just like I ended that writer woman. Harry," she yelled, "Throw that piece of dirt down here. He can drown with these other ship's rats."

A human shape crashed down the steps behind Chloe and slumped on the floor. Then a second pair of heavy boots descended, and Harry Salisbury joined us. He wore overalls and a baseball cap.

"I warned her to stay away from this barge," he said.

Gone was the smartly dressed, well-spoken ex-navy officer.

"Get up," he yelled at the figure on the floor.

The person attempted to kneel, then fell forward again. Their face was covered with a black hood, and their hands were lashed behind their back.

"Get up," Harry said again. He kicked the prone figure, who scrumpled into a foetal position.

Harry grabbed the ropes tying their wrists, and they cried out as he pulled them to their feet.

I clearly made out the tattoos on their arms.

Lance Evans.

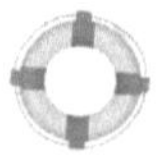

Harry shoved Lance, and he fell against the side of the barge and slid to the floor next to us.

"Three ship's rats," said Chloe. "Or maybe"—she traced the point of the knife next to my eye—"three blind mice?"

She cackled, and my blood ran cold.

"Harry, start the engines," she said. "These stowaways are heading on their final voyage. To a watery grave." She laughed maniacally, and I squeezed my eyes closed. I had to survive. If not for me, for Emily, who I'd dragged away from her early bedtime and her book.

How are we ever going to get out of this scrape, Shiraz? Poor Emily; she didn't have to come with you. I need to keep Chloe talking.

"Why, Chloe? You have three beautiful children. They need their mum with them. Not in prison."

"Who's going to prison? Not me. You two and this piece of filth on the floor are about to have an unfortunate accident. All's fair in the battle arena."

"Battle arena? What d'you mean?"

"Afghanistan. Special forces. Peacekeeping, they told us. How can a military presence like ours be peacekeeping? They trained me to be a killing machine, to take out key members of the enemy before they realised I was anywhere near them. Unarmed, close quarter combat." She looked me in the eye, and the muscles on her forearm tensed as she gripped the knife. "I'm removing dangerous combatants now. Phase four of this operation is coming to a successful end."

My entire body trembled, and I glanced in every direction for an escape. "We're not dangerous combatants, Chloe. We're marine rescue volunteers, remember?"

"You're dangerous combatants, sabotaging the operation," said Chloe. "You and that piece of trash on the floor. He disobeyed orders, and he'll pay."

She aimed a kick into Lance's side as the barge engines vibrated. Emily's tears fell onto my hand, and I determined somehow we were going to escape this situation.

Keep her talking, Shiraz. Keep her talking.

"What operation, Chloe? This isn't Afghanistan anymore. We're on the south coast of England."

"Battle arenas come in many shapes and sizes, marine rescue woman. This is one more in a long line."

The barge jolted, and it moved slowly.

Don't stop, Shiraz. Think of things to say. You have to find a way to escape.

"Why drugs, Chloe? Why the dolls? Whose idea was that?"

"Mine, of course. I made a deal with an Afghan warlord." She laughed. "The Taliban's opium ban had decimated his business, and he had stockpiles he needed to smuggle out of the country. He took me through this dusty town to a factory and showed me a complete refinery operation, export-ready production of one hundred percent pure heroin. Then he revealed another factory he owned, where they produced these dolls. The dolls that were specifically manufactured for concealment of drugs. In that moment, I knew what my next operation would be."

"Where does Lance come into this? What's he done wrong? Isn't he your partner in this? Your husband?"

"Husband?" She spat at Lance, who gibbered on the floor. "Pah! He's nothing. My real husband died a hero, no thanks to our senior officers, who killed him like you'd crush a cockroach. He wasn't a traitor like that waste of space."

The vibrations slowed, and the engine idled. I wondered if she'd throw us over the side here and now.

Keep her talking, Shiraz. Do whatever you can to buy time. You have to think of something.

"And Harry Salisbury? Why is he involved? Was he in Afghanistan too?"

"A very useful man, Harry. Did he tell you he was a ship's carpenter? He built packing cases from leftover wood from his barge fitouts. Then we loaded them onto Lance's truck and drove them to the factory in Afghanistan full of blankets, medicine and clothing for the relief effort. Only, what nobody realised was, once the packing cases were empty, they'd be returning full. Full of my future." She laughed again. "They returned to Holland full of heroin inside the dolls. A perfect operation. My best, even though I say so myself."

I ran out of things to say, and squeezed my eyes closed, as tears ran down my cheeks.

"What are you going to do with us?" asked Emily. I started, as this was the first time she'd spoken, and I heard a quiet confidence in her voice I wasn't accustomed to.

"Where d'you think we're going?" asked Chloe. "This isn't one of your marine rescue training exercises. You're going to need to swim well where we're headed."

"Marine rescue will save us," said Emily. "I'll call the coxswain." She stepped forward and held her phone out. I wanted to tell her to keep her hands by her sides. We couldn't risk angering her more.

"Drop your phones, both of you." yelled Chloe, pointing the knife at each of us in turn. "No one's coming to help. By the time they reach you, you'll have drowned. Dead, like the writer woman and the church man. And your friend on the floor here." She aimed another kick at Lance, who screamed and bunched himself tighter into a ball.

"Our friend?" I said. "We'd never met him before the Easter egg hunt."

The noise of the barge engine increased to a deafening level, and Chloe shouted at the top of her voice.

"Your friend"—she kicked him again—"believed we were simply shipping goods under cover to avoid import duties. Once he discovered what was inside those dolls, he said he wanted nothing to do with it, and threatened to tell the police. Clearly he wasn't part of the team, was he? He's a traitor, and traitors deserve to die." She kicked Lance once more.

This woman is completely insane. She killed Jack Walter, killed Betty Stanton and now she's going to kill us and Lance. What to do, what to do?

Chloe shouted up to the wheelhouse. "Harry, are we far enough offshore yet? These three water rats are becoming impatient."

There was no answer above the noise of the engines. I panted, and cold sweat beaded over my face. We had moments to find a way to escape, or die a horrible death by drowning, miles out to sea. The barge engine's reduced to idle again, then stopped. My ears rang in the sudden silence.

"Harry," yelled Chloe. "Are we here? Is it time to throw them over?"

No response came from up in the wheelhouse. Chloe backed away from us towards the steps and yelled up, "Harry, can you hear me? Come down here and help me drag these three rats upstairs."

Silence.

"Harry, you're disobeying the orders of your commanding officer. D'you want to go the same way as these three?" She glanced at us, still pointing the knife in our direction, and placed her foot on the first rung. "If you move, marine rescue woman, I'll slit your throats here and now. Understand?"

She climbed the first three rungs, and her head vanished through the opening at the top. "Harry?" she yelled again. "Is this where we'll throw...?"

WHACK

Chloe tumbled backwards and fell in a crumpled heap in front of us.

CHAPTER THIRTY-SEVEN

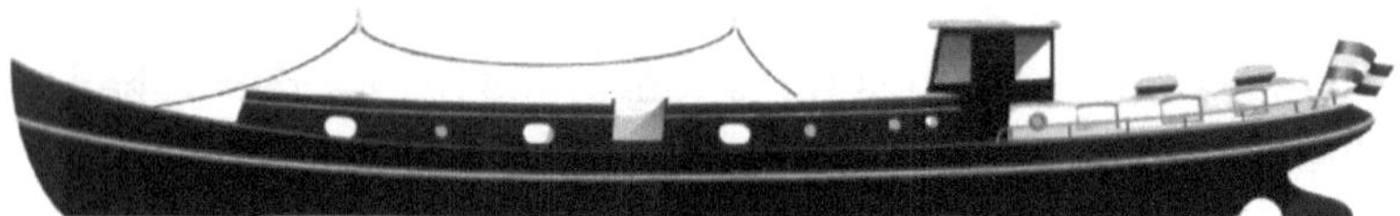

Emily and I shot a glance at each other.

My mind raced.

What just happened? Did Harry knock her out? Is he a traitor like Lance?

A pair of dark shoes descended the steps, and I tensed. The back of a Macintosh coat followed, then a head wearing a trilby. The figure turned towards us and brandished a long, black torch. "Anyone else?" he said. "Or just the two of them?"

"Oscar!" Tears ran down my cheeks. "What on earth? How did you…?"

"Special forces?" he said. "No match for ex-police forces. People should be careful climbing boat ladders while holding knives. Three points of contact while on board, right?"

Emily sank to her knees and sobbed.

"Explanations later," said Oscar. "Let's tie up both your captors before they regain consciousness. I've dealt with the chap upstairs. He can wait down here in the hold too."

"What about Lance?" I pointed at the hooded figure who remained curled in a ball on the floor, moaning.

"Leave him there," said Oscar, pulling Chloe's hands behind her and lashing her wrists together. "And once we've secured them all, I'll have to work out how to drive a Dutch barge. We're drifting in a shipping lane, and it would be a shame if you were saved from drowning and then sunk by a passing container ship."

Oscar stood behind the barge's huge wheel as the engine chugged us back towards the marina, and I took up position next to him. Emily sat in the wheelhouse holding Chloe's knife, pointing down the hatch to the hold where groans and yells indicated our captives were regaining consciousness. Although, to be honest, I'm not sure whether either of us would've used the knife in anger. We weren't trained in unarmed combat like Chloe was.

"They're not going to escape, are they?" asked Emily.

"Of course they won't," said Oscar. "I haven't forgotten my marine rescue knot training. And we only have to keep them captive until we return to Brighthaven Marina. I've rung Inspector Buchanan. He's meeting us there, and Sergeant Will Bishopstone's on his way too. Jack Walter's death happened on his patch, remember."

"Explanations later, you said?" asked Emily. She clawed her free hand through her hair. "I thought we were done for. They were going to throw us overboard like Jack Walter. Then you turn up at the last minute like some kind of movie hero and save us."

Oscar spoke loudly above the rumbles of the engine. "I sat in your car, shaking my head as you two disappeared into the darkness on that pedal boat. I knew, Shiraz, you were determined to find evidence to support our theories and, secretly, I hoped you would succeed. Then, moments later, as I was scanning the water waiting for your return, I noticed the wheelhouse lights of the end barge come on, which I presumed from your description was the one you'd boarded. So I stepped out of the car and walked to the beach. I wondered if you'd switched them on yourselves. From across the water, I heard the barge engines starting, and at that point I knew you were in trouble."

Oscar steered the barge to starboard as the lights of a vessel significantly larger than ours approached, and I watched its red navigation light pass in the dark.

"I had to do something," he continued, "and I thought of calling Inspector Buchanan, but I wasn't completely sure what was happening, and didn't want you both to be arrested for breaking and entering. And my next thought was to grab one of those pedal boats and pursue you."

"You dragged one down to the water by yourself?" I asked.

"I surprised myself how strong I was in an emergency. And those pedal boats aren't heavy; just awkward. Anyway, I launched it, getting my trousers and shoes wet in the process, and pedalled like mad after the barge. I reckoned I didn't have a hope of catching up with you, but then the barge slowed and drifted briefly. I took my chance and pedalled as hard as I could until I was alongside. I grabbed at a tyre hanging over the side and, as I gripped it and tried to climb on board, the barge engines became louder, and it took off again. One chance. That was all I had. One chance to jump on the barge and not fall in the water myself. I pulled myself up the rope attaching the tyre, and the pedal boat bumped along the side of the barge and disappeared astern. But now I was on the deck, and I had no idea what was happening. I saw a man in the wheelhouse steering the vessel, and I crept towards the windows and peeped in behind him. You were nowhere to be seen, so something wasn't right."

Oscar sounded the horn five times at an approaching vessel, and it altered course to avoid us.

"So I pulled my torch out of my coat pocket and quietly opened the door behind him. Not only were the engines so loud he couldn't hear me but, of course, he had no idea anyone else was on the barge. Then, even above the engine noise, I heard someone give a huge scream from below, like they were in severe pain."

"That was Lance," I said. "Chloe kicked him in the ribs several times."

"I'd no idea who else was on board, but I knew you were. So I crept up behind the man at the wheel, brandished my torch and shouted 'Hey!' You should've seen the look of shock on his face when he turned around. Followed by a look of agony as I whacked him over the head."

"Wow."

"Then I pulled the throttles back and the engine idled. I figured that would entice anyone down below to show themselves. And I heard a woman yelling, who wasn't either of you. When she shouted, 'Are we throwing them over now?' I had to stop her. I was about to climb down the steps, when someone appeared who I didn't recognise, their face smeared with camouflage paint. Without pausing, I whacked them with my torch as well."

"You're amazing, Oscar. You have totally saved our lives. We owe you big time."

"We'll discuss this another day over a drink at the Smuggler's Tavern. Right now, we have a barge to moor up. Could you both prepare lines and fenders on the port side? I'll dock her in the same place she was before."

CHAPTER THIRTY-EIGHT

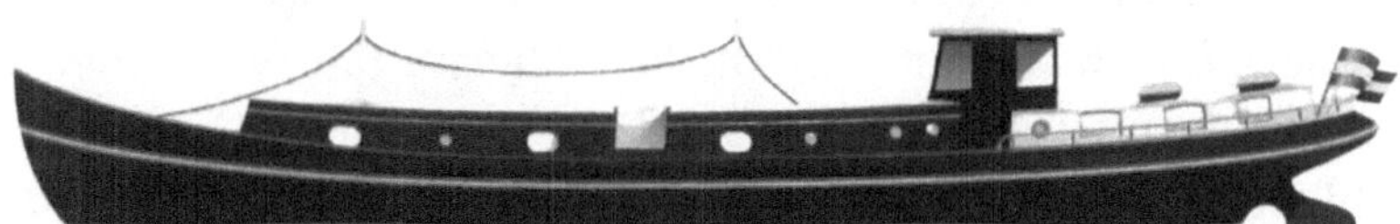

Oscar sat with us in Inspector Martin Buchanan's interview room.

"We have Chloe Brown, or Evans, and Harry Salisbury in custody," said Martin, "thanks to your efforts, Oscar."

"Not my efforts, Martin. Thank Shiraz. She was the one who suspected there was more to the third barge than merely an unconverted floating home."

"It was a team accomplishment," I said. "We all put our heads together to work this mystery out."

"Thank you all, then," said Martin. "Lance Evans is in hospital with four broken ribs and a ruptured spleen. The doctor permitted me to interview him, and he spilled the beans about everything. And when you hear what he had to say, you'll understand why he turned against the other two."

We crowded in to listen.

"Chloe Evans, also known as Chloe Brown, her former married name, and sometimes Charlotte Brown, was a soldier in the British army. She'd become increasingly disillusioned with life in the service, having failed to qualify more than once for entry to the special forces, despite her skills at explosives and unarmed combat. Her role had changed from being senior officer in an elite platoon to more of a peacekeeping role, even unloading trucks full of supplies for the people she'd been trained to think of as enemies. So she hatched this scheme to benefit from a contact she'd made in Afghanistan, which she believed would secure the financial future of her and her children."

"Gosh," I said. "I would never have guessed her background when I first met her on the beach in her swimwear. Although, I did notice at the time she had a very toned physique. But why did Lance tell you this? Surely he would've wanted his children to benefit from Chloe's operation, as she called it?"

"Hunter and Gracie weren't Lance's kids. Their father was another soldier who was killed in an army training exercise two years ago. Chloe blamed the British establishment for his death, and she grew more and more bitter as she turned against her former comrades. That was the catalyst to make her finally enact her plan. She met Lance in a bar while she was drinking to cope with the bereavement. They began a relationship and had a baby together, but Lance told me she constantly belittled him and reminded him they were only together because he physically resembled her former husband."

Inspector Buchanan referred to his notes. "Lance said she was having nightmares, she became distant, erratic, and incredibly emotional. A doctor prescribed her something called Citalopram, but she didn't always take the medicine, and she'd flare up at him and the kids without warning. She became, in Lance's words, a ticking time bomb. He stayed with her for the sake of the baby, but she grew more and more erratic."

"I should've spotted that clue about Lance not being the kids' dad," I said. "When we'd rescued the kids, Hunter told us a story that he'd seen a sea monster with tentacles that could drag a man under as big as Lance."

"Of course," said Emily. "Most kids when talking about their father would call them 'Dad' or 'Daddy', not by their first name."

"And how did she inveigle Harry Salisbury into this plan?" I asked.

"Harry's heavily in debt and in dire need of funds. He can't convert barges quickly enough for it to be a viable business. He needed cash, and he needed it quickly. Chloe was looking for someone to transport the drugs from Holland to England, which was their eventual destination. And Harry saw this as a way to give his business a swift, one-off injection of cash. We're not clear how they met, but he became Chloe's partner in Europe."

"Wow," said Emily. "Money tempts people so easily."

"It does. Lance told me he trucked the dolls from Afghanistan to Holland concealed inside empty packing cases which Harry had made from tongue and groove offcuts. In Rotterdam, they were loaded onto Harry's barge. At this point, remember, Lance believed he was merely importing goods to avoid duties. Then the barge sailed from Holland to Brighthaven. Once safely docked at Brighthaven, the drugs were cut using various substances to increase their street value. Flour, talcum powder and so on. Lance didn't know about this part of the operation until later. They were then repacked in the dolls, and the dolls replaced in the packing cases. The word *Poppen* was stencilled on the outside, to increase the subterfuge that these were nothing but cases of toys imported from Holland. *Poppen* is Dutch for 'dolls'."

"Oh, yes," said Emily. "We never did look that up on Google translate. Um, may I interrupt? Not all the dolls had drugs in them. We, err, found one which was empty."

"Correct," said Martin. "Lance told me only one in ten were filled with drugs. The idea being, if they were ever examined, the authorities would inspect one of the empty ones. Anyway, they then had the challenge of removing them from the barge. Harry told them about the cameras, and Chloe didn't want to risk carrying all the packing cases out of the marina by hand, which would have made someone ask questions. Nope, those cases had to leave by boat. But there were far too many to move all at once. A bargeful, if you'll pardon the expression."

Oscar cleared his throat. "I'm intrigued how they chose All Saints barn as the storage location for a wholesale drug importing operation. I haven't made that connection yet. Did Lance share that piece of information?"

"He did. Harry knew about the old smugglers' tunnels. His hobby was local maritime history. But they hadn't been used for centuries, and the entrance at the back of the cave at Smuggler's Cove had been sealed decades ago for safety. Chloe, of course, was trained in the use of explosives and she blew open the passages and made them operational again."

"Gosh," said Emily. "We were lucky they didn't collapse on us and bury us alive. No one would've ever found us again."

Oscar tapped his fingers together. "So they discovered the tunnels led to the barn. But that didn't help them. Because they needed the man in charge of the barn, Jack Walter, to be part of their operation. And there was no way a traditional, churchgoing gentleman like him would want to be involved with drug warehousing and distribution. How did they persuade him to co-operate?"

"You're right. Jack was, as you say, a traditional, churchgoing gentleman. But maybe he was too traditional. Lance told me Harry approached him with the suggestion of recreating the tradition of the tithe barn. Harry asked if the barn could be used to store valuable goods, in return for the church receiving ten percent. The church would receive the duty instead of the tax man, like in days gone by. The money Harry was offering would pay for new church boilers, repairs to the building and even refurbishment of the church hall. It was a sufficiently large enough sum for any scruples Jack may've had to be overlooked."

"Incredible," said Oscar. "Chloe planned a well-managed operation."

"Jack opened the barn for Lance and Chloe, then Harry sailed the barge around to a position off Smuggler's Cove and brought the packing crates ashore by rowing boat. But there was a problem. They had over a hundred crates. And the rowing boat only held three at a time. So the three of them had to cart the crates ashore in multiple journeys over a number of nights."

"Gosh," I said to Emily. "Marion at the bed and breakfast must've been babysitting their kids while this was all going on. I reckon we caught them during their final shipment. If we'd left it another hour, we'd have been none the wiser about any of this."

"Yes, and we'd still be scrabbling around looking for clues to Betty's murder."

"Which neatly segues us into that matter," said Martin. "Chloe had apparently seen Betty's publication in a store in Redcliff while shopping for books with her kids."

"Hatcher's Book Emporium," I said. "It must possess the only copy ever sold."

"Exactly," said Martin. "Chloe was idly browsing through books by local authors while her kids read stories in the children's section, when she came across a photo and description of the exact doll she was using to conceal her drugs. She realised that if Betty's new book became widely distributed, the game might be up. And when Harry persuaded Betty to visit his barge and see life on board first-hand, Chloe saw an opportunity to dispatch her. Without Betty promoting them, the books and the photo of the doll would always remain unopened in her garage."

"Hang on," said Emily. "Betty was the only person who Chloe killed, or tried to kill, without drowning them. Why did Chloe feel the need to deliver the fatal blow in such a violent way?"

"You're very observant," said Martin. "I could do with brains like yours on the force. Betty wasn't expecting to see Chloe; she thought she'd be meeting Harry. Chloe had to deal with her quickly, while Betty was standing around wondering why Harry hadn't kept their appointment."

"Gosh," I said, "she didn't have time to be surprised at Chloe appearing before she was stabbed in the back of the head with a twelve-inch knife."

"And Jack Walter?" asked Emily. "Why did they have to kill him?"

"As soon as they'd finished with the barn, Jack was no longer useful. And Chloe was worried he'd seen too much. All Lance told me was that Harry somehow lured Jack into his rowing boat. The poor chap couldn't swim, and he drowned within sight of Smuggler's Cove."

"Wow. Two murders. What's going to happen to the killers?"

"Chloe Brown and Harry Salisbury have been charged with murder, attempted murder, kidnapping and importation of a controlled narcotic. That little list should keep them in prison for decades."

"And what about Lance?"

"That's a good question. He maintains they were going to drown him when he threatened to expose their drug importation scheme, so, on the face of it, he seems to be less of a guilty party. But he has implicated himself in his account, and though he may not have been directly involved with the murders, he's not innocent by a long way. Anyway,"—he turned to us—"thank you again for all your help, in more ways than one. Oscar, it's been fantastic to renew your acquaintance."

"Any time, Martin. I do enjoy getting my hands dirty, to coin a phrase. What's your next case? Anything I can help you with?"

"Thanks, but I'm sure I won't need your consultancy on such a minor matter. The Brighthaven beach vendor's complained someone stole two of his pedal boats the other night. One was found tied up in the marina, the other was washed up between here and Headland Bay. It was probably teenagers taking them for a joyride. That's not something I'd need your insight to solve, is it, Oscar?"

Oscar shrugged and clenched his teeth. "Sorry, Martin. I can't help you with that one."

CHAPTER THIRTY-NINE

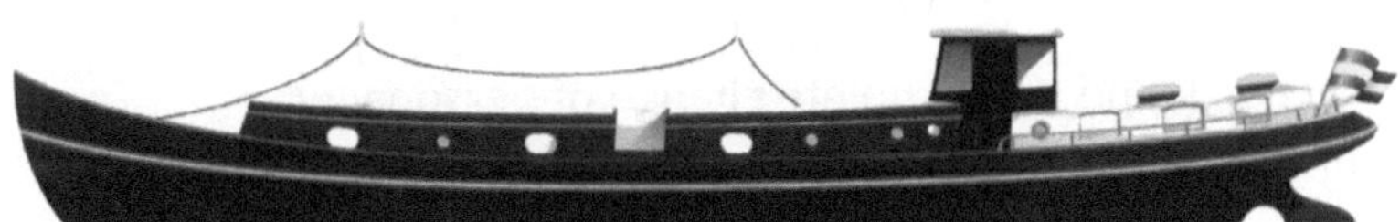

One week later

Oscar, Emily and I sat at a window seat in the Smuggler's Tavern taking in the vista of Redcliff Bay. Easter was well behind us now, and the summer holidays were still far enough in the future to be nothing more than a schoolchild's dream.

"One or two ends remain untied," I said, topping up Emily's glass of Chardonnay. "D'you remember, when the kids went missing, Lance vanished? We never worked out where he went. And he wasn't helping us look for them."

I think he'd gone to make sure the barn was locked," said Emily. "When we began searching every nook and cranny in the vicarage garden, we must've thrown Chloe, Harry and Lance into a panic that the packing cases would be discovered. That's why Harry took charge of the hunt. He needed to make sure we stayed away from the barn."

"I suspect," said Oscar, clasping his hands around a pint of golden Badger's ale, "they were on heightened alert already. Clearly when Jack Walter agreed to let them store the dolls, he failed to mention the Easter egg hunt. I'm sure they all attended it to keep an eye on the barn and make sure nobody entered. And they could hardly tell us not to search for the kids when they went missing. That would've seemed very suspicious."

"Imagine what Chloe thought when I found that other doll in the cellar. She looked absolutely terrified. I assumed at the time that was because she thought something dreadful had happened to her daughter. But the real reason was fear we'd discovered the packing cases."

"I still find the complete change of personality unbelievable," said Oscar. "You say she was a caring mother, looking after her kids, breastfeeding her baby, and then suddenly she turns into a drug-smuggling killer. She must've been a very good undercover combatant."

"I think she's suffering from mental illness exacerbated by what she witnessed in Afghanistan," I said. "Post-traumatic stress, or whatever it's called. I can't imagine what it must be like being a soldier serving on the battlefield and then returning to normal, humdrum, civilian life, bringing up kids like any other suburban parent."

"She's not going to be able to care for her children now she's in prison," said Emily. "What's going to happen to them?"

"They're staying with grandparents, I understand," said Oscar. "I'm not sure what the long-term plan will be. I'm also wondering what will happen to Harry's barges. He won't be in a position to refurbish them now he's locked away."

"Err, about that..." I chewed my bottom lip and glanced at Emily.

She frowned and tilted her head to one side.

Time to bite the bullet, Shiraz.

"Emily, I've had a wonderful four months living with you above the Wicked Whelk, and it was so kind of you to help me when I had nowhere to live, but…"

"You know you can stay as long as you like," said Emily, laying her hand on my arm. "I love your company."

"Don't worry; I love yours too, but we each need our own space. And yesterday, I received a phone call."

"You're not leaving Redcliff and flitting off back to London?" Emily squeezed her eyes closed, and her mouth turned down. "I won't let you."

"Of course not." I rubbed her upper arm. "Redcliff's my home, and you're my friend. My best friend. We're going to become qualified crew members together."

She smiled and wiped her eyes.

"No," I said, "but it's time for me to find my own place. And this phone call came from, believe it or not, Harry Salisbury's brother, who'd found my number on Harry's barge. He told me Harry was technically bankrupt. The barge he lived on was fully mortgaged, and he'd borrowed money from his brother to fund the refurbishment of the other two. Presumably he intended to repay him with his share of the drugs operation. Now, naturally, his brother wants his money back, so he's begun investigating whether he can sell Harry's assets."

"Ye-es…?" said Emily.

"And… I've agreed to buy his barge."

"The one he lived on? The finished one?"

"Yes." I clenched my fists in front of my chest. "I'm so excited."

"Gosh. Can you afford it?"

"Emily, money's for spending. I've more than enough. Monty's looked after me very well following our split. Which is fair, as it was entirely his doing."

"But the barge is in Brighthaven. I mean, I'll come and visit you, but it's a long way to go for a cup of tea. And it's not exactly convenient for marine rescue training. Are you sure about this?"

"I don't want to live in Brighthaven, Emily. How will we have our girly chats after training? Or catch up for coffee, or one of your amazing breakfasts? How will I help out in the café?"

"I don't mind if you can't manage the last one."

I laughed. "Nope. I've already asked the Redcliff Harbourmaster if there's any chance I might moor a Dutch barge in Redcliff Harbour and, as luck would have it, a spot's coming up next month."

"Seriously? Wow. We'll be practically next-door neighbours."

"I know. Won't that be fun? I really can't wait."

I paused. "There's just one favour I need from you both. I may ask you to reprise your roles from the other night. We'll have to drive the barge around from Brighthaven to Redcliff. Would you take the wheel again, Oscar? And, Emily, would you be my crew?"

"I'd love the opportunity," said Oscar. "Any chance to skipper a boat."

"I'm very happy to be crew for Captain Shiraz," said Emily. She grinned and nudged me. "So long as we don't have to practice our man overboard skills."

"That's settled, then. I'll let you know the date when we can relocate her."

"What an excellent result," said Oscar. He raised his glass. "To Shiraz's new home. I can't wait for the housewarming. Or should I say, bargewarming."

"Me neither," I said. "But, Emily, I'll employ you to do the catering. Nobody wants to taste my cooking."

We laughed and clinked glasses.

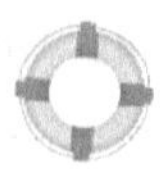

Shiraz's adventures continue in book 5:
A Spook in the Dark at Alnchurch Park

SHIRAZ'S NEXT ADVENTURE

Hi, it's Simon.

Thank you so much for reading *A Smuggler's Cave and a Watery Grave*, the fourth in my *Shiraz Jones Marine Rescue Mysteries* series.

If you'd like to read more of Shiraz's adventures in Redcliff, why not:

Sign up for my newsletter at simonmichaelprior.com

Follow me on Amazon to be notified of new releases.

And please consider leaving a review to let other readers know how much you enjoyed it. A few words will suffice. Even if you didn't buy the book from Amazon, you can still leave a review there if you have a valid Amazon account. I read every one with interest and gratitude.

Now, if you wish, you could continue onto *Shiraz Jones Marine Rescue Mysteries* book five:

A Spook in the Dark at Alnchurch Park

Available from Amazon and all good bookshops.

MORE BOOKS BY SIMON

Available on Amazon and from all good bookshops

Shiraz Jones Marine Rescue Mysteries

A Murderous Clamour at Redcliff Manor
A Deadly Affair in the Pirate's Lair
A Landslide, a Bride and a Fatal Ride
A Smuggler's Cave and a Watery Grave
A Spook in the Dark at Alnchurch Park

Fun Travel Memoirs

The Coconut Wireless:
A Travel Adventure in Search of the Queen of Tonga

The Scenicland Radio:
A Travel Adventure in Search of the New Zealand Experience

The Pomegranate Busker:
A Travel Adventure in Search of New Zealand Rock Stardom

The Anticlockwise Proposal:
A Travel Adventure Around the World in Eighty Diamonds

A Capybara for Christmas:
European Travel, Japanese Adventure, Maximum Mayhem

Historical Memoirs

An Englishman in New York:
The Memoirs of John Miskin Prior 1948-1949

DISCLAIMER

A Smuggler's Cave and a Watery Grave is a work of fiction, based on the experiences of Simon Michael Prior, a search-and-rescue skipper with one of the many volunteer marine rescue organisations seafarers depend on.

Although the book is set in England, the town of Redcliff-upon-Sea, the vanished settlement of Golden Beach and the surrounding locations are fictional. Hebble Bridge and Milltown are fictional locations. Montague Jones PR Ltd is a fictional company. *Red Carpet Superstars* magazine is a fictional publication. Which is a shame, as it sounds like a good read.

Names, characters, places and incidents are either products of the author's imagination or are used fictitiously. Any resemblance to actual events or locales or persons, living or dead, is entirely coincidental.

I had to say that.

ACKNOWLEDGEMENTS

This book wouldn't have been possible without the help of the following people: The wonderful beta readers: Alyson Sheldrake, Dawne Archer, Lisa Rose Wright, Louise Pierce, Rebecca Hislop and Val Poore; your feedback improved the final result so much.

Thank you to Victoria Twead, Matthew J Holmes, Meg LaTorre, Craig Martelle, Angela Ackerman, Becca Puglisi, David Gaughran and Dave Chesson for informative courses, tips and useful tools.

Thank you to Jeff Bezos, for giving independent authors a platform on which to publish our writing.

And thank you so much to the skippers and crew of the AVCGA Volunteer Coastguard. I couldn't have done it without you.

ABOUT THE AUTHOR

Simon Michael Prior experiences constant adventures, hazards and exciting situations as a marine rescue skipper and a commander of rescue operations.

Although Simon is absolutely nothing like Murph, Redcliff Marine Rescue's burly, grumpy coxswain, many of the scenes in his stories are inspired by events he encounters during his duties.

Simon has also lived on two boats and sunk one of them; sold houses, street signs, Indian food and paper bags for a living; visited almost fifty countries and lived in three; qualified as a scuba diving instructor; nearly killed himself learning to wakeboard and built his own house without the benefit of an instruction manual.

He now lives in it by the sea with his wife and twin daughters, where he spends his time regurgitating his experiences on paper before he has so many more that he forgets them.

Website and newsletter sign up: simonmichaelprior.com
Email: simon@simonmichaelprior.com
Facebook: @simonmichaelprior
Instagram: @simonmichaelprior